THE GIRL IN JAPAN

A Young Soldier's Story

JOHN A MCCABE

Assiduous Way™
DOYLESTOWN

First Edition: April 2022

Assiduous Way Books, Assiduous Way, the colophon, and logo are trademarks of Assiduous Way LLC. For information about bulk or educational purchases, please visit AssiduousWay.com ("Sales"). The Assiduous Way Speakers Bureau can make your live event even more special by bringing authors, artists, and others to deliver inciteful and impactful presentations to your audience. For more information visit AssiduousWay.com ("Speakers Bureau").

Cover copyright © 2022 Assiduous Way LLC.
Book & cover design conceived by Don George. Cover graphic design by Rebecacovers.
Author Photo © 2022 Don George.
Portrait of Reiko, © 2021 Assiduous Way LLC, commissioned work by Keith McCabe.

The cover images of Marines with mushroom cloud and Cherry blossoms are used under license from Shutterstock.com as are the Maps of United States and Japan internally.

ISBN 978-1-958133-00-2 (hardcover) | ISBN 978-1-958133-01-9 (paperback) | ISBN 978-1-958133-02-6 (ebook)

Library of Congress Control Number: 2022936195
LC record available at https://lccn.loc.gov/2022936195

20220416_6

'Tis strange - but true; for truth is always strange;
Stranger than fiction; if it could be told...

Lord Byron, 1823

DEDICATION

There is sanctity to our remembering our lives. It escapes most of us that we live in a vast and constant cosmic reality. We may believe that we are unable to recall our feelings exactly over decades. I know, however, that when it comes to this memory, I know how I felt standing unprotected except for the last-minute field issue of black lenses in test range goggles and my steel helmet.

We were amassed in the open desert at a curiously unannounced distance from an atomic bomb detonation. A voice laden with guilt from a civilian man announced to us that the government was testing a weapon the exact same size and type as the one dropped on Nagasaki more than fifteen years earlier. He was constantly looking past us and straight out toward the nuclear test range and the army's assumed ground zero all the while that he struggled for the words and phrases of his academic sounding nuclear dissertation.

I learn later in life that we were unwitting accomplices in a hugely secretive medical experiment. We innocently participated in decades of documentations on weapons effects from live studies like rats in the cages of experimentation with no way to escape. Somewhere in the bloated hidden government files are soldiers' names who were within ten feet of me in the trench. They are buried reports of men who died from breast cancer, like Barry, a tough Jewish kid from Brooklyn and Sanchez a chubby Latin American teenager from L. A.

To all of us, I dedicate this book.

THE GIRL IN JAPAN

PROLOGUE

I am Joe McGrath and I return now to that very hot day under a blazing Nevada sun. I am wearing the army olive drab combat uniform, and it is miserably hot beneath my steel helmet. I know I am about to see something awful. I expect it to be like watching newsreels of the horrors of war destroying life. Golda Maier said, 'I can forgive our enemies for what they did to us, but I cannot bear the thought of what they made us do to them to survive,' and thoughts, like arguments, are gathering like webbing in my brain.

I tune out the speaker's explanations of what will happen. I have become hypnotized in the breath-like movements in the air above the surface of the Nevada desert. I knew it was impossible for the living panorama of scenery to lie perfectly still like a painting on a wall. As always, the desert appears to be alive and breathing in and out of its vast parched land. Nevada was claiming its space in the universe.

To me the big bomb about to be exploded belongs somewhere in the grit of immorality. It is like the riveting matter of a confession held within us, not yet told honestly, not yet seeking nuclear absolution. We are the victims and the perpetrators, as if the same.

The allegiance I have held is now challenged by a monstrous evil, an unfortunate reality, and I stand as if paralyzed, equipped only with the limited offsetting power of curiosity. Though all is fast becoming foreign, I am still me and cognizant of what is happening but not of what the bomb will look like through the lenses of pitch-black goggles. What will it sound like, or what will it reveal of the city, Nagasaki, mentioned by the army's spokesman on nuclear science?

Dr. Spencer's presentation and what seemed like a rehearsed lecture failed to gain the attention of most of its youthful audience. Nevertheless, he spoke to us soldiers as if he were hiding a truth that he was ashamed of, or a past he regretted.

I am anxiously breathing in and out little puffs of air. My mind is spinning in expectation of something too disturbing to discuss with those around me. Before putting on the claustrophobia inducing goggles, I am mesmerized by the desert's dust devils, those persistent natural cyclones twisting and curling as they lead my eyes to what is so hideously called ground zero.

I look around at my comrades and wonder what the hell we are doing here and why the hell they are showing this dreadful thing to us, and I see clearly that the authorities among us are lunatics. I see that, and I am nineteen years old, and I belong to them by law. I am a reluctant guest to a party of horrors by my local draft board

Once I imagined the citizens of German towns being marched in single file through the Auschwitz type camps. In my writer's mind, I saw them, and I even smelled the camps in my bleak meditations.

Now is a time to take Americans and peoples of the planet to atomic detonations that were just as real, just as historically chronicled in our global guilt and our despondent love.

Does anyone not need to know that in 1945 two city's people including thousands of children were destroyed, some evaporated alive, eyes melted, thousands in unspeakable devastation that cannot be described.

The nuclear weapons, those exploded, even in the controlled atomic and hydrogen bomb testing by nations who stockpile them are a form of constant psychological warfare. Therefore, we are all in their grip and under continuous injury. The narrative explores if we soldiers were being recklessly toyed with in an olive-drab world of nuclear experimentation.

That army that I was forced to enter because of draft papers with my name on them controls my repeated exposures to radiation and force fields. The same process identifying me as a number holds me there in the impersonal captivity of the Draft. I served under the heralded cause of a nation I extol willingly and militarily because of its countering appeal to the idealistic. It is America.

CHAPTER 1

1962, NEVADA USA

"Never, my Children, give up Hope."

The black sergeant's sweat-soaked face appeared shades darker in the sunlight. He stared at the opposite side of the trench; his eyes possessed by fear. A deep, serious voice from the loudspeakers began firing out commands up and down the line. Following an instinct, Joe looked up just as a black projectile crossed over the trench about five hundred feet above them. Seconds later, the men were surrounded by that horror-filled precursor, that flash of artificial light, bright beyond anything natural. Joe, Hank, and the horrified sergeant saw their hands turn into negatives, as if the trench had suddenly become an X-ray machine. Sergeant Nathaniel Masters shuddered at the sight. "Mercy, mercy, mercy," he moaned.

Joe instinctively pressed his now strange hands harder over his eyes. He had seen the bones in them as black forms, and the hands pressing on his eyes felt alien. Those black bones, hidden now by his skin, were not his anymore. He wondered if he would go blind from having his eyes see the bones during the blast.

The first shock wave, the one that dilates the heart, pounded through the earth and drove into their backs as the global curse of chain reaction hurled otherwise innocuous neutrons into wildly rapid strikes at nuclei, splitting them into atomic abuse promulgated by the conceited and prejudicial. An atomic bomb was once again exploding, wherein its substance would grow into torrents birthed from the indistinguishable substance of uranium rocks. It would become a crude and massive creature, like a mythical dragon blowing and destroying within and without its overheated chamber of blackened radioactive filth.

The sound, so incredibly explosive beyond anything imaginable, crushed Joe's spirit with fear. Joe felt as if he should have been hurled through the air or shattered into a violent vapor, like the dust and dirt that was rushing over them and threatening to bury them alive.

Holding his hands over his eyes like a visor and squinting, Joe saw Hank swatting at the dust and scrambling to stay above the dirt that was swirling into the trench. They yelled to each other "Stay down!" knowing that something from that indefinite fringe of reality was forming over them, something with more intensity than the very core of their beings had yet known. The bomb, like a ruined world extruded from the abuse of matter, was enough to shrink any teenage soldier into asking passionate questions either to another desperate Cybele or to the heart of his true God.

Zero plus 3 minutes, 36 seconds: When the atomic bomb blast silenced, the soldiers felt as if they had to rise above the threat or be enslaved by their own fear. They got up, first a few at a time, then the whole population of the trench. They stood starring at the atomic monster, half their irradiated bodies rising out above the crude, inadequately shallow earthly protection. The trench was only half as deep as it needed to be if the men were standing, but a deeper pit might have resulted in their being covered alive. Unrecognizable by the dust, the boys looked out, none of them moving other than to face the blast area.

To Joe, it seemed a strange vision of some futuristic battlefield, a nuclear Gettysburg on the hidden far side of the moon. His eyes discovered the hill at ground zero remade into a mushroom symbol, a shape to match the spirit of the foredoomed desert after its nuclear death. The victims were the same, young men, just young men, again. In Joe's mind, in a single, arrested scene, only two things existed: the stunned, irradiated, dust-faced young soldiers standing in a shallow ditch on the surface of the world and that atomic bomb mushroom now towering on the same surface. The armored personnel carriers moved up in front of them between the trench and ground zero, the noise of their diesel engines somehow unnoticeable.

Joe sensed something like an invisible being in the trench with him. It was as if he were two people, the person before the radiation and an invisible person that was either still Joe or some unnamed spirit.

He dismissed it in the increasing rumble of the APCs and the grating squeals as they opened their steel doors. The hydraulically controlled boarding ramps lowered without any human hand touching them, and the dust-covered, irradiated soldiers ran up the ramp into red electric lighting within the menacing machinery. When loaded, each vehicle closed its ramp, swallowing twelve soldiers in a macabre scene beneath the mushroom cloud now eleven thousand feet in the air. The dusty tracked vehicles turned about and lumbered across the test range. When they came within five hundred meters of ground zero, they heard the hydraulic noises of the transport machine opening the steel ramps to release their human cargo, the young soldiers yelling as they were trained to yell even from ancient times and now into the atomic age.

When all the men had disembarked, Joe and those around him stared upwards at the enormous nuclear cloud that filled the sky. The head of the mushroom, borne like a massive Indian thunderhead, was elevated above a strange hole in its core. Joe felt a nightmarish fear as the hole opened to the darkness of the universe. The cloud began to migrate down range, tumbling over toward the gawking infantry. There was no time to talk, for as soon as the APCs were empty, the sergeants shouted, "Move out!"

They ran and leapt over smoldering fresh craters and rivulets of atomic lava, its flowing surface gray-black-crusted and molten. Joe saw his foot about to sink into the gray-and fire red-crusted lava flow as he jerked himself further over the threat. Only his heel touched the shocking inferno. Thinking he would lose the heel to the molten fire; he was glad to be wearing thick heeled combat boots. As he ran onward the gray-black crust scene stayed vividly in his mind. He unconsciously imagined all the desert dust turning nuclear gray.

In Joe's mind, and in his new reality, the dust was quickly making all the men gray. The atomic army was out on the nuclear range to accomplish its senseless mission, and they did the best they could. Pretending to be advancing on the enemy, accompanied by live artillery, and acting as if they were engaged in a real battle, the young soldiers and their sergeants ran unprotected from the radiation across ground zero to their designated target.

As they raced forward, Joe's bulging eyes encountered desert life-forms that had been routed by the explosion. The reptilian survivors stampeded toward the soldiers, scurrying through the dust, and flipping themselves over the lava-like streams. They ran as fast as they could in a direction toward the bleachers that were now more than three miles behind the infantry, where the perpetrators were acting the part of concerned spectators. When the running men reached the other side of ground zero, they saw more lizards racing away from the bomb site, and eventually the infantry caught up with them.

Joe watched with astonishment how the two species ran in tandem, and he imagined their movements looked somewhat alike from above. Each ran in spurts and, after each sprint, the men flopped into prone firing positions while their counterparts froze in place for a few seconds, then both continued to advance. For a short time, the desert floor was covered with soldiers and lizards. As each platoon reached the base of the assault objective, Masters and the other sergeants waved them to a halt. For the soldiers, the forward charge had ended, but the lizards continued to race at full speed. The horizon seemed to be waiting for the innocents to arrive.

The moment the exhausted men saw the signal to halt, they stopped in their tracks. Some of them stood in place, while others dropped to the ground. Joe looked around for Hank and began to walk slowly toward his friend. There was a pause in the whole Army out there in the mangled desert as if their world had to catch a breath and reconnect with their previous existence. In a time that was initially still in between worlds, when only the mushroom cloud was stirring, Sergeant Masters waved his troops to stay in place. When they all stood curiously still and as more of them dropped to the ground, the sergeant began to walk away.

The sergeant moved on ahead. He nearly disappeared over the crest of a slightly elevated desert landscape to their front. Masters started blowing a whistle. He walked back to stand on the higher ground. He had his radio at his mouth. Suddenly some civilian men came to where he was standing. They were obviously Native American tribesmen. Their land, now contaminated beyond human usage, was being blown over by the nuclear dust. Their hair and bodies were made gray by Joe's imagination. Three jeeps and an Army ambulance made their way through the dumbfounded troops gaping at the scene. Way off in the distance, the soldiers could see the commotion but had no idea what was transpiring.

Two men in silver protective clothing immediately began to take radiation readings off the civilians. The most injured civilian man got their full attention first. The ambulance with its big red crosses drew the attention of the soldiers' eyes. Four MPs with .45 caliber side arms produced handcuffs. The Western Shoshone tribesmen were shackled, even the wounded man. Masters walked from man to man. He shouted to one of the military police, "Hey, go easy there, Specialist. These men are Indians . . . civilians . . . they're here by accident or they were uninformed about the test. They ain't criminals today! It's their land. You don't need cuffs. No cuffs!"

Masters' orders were being ignored. He yelled again, "Forget the cuffs, man. You can see they're harmless, you dumb bastards . . . I'm telling you this is their fucking desert you're on."

An officer in the military police pulled up in a fourth jeep with his driver. He stood directly in front of Masters and said, "You can go back to your platoon, Sergeant. We have this contained now."

Masters, his eyes bulging, stood his ground. The unmistakable Cherokee profile of his nose glistening in the brilliant sunlight stood out like the edge of a lance.

"You're done here, Sergeant," said the officer. Obviously reading Masters' name off his uniform, he added, "Sergeant Masters."

Masters kept quiet, staring at the major's MP armband.

"Move on, Sergeant!"

The Native Americans were crammed into the ambulance under armed guard. The jeeps drove in front and behind the ambulance.

Masters quickly got control of his platoon and said, "Show's over! Don't bunch up! One A-bomb will get y'all. Saddle up! Move out!"

Joe walked head down in an overheated daze. With the mechanical, rattlesnake sound of helicopter blades waffling in the desert air, he again sensed something. He looked up and again he saw the two men in silver, full-body, protective clothing. Just behind the two men, the colonel he remembered seeing in the cafeteria when they first arrived was standing beside a civilian man in fatigues. The man in fatigues was Dr. Spencer, the blond-haired man with the tattoo on his hand who had given them the atomic bomb speech before they watched the first bomb being detonated. The colonel had his arm on the other man's shoulder as if to praise him.

Much closer to Joe, the two men in protective clothing had formed a foreboding gateway for the soldiers to file through. They held Geiger counters against each man as he passed, probing legs and upper bodies and calling off to each other the Roentgens count. Joe passed through the men in silver, their suits reflecting brightly in the desert sunlight. "This is science fiction. They're like Saturday matinee aliens," he thought.

Joe continued watching the colonel and Dr. Spencer as he, too, walked toward the silver covered aliens. The colonel and the scientist were side-by-side in conversation, walking toward their vehicles. Hank looked around the desert scene for Joe. The sweat on his skin glistening like that brilliance of wet African rosewood in the bright sun. He noticed that they were segregating those in need of decontamination by directing them off to the right side. He saw that they were letting a greater number of men gather on the left. Sergeants were assigning details to sweep off the armored personnel carriers with brooms that seemed to appear out of nowhere.

The diesel engines sounded very loud again. A soldier from California was already up on one of the armored personnel carriers with a broom. Joe picked up a broom and started sweeping the olive drab steel but stopped when Hank came over to take the broom from him. Hank also waved at Garces to come down. In reply to Hank's suggestion, Garces, always joking, flicked some of the dust at his friends.

"Get off there with that fuckin' broom, Garces. The whole thing is radioactive, you dumb shit. Didn't you see those Indians? They were already messed up. Do you want more of that crap on you?" At that, Joe jumped back, afraid of the gray dust. Joe and Hank walked a good distance away from the vehicles.

Sergeant Masters, watching it all, stood uncharacteristically silent and still. As Joe and Hank approached, he said, almost under his breath, "It truly is the Atomic Age, and the 4th Infantry is now prepared for nuclear war at the expense of many and this desert land as well. Human beings are the dumbest fuckers ever created. God help us."

~ ~ ~

Automatic Rifleman, E4, McGrath Joseph R, and Squad Leader, Acting Sergeant Daniels Hank, flew almost without any conversations on board a C120 Troop Transport Plane with the secretly deployed elements of the 4th Infantry Division. Their faces were camouflaged and as they sat inside the fuselage for hours inflight to support the legitimate Laotian government Forces Armées du Royaume. The secret mission orders stated that they were operating from out of a base camp at Phou Khao Khouai, in a U.S. tactical nuclear strike to drive the insurgency of the Pathett lao, the generic name for Laotian communists, back into China.

On the rear deck of the plane, Joe saw a piece of discarded candy that had fallen out of someone's backpack. He was struck with a flashback of being a boy during a Fourth of July Parade back home and standing on the sidewalk as the parade marchers would throw candy at the waiting children. Just a pleasant memory among his many fears, he thought. Then the plane was suddenly banking into a descent to the airfield below as Joe was suddenly overwhelmed by his very real fears.

~   ~   ~

Nine days later, three Davy Crockett nuclear mortar/missile rounds were planned to be launched in the final attack before the entire attack and secret mission was aborted. One of the atomic mortars blew up where it was going to be fired which caused an emergency need to fully withdraw. This is not what they had rehearsed with live atomic detonations in Nevada. Threatened with being overrun and defeated by Laotian/Vietnamese once called Viet Minh forces and eventually The People's Army, the U.K. and U.S. soldiers were abruptly air lifted to Long Cheng.

Numerous U.S. infantry were believed irradiated, and in the chaos, Joe McGrath lost his helmet, cigarettes, lighter and his compass among other items from his torn clothing during the abrupt airlift withdrawal. He still had two of those wrapped candies he picked up and stowed in his O.D. (olive drab) shirt pocket. He was eating one of the candies during the air lift. As if a memory trigger, the candy on the streets of the north end of Philadelphia appeared and he became lost to it all and fell asleep.

His exhaustion and the losses and the horror became bewildering, He feared the radiation and he had a crippling pain in his back after the force field from enemy artillery blew him onto the ground during the withdrawal. He saw his helmet when it was falling off his head. His I.D. cards, driver's license and money were also lost somewhere in the thick blackened green jungle landscape of Northern Laos. Just like the presence of about three thousand secret Soviet anti-aircraft Russian soldiers defending Hanoi in North Vietnam were never revealed, Joe McGrath and Hank Daniels' outfit would also remain locked in secrecy for years.

As the airlift progressed, Joe finally awakened and listened to his best friend Hank breathing and saw in him the kid who was always with him and running from cops and bad guys and laughing on the streets of North Philly. The memory was so distracting and in contrast to his surroundings and the recent debacle, he found hypnotic solace in the past.

When the forces from the discrete Battlegroup finally arrived back in the United States, they had been cleared of any immediately measurable radiation poisoning by a secret hospitalization and extensive blood testing.

He took a thirty-day leave from duty and went home. It was summer in the city and he was anxious to meld in with home and friends once again, to become that carefree teenager that loved his country and his city. But he could never be that kid again because now he carried the threat of ten years in federal prison if he revealed anything about the nuclear events which he had survived.

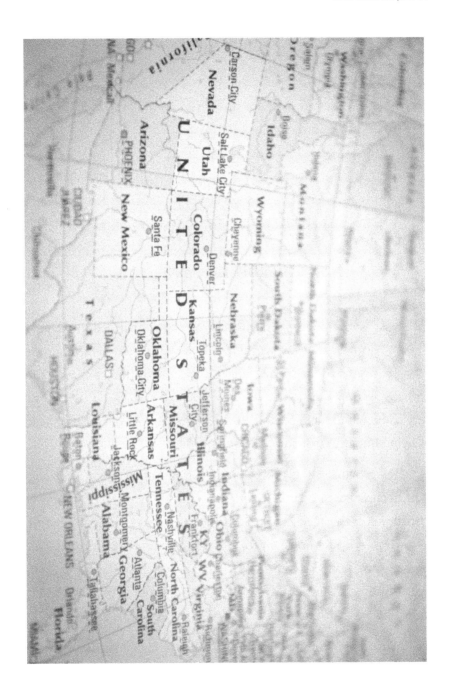

CHAPTER 2

1968 JAPAN

Reiko Fumioka sat primly on the edge of her bed in the girls' dorm so as not to wrinkle her yukata, a summer kimono. At five-feet-four-inches tall, she had grown into a remarkably attractive woman although she held resolute concerns that she was very plain and that her complexion was flawed from the postwar years of being undernourished as an orphan.

Reiko had lived at the Catholic Nuns' School and Orphanage for fifteen years. She lost her parents in the 1945 atomic bombing of Hiroshima at the age of one, and her grandparents had both died the following year. Her uncle Shiro, a Buddhist monk unable to raise her himself, had placed Reiko in the orphanage. He had watched over her and directed her upbringing under the tutelage of the Western nuns since that time.

Her eyes fell on the brown envelope that lay on her neatly made bed. Her name was handwritten on the front in bold *hiragana* strokes and the syllabic calligraphy in thick black ink evoked the oppressive presence of the stern Mother Superior, Sister Marie Baptiste. Reiko knew every girl was given such an envelope when departing the orphanage which contained her records and Mother Superior's personal comments, do's, and don'ts.

She knew, too, that she would never open her folder—although she had not yet decided whether to take it with her or leave it on the bed. She sighed, then picked up her *Redbook* magazine and flipped through the pages, stopping to focus on an ad for lipstick, attracted by the colors. The noon bell tolled its dull, metal-to-metal knocking and shortly afterward a student one-year Reiko's junior came to the doorway and announced Uncle Shiro's arrival.

"Thank you, Katsuko," Reiko responded, standing to brush imaginary wrinkles out of her kimono.

Katsuko asked in English, "Fumioka-*san* will marry if chosen?" During the last week of the school year, students were always required to speak English. Many of them struggled with the language structures, but they posed no problem for Reiko, whose English was always correct, if somewhat measured and formal at times.

"No. I have never . . . imagined . . . being a wife," Reiko replied, blushing slightly. "I cannot think of myself that way."

"Then you will become a nun like Qing and the others?" Katsuko persisted.

"I might," Reiko smiled. "Frankly, I find most . . . flirtations . . . unbearable, but I might like to be the . . . female complement to a handsome, caring man of virtue and purpose. I do not know. You always said . . . my love of solitude . . . was part of a truly artistic nature. How does one know if one is destined to be a nun, or a wife, or what?"

Katsuko smiled mischievously. "One asks those who have already become nuns or wives or what."

"Oh, I will miss you, Katsuko," Reiko sighed. Her lips trembled as tears filled her eyes, but she was determined not to cry. Contrary to what the Western nuns expected of "the Orientals," as they called the children in their institution, there were often tears in the orphanage—but Reiko had sworn this would not be one of those times. She swallowed hard and breathed deeply to maintain control, and Katsuko did the same. The girls bowed, touched by each other's sadness. Katsuko quietly left the room.

Reiko glanced around her small living space to make sure she had packed everything, more as a matter of tidiness and respect than of concern for her personal belongings, which were few and of little value. *If I perhaps do leave something behind, it may be that one of the other girls can make use of it.* Reiko left the room without the envelope.

A four-door, shiny black car was parked beyond the entrance to the orphanage, and a man in a chauffeur's uniform stood beside the rear door. Reiko walked slowly across the pebbled ground, careful not to stir up any dust with her sandals. The old monk, his lips curved into the faintest smile, seemed to read the sound of her footsteps, as if the barely audible disturbance of the little stones spoke to him about the present emotions of his niece. As she approached the car, the driver opened the door for her and she saw her uncle in the back seat, draped in orange robes that beckoned to her like a warm flame.

The driver took her suitcase and held the door for her to enter. Uncle Shiro leaned forward and smiled broadly, and whatever fears she may have had vanished under that sunny look of welcome. She suddenly knew this was the right thing to do. Bowing to the driver and then to her uncle, she lifted herself gracefully onto the seat and drew in her legs, taking advantage of a moment when she faced the window to wipe the remaining wetness from her eyes. The silent driver deposited her case in the trunk, slid behind the wheel, and began to drive her northward to her new life.

~   ~   ~

Speaking in Japanese, Reiko and Uncle Shiro exchanged small pleasantries but discussed nothing of importance because of the driver. They sat mostly in comfortable silence, enjoying the view and the long ride. While still a bit apprehensive about leaving the orphanage, Reiko felt excitement building as she embarked on a new adventure and she eagerly drank in all the sights along the Inland Sea's coastal road.

They had not been traveling long when the car passed a road sign that declared:

ひろし ま (Hiroshima)

To Reiko's surprise, the driver turned in the direction pointed out by the sign's arrow. She turned to her uncle, a question forming on her lips, but he spoke before she could ask.

"Since Hiroshima is on the way," he explained in a mild voice, "I thought we would revisit your birthplace and the place where your parents died." Tears sprang unbidden to Reiko's eyes at the mention of her mother and father and she stared at Uncle Shiro with dismay. "Please understand," the monk continued. "I do this not to sadden you, but to give you true peace and union with your parents." Though she was disturbed by her uncle's plan, Reiko bowed her head in obedience and the car carried them into the rebuilt city which originally dated to the 6th century.

After they arrived in downtown Hiroshima, Shiro issued directions to the driver until their route intersected with a narrow, empty street. The driver parked the car and opened the back door, helping first Reiko and then the old monk to exit, then returned to his seat and settled in behind the wheel. Shiro turned the corner and walked into the deserted street. He stood still for a moment, looking around, and then walked back and forth. Reiko followed close behind, wondering what he was doing. Dressed in her beautiful blue kimono, she floated over the bare concrete like a butterfly that had lost its way.

Shiro stopped suddenly, and Reiko, caught off guard and unable to check her forward motion, stumbled into him. Turning quickly, the old monk caught her shoulders to prevent her from falling and then pivoted so they were both facing the same direction. "Here," he said, his eyes riveted to the center of the pavement. "This is where they died. This is the place where, in an instant, the lives of your parents, my sister and brother-in-law, were taken by the blast. This entire area was destroyed, and it always takes me a moment to get my bearings and remember where their home was."

The sounds of Hiroshima filled their surroundings.

"They were here the morning the bomb exploded. During the war they both worked at night and slept during the day. That is why you were outside the city on the small farm with your grandmother and grandfather who cared for you during the night while your parents worked in the factory. Each morning, your parents would come to get you but one day they were late coming for you. You are alive because your parents were working nights for the war effort, and your grandparents babysat you."

Shiro staggered a bit as he paced back and forth over the area of concrete that was the only headstone Reiko's parents would ever have. "Here is where your parents were at this spot. I saw their burnt feet under the debris," he said softly, almost as if he were speaking to himself. "They were together, side by side."

Reiko stared at the concrete, feeling a strong desire to step onto the spot. She looked at Shiro's now creased and furrowed face and knew he was feeling the pain afresh. Her throat tightened. "And your parents, my grandmother and grandfather?" she prompted.

"They were so overwhelmed by sorrow at the devastation and loss of their only daughter that they died of grief the following year, one after the other." Completing his statement, Shiro bowed low over the concrete, offering a sign of respect to their dead relatives. Reiko's face crumpled as she began to feel Shiro's sorrow mixed with that of her own. Shiro inhaled deeply and noisily, and then exhaled explosively. "So!" he snorted, "The two of us became orphans at almost the same time!" He broke into a forced grin and reached for Reiko's hand, clasping it warmly as he began to walk away. Reiko went willingly, relieved that he did not want to remain any longer at that hallowed, yet horrible, reminder of their shared loss.

At the end of the barren street, they came upon a smooth stone wall built above a riverbank. The shallow water ran silently through the ravine and colorful birds flitted above the overgrowth on the opposite bank, filling the air with their repetitive songs. Uncle Shiro dusted off the gray flat stones of the wall with his robe as they sat down.

"Do you come here often, Uncle Shiro?" Reiko asked.

"My heart often returns to this place, even when I am in the monastery, If you could climb a tree over there, you could see the monastery," he replied.

His answer was indirect, but Reiko accepted it. She smiled, and he smiled in response. It was a certain knowing smile they had shared, a thing of family. Even though he could not be with her, during all those years in the orphanage, he had kept her world from being as lonely as it might have been. Through visits, letters, and gifts, Uncle Shiro had made certain she knew she always had family.

"Was there any other reason for us to come to Hiroshima?" she asked.

Like a teacher listening to his favorite student, Shiro's face filled with satisfaction.

"You are very astute," he praised her, obviously pleased with her question. "We are also here because I wish to tell you more about what our family experienced here in this city."

Shiro stood and brushed off his deep orange robe. As he stood in the sunlight, he reminded Reiko of the saintly statues pictured in stained glass motifs in the Catholic chapel at the orphanage. Facing toward the center of the city and blinking at the glitz displayed in the modern Hiroshima skyline, he said, "I brought you here to hear my personal account, so that I may give you what I carry in my memory. It is a sacred matter. We monks are taught to seek upwardly. We seek, begging to become selfless. I pray that what I say will be worthy of this sanctified tragic history."

He was now staring at her face, an unusual gesture for most Japanese, and his eyes grew wide, as if they knew this was irregular behavior. He wet his lips with the tip of his tongue, then lifted his arm and pointed toward the center of the city. "A great shining darkness occurred here," he began. "It happened even when it was too late for us. Japan was already defeated. These were senseless deaths, especially the thousands of children. The children did nothing to America."

The old monk held his hand across his eyes while scanning the area for others. Satisfied that they were still alone, he spoke again,

"We Japanese were burnt to death here, like your parents, because we had chosen to go to war, even though we had been taught that it was our responsibility never to waste any living thing. But instead of following this teaching, our leaders sought conquest by following the old ways -- and we obeyed them like feudal serfs. Because of their zeal to taste victory, and our failure to restrain them, we brought this horror upon ourselves."

~ ~ ~

Shiro stared at the river landscape with unseeing eyes; his terror-stricken pupils gleaming like polished dark gemstones as his face took on a pale, glazed, almost inhuman rigidity. Reiko knew he was remembering Hiroshima on the morning of August 6, 1945, and that he was being emotionally turned to stone by what he envisioned. He spoke quietly through clenched teeth, his voice strained, and Reiko closed her eyes to concentrate on his words.

"Hiroshima, every inch of it and everything in it—buildings, schools, trams, trucks, homes—the very structures of the city and its inhabitants—in an instant, the whole city became like compressed, air-blasted sand from a gigantic sandblaster."

Shiro stopped speaking. The sudden silence, broken only by the wind's soft sighs, caused Reiko to open her eyes. She looked out over the quiet water immersed in vivid imaginings triggered by his descriptions and the realization that she was at the exact 1945 ground zero. She waited for her uncle to continue. When he did, she felt trapped in a nightmare, expecting some vapor to be exhaled from the ground. For her, the atomic bomb was forever present, perhaps buried in the very earth it had scorched to a place of death and gray ash.

When Reiko emerged from her trance, Shiro was still talking. "I had a view of the destruction as it happened. It came from between those rivers," he said, lifting his arm and pointing downstream. "A ball of fire so huge, so hot, as if it could melt the sun. I heard the bomb—an astonishing, unbelievable noise that threatened to shatter my ear drums—a split second before I saw it. A shock wave of incredible speed, taking everything with it in a force so great it ripped and pulverized all things. That horrible wave of destruction advanced on the city at lightning velocity, carrying thousands of degrees of heat, searing the ground and the atmosphere, obliterating all forms of matter in its path, including our people—mothers, fathers, and the children." His voice trailed off again.

Shiro felt his emotions rising and paused, taking deep breaths and exhaling audibly, to calm himself. "Perhaps we should walk for a few moments," he suggested.

"That would be good, Uncle," Reiko answered in a subdued voice.

They rose and walked along the stone wall for a short while, not speaking, both lost in their own thoughts. Reiko sighed deeply, and Shiro, looking at her mournful face, reminded himself grimly that he was telling her this not to hurt her, but because there were things she must know. After several silent minutes had passed, they settled themselves on the flat stones once again, and Shiro, despite being reluctant, resumed.

"You see, when I think this way, just about now there comes upon me a peculiar impulsiveness, a reckless thinking, and then comes a stream of imbecilic thoughts about the guilt of surviving, so odious to the soul." His dark eyes widened, and his face expressed sheer blank fright. "I have a strange disorder that my mind can barely escape, as if it were all a waking nightmare of my choice. I feel the guilt of one who did not die with the others, of one who escaped when no one should have." He gazed at Reiko with tortured eyes. "I leap back from it just before going mad," he confessed, "and force myself into the narcotic effect of the present."

"Oh, Creator God!" Reiko whispered.

"I saw the American bomb when it exploded," her uncle said, "and that will stay within me for the rest of my existence. There is no force in nature like the atomic bomb, Reiko. It destroys and alters forever every molecule of matter gripped in its power." He stared out over the river.

"Yet, you survived, Uncle," Reiko said quietly, laying a comforting hand on his arm. She was gratified to see a composed look return to his face, taking it as a sign that he had been released from his terrors.

"Did everyone wish for death, as we have been told?" she asked.

"Many," Shiro answered.

"Did you know what the bomb was and that it came from other human beings?"

"I did," Shiro replied, "but many had no idea what was happening. They seemed to identify only what they knew: fire was fire, force was force. But I knew. I had learned from other monks that there was a secret weapon coming to defeat Japan and I heard the plane. I recognized that weapon as man's inhumanity to man. I knew immediately it had that evilness about it, and that was what terrorized me. I was stripped of all sense of security and suddenly did not know what it meant to be Japanese. In an instant, we were the victims of our own race, a nest of ants crushed under the fiendish stomping of other human beings."

"You, Uncle Shiro, are not an ant but a giant," Reiko gently chided.

"I saw my people annihilated and my place of birth made into a molten, mysterious death camp," Shiro said. "We were being exterminated. The street names, which called to mind the families who lived there, became semi-obliterated grave markers, now calling to mind those who died there. The stench was ghastly, worse than all the human vomit and waste. People grew sick and died every day, until the toll rose by the thousands more than the initial blast. Severe burns became coated in disgusting pus, and maggots appeared on the suffering. Flesh melted to flesh, and one saw children and others with their chins fastened to their necks, or their fingers fused together."

Shiro was breathing heavily, and his back and shoulders arched back.

"Those hands became like crab claws, welded together and deformed, sometimes so much so that they were useless tools. Monstrous deformities that never healed normally, such as elevated, elongated bubbled areas, formed on faces and any other unshielded flesh. There were some who appeared unhurt, but more were sickened genetically, a disease that did not show until the next generation. All living things faced the atomic demise of otherwise natural science."

"The vegetation grew back almost immediately, and even though they suspected it was not good for their health, the people ate it—even the grass—for they were hungry. Initially people were so dried out by the heat of the blast that the dehydration alone was killing them. They tried to rehydrate by drinking water, but they died anyway. Drinking was not enough; they needed special hydration treatment. But, of course, they did not know that -- they thought the water had gone bad and was killing them."

For a moment the two were silent while Shiro gave Reiko time to absorb what he had said. He was glad that the spot he had chosen for their conversation remained isolated and that privacy was not a problem.

"That was what our enemy held for us, and I thought for the first time of how deeply we must be hated by the Americans, and I was afraid of what we meant to them. I wanted to know how such hatred was born. We are a good people, a polite people, almost to a fault. If you walked among the dying as I did and heard their requests for water and aid, you would hear nothing but politeness. How, then, could such hatred come to be? Nothing made any sense anymore—that is one reason I remained a monk—I would be lost out in the world."

"We did not learn until after the surrender how our troops and military leaders committed hateful war crimes."

Reiko, caught within the mental torrent of her uncle's mind, felt the blackness and horror of his memories. A complete loss of light darkened her interior being.

Shiro allowed his niece a few moments of silence and then said, "I have finished with the telling. Do you have any questions, Little One?"

"Just one, Uncle, if I may," Reiko answered. "Being so close to the explosion, how is it that you survived?"

"I was very fortunate," Shiro replied. "The monastery was a natural atomic bomb shelter. Though I was briefly blinded, we were nested in the rock formations just far enough away and at low ground levels. It protected us. Our community's mortalities came later from the radiation, not the blast. So far as I know, I escaped from that as well. No one knows why radiation goes into one person and not another."

"I consider it my good fortune, also, that you were spared," Reiko said.

"Thank you, child," Shiro said.

They bowed deeply to one another, then linked hands and began to walk back the way they had come.

"I have to go away from my home and from my birthplace, two separations in one day, and start a whole new life," said Reiko.

"It is so, Little One," Shiro answered sympathetically. "But you are strong and the ride will help you prepare."

"It is not easy to be alone, is it?" she sighed and felt Shiro give her hand a comforting squeeze as they approached the car. On the ride north there was only the whir of the air conditioner and the hum of the tires. Lost in their own thoughts, Shiro and Reiko looked out at the passing landscape.

CHAPTER 3

That evening Reiko met the bishop. The bishop and his home did not seem to be the bureaucratic center she feared it would be. She had imagined a religious opulence, a house of quiet luxury with recorded music and somber rituals but the bishop was not of that ilk. The simplicity of the man and his humility matched his appearance. It became her image of him and the fact that he combed his hair with his hand with unconcern, and that he had thin and soft blonde hair that was unmoved by his attempts and how he stood and walked with never perfect posture and almost always silently comforted her. He was addressed as your excellency, but acted without pomp, which pleased her. She did not want to become once again a dependent and totally supported ward of the local congregation. She wanted to be useful, to cease living the misery of a presentable beggar orphan, as she and the other children often described themselves.

The first evening she wore some of the new clothing her uncle had given her -- clothing in a box with a Tokyo department store name. It made her feel new and different. Her uncle had left after dinner and the orphanage was ninety miles and a lifetime away. She felt so many conflicting emotions that she spent an uneasy night. Before her duties began the next morning, she took the first of many, many walks along the beach of the small coastal town in central Japan to calm her nerves.

As she walked in the damp sand, the surf grew louder. The crashing waves advancing and retreating pressed the incline of beach sand flat and cooled Reiko's bare feet. Again, and again she watched her feet splashing the water until she turned to leave. In a few steps she stopped and turned back to the sea. *How much have I lost in my life, not having parents, not growing up in a Japanese home, not being happy so many days and nights and years? I am alone because of the atomic bomb, because of war. What will become of me now? Uncle Shiro is far away.*

"*Ima nan-ji desu?*" she whispered, asking herself what time it was. Thereafter on the beach walks, she always dismissed her English and thought in Japanese. "*Juu-ji,*" she said, looking at her watch that read ten o'clock. It was time to have tea with the bishop and to resume work on his manuscripts and correspondence. It was a sunny day, and the wind blew cool ocean air through the shoji door when she opened it. The few flowers she had picked along her beach walk blew against her kimono as she entered.

Glancing up, the bishop's eyes seemed to notice how much the flowers enhanced Reiko's face and hair. He was, however, an American and a bishop so that those distinctions caused a cultural difference that left a clear distance between them even in the friendliest of encounters.

As they took their tea, the bishop spoke to her of the garden and how he had inherited it from another priest. He asked her if she would like to take charge of the garden surrounding the turtle pond. She agreed with a look of surprise and joy. "I do not know much about tending to a garden."

"You will learn, and the garden will prosper under your guidance," the bishop insisted. "That will be on your official list of duties."

"Oh, yes, Reiko. You will surpass anything Father Grafton would have imagined. Everything you touch will turn into beauty, while my green thumb is a weed-growing phenomenon."

She smiled demurely, trying not to show how depressed she was to be so alone in such a foreign place, with no friends and nowhere to go to escape her fate. Eventually, as time went by, Reiko spent hours and hours gardening, and teaching herself how to do so.

~ ~ ~

The boy who delivered groceries to the bishop's rectory was typical of the male dominating yet nontraditional Japanese teenagers in post war Japan; he wore jeans and T shirts with his hair in long waves of greased and a distinctly American-looking pompadours. The hair was combed unquestionably like the characters in Americanized Japanese films. When he arrived at the side driveway of the rectory at the kitchen door, he always left the delivery truck running and the radio playing American popular music turned loud. No matter who answered the rectory door to let him in, he never turned off the radio.

Almost every Saturday he showed up. To Reiko he was the world she all but missed growing up. Only a handful of the teenagers in the orphanage were influenced by the big changes coming from the West to alter forever Japanese youth culture. The boy was a multiracial, Japanese American (Caucasian) teen, the embodiment of the Allied Occupation and American culture. Those among the young who blamed their Japanese parents and the older Japanese generations for the horror and depravation of the war years were in full revolt and determined to be westernized even if it made life more difficult. Reiko had no parents to blame but, like all in her generation, she knew of the changes and cultures even though she barely lived in her country's teenager rebellion.

The boy went by the name Frank, and he had mostly only two words to say to Reiko or anyone else, "cool" (*ikasu*)" and "dangerous" (*yabai*). Although the Bishop and his home did not seem to be steeped in tradition or stifling religious opulence, somehow this boy irked all around him even though he was permitted no more than entry to the pantry area and the driveway.

Only Reiko alone acknowledged and welcomed him. When the Bishop acted as if the boy was an unimportant necessity, it pleased her. Only in Frank's company did she feel like a young woman, one who did not want to be considered merely a feminine religious assistant not even, even if it meant denying her Japanese heritage when the boy was there.

"What's your name, girl?" the boy asked one day.

"Reiko. Are you Fraang?" she asked, deliberately mispronouncing his name.

She was looking at his imitation cowboy boots and then, when he turned to pick up the grocery packages, she made quick study of what she saw. When he turned back in her direction, he caught her looking.

"How come you live here, girl?"

Reiko was miffed by the unexpected question, and she remained silent, looking again at his cowboy boots.

"Girl, you are dangerous, really dangerous."

She stared at him, speechless. Then, when he walked through the pantry door and brushed against her while he set the packages down, she found that she immediately felt his aggression, and imagined him expecting her to be the passive female, that Hollywood archetype she heard about in Japanese films. Wondering if she liked it, she found words. "Are you always listening to that music on the radio?"

"Yeah, you like it?"

"Yes, I hardly ever hear that, and I do like it. The Americans are always playing rock-n-roll. The ones, who live near the airbase, play it loud."

"Yeah, the Yanks."

"You look…"

He knew what she was about to say about his looks, "Don't worry I am used to it. I am a half breed, half-American, half-Jap, or that's what my father said."

"Your father is an Airman from America?"

"That's cool, uh?" As Reiko bent over to remove the grocery items from the bags, he brushed by her with the lightest of touches on her back. She said nothing but giggled under her breath.

As months went by, she became familiar with him because he treated her the way the dynamics of the cultural experiments by youth were going on in Japan. He saw himself as the leader in the constant hunt for girls. His knowledge of American cinema and its romantic Hollywood culture was the strongest point in his character, his only source of identity. While Reiko maintained her orphanage innocence about people, she hungered for the excitement of the new Japanese culture. The first time they kissed, she was dressed in western clothing, nothing like what her uncle Shiro would approve of. They were riding in the grocery store delivery truck. Frank had made the excuse that the store delivered the wrong brands on about six items, and he wanted Reiko to go and pick out what the priests and the Bishop would expect for their dinners.

Half a mile away from the rectory, when he stopped the van near the river, she asked, "Why are you parking here?"

"Frank has a cool Idea," he said.

"What's that?" she asked looking straight ahead and cautiously out the front windshield, avoiding his eyes.

'Let's take a walk in the trees over there by the beach."

"You really want to?"

"Dangerous ... you and those trees are dangerous."

She smiled and then she wondered what she was doing.

"Do you like Elvis?"

"What?"

"Elvis Presley!"

"What about Elvis? His songs sound nice, or they are wild, but he's weird."

"I guess you don't see the movies, do you?"

"I have seen a few."

"What ones, American or Japanese?"

He put his hand on her knee. She felt awkward and opened her door to get out. He kept his hand on her as she turned, keeping her leg closest to him from moving. She turned back and he kissed her. She drew back momentarily before she kissed him.

She used to kiss a boy in the orphanage but that was different from this. This kiss had more going on for her to wonder about. The boy in the orphanage was childish. This boy Frank was half American and she knew that his adoption of the American culture was partly why she was attracted to him. And that's why he was dangerous to her. Under his guise as an American influence, he was more the man, the male, the hunter-of-girls conquest, the Japanese superior male. Her first instinct was anger, her second was laughter.

He protested as she drew back with ill-concealed mirth. "What's so funny, Reiko? I thought that we were getting along just fine."

"Oh, Frank. You are such a—man after all. Just drive to the store and take me and my groceries home."

On the silent ride home, she mulled over the conflicting emotions. She knew if she didn't act like herself, the active person, the independent woman person, she was meant to be, she would never survive. Oh, it would be easy to simply give in and be easy and be the female like the ones in the films. Later when she was back at the bishop's home, the memory, the scene in the truck, and Frank's advances represented his stark and alarming prowess and sexual power.

Her emotions were locked in her feelings as she lay in her bed at night. Nights long after she avoided Frank, no longer found him attracting her, she still pondered her sexuality and her kissing him. His Japanese male dominance, no matter how altered by the American blood and the times they lived in, was too readable, too unmasked by her intellect. She began to expect disappointment. He said it all one day when she rebuked him, he used the expression, "That is without coolness, Reiko."

CHAPTER 4

1968, PHILADELPHIA PA USA

Joe arrived at the veterans' administration hospital. He pulled his car into the entrance and found a parking place. He sat for a while staring vacantly, willing the mushroom cloud memory and the anxiety in his mind to subside. Finally, he crossed the parking lot to the sidewalk, turning to follow along the tall bars of black iron fencing. He stopped and looked up at an etched iron plate on the fence that read PROPERTY OF THE UNITED STATES OF AMERICA. He continued to an outdoor bench just past a bus stop area in front of the hospital entrance. Again, overwhelmed, he sat down on the bench. He lowered his head and stared at the ground as more memories stirred and images from the Army filled his mind:

The infantry is charging over rivulets of molten, red-burnt nuclear lava. His foot is sinking repeatedly into a flowing inferno. He jerked it back every time and kept running carrying his Browning automatic rifle across his chest. Frantic lizards dart across the ground. He sees two men in silver-metallic suits probing with olive-colored rods, pointing at soldiers' bodies, and calling out radiation measurements.

Several minutes passed before the mental tempest of nuclear memories was over. Joe adjusted his sunglasses and rose to his feet. He approached the front doors, his mind still swimming, to find his path blocked by a security guard. The short black man rubbed a palm smugly across the breast of his uniform, produced a pen, and reached back to his stand for a clipboard.

"Your name, sir?" he asked stiffly. "Are you staff?"

"No," Joe replied. "My name's McGrath, Joe McGrath."

"Got an appointment?" The guard asked, writing Joe's name on the clipboard.

"No. A Dr. Stevenson said to come any time."

"No appointment." The security guard placed an "X" beside Joe's name, then put his pen away and looked straight ahead, as if Joe were no longer a person. Swinging his clipboard like a gate, the guard waved Joe forward, treating him like an automobile or a delivery truck as he pursed his lips and allowed McGrath to pass.

Joe stopped just inside the door to get his bearings. He noted the locations of the admissions desk, the elevators, and the restrooms, and then looked over the other visitors. No women were present, just a group of tough-looking city guys, one on crutches and four in wheelchairs, most dressed in worn clothes. Obviously familiar with each other, they looked back at him with undisguised curiosity. They seemed neither hostile nor friendly, just interested. Joe felt out of place, not only because of his sunglasses and business suit and tie, but also because he knew he did not look sick or injured. He removed his sunglasses and slid them into his pocket.

Crossing through the waiting room to the admissions counter, he stood behind a sign that read "Please form a line here." The clerk, a heavy-set black woman, put down her candy bar with a guilty look, chewing and swallowing hastily. "I'm sorry," she apologized with a smile, daintily wiping the corners of her mouth. "It's *their* lunch hour," she said, waving a hand to indicate the steady flow of doctors and nurses by the elevator, "but I have another hour to go, and I'm *starving*. How may I help you?"

Automatically returning the clerk's friendly smile, Joe moved forward and gave her his name. After telling her why he was there, he patiently answered her questions as she filled out a form.

"At last," she pronounced, "the final question: Whom should we notify in case of emergency?" She enunciated each word carefully, as if intelligence levels were measured by pronunciation.

"No one in particular," Joe replied.

"You sure? You should put someone down."

"Yes, I'm sure. I'll think about it and let you know," he said, expecting her to insist.

"Thank you," the clerk said, completing the form. She looked it over to make sure she had all the information and then motioned him toward the waiting room. "Please take a seat in Section H, Mr. McGrath, and someone will come get you."

Joe found an empty seat in Section H and looked at the clock. It was 12:35 PM. He removed his tie and stuffed it in his pocket, then unbuttoned his shirt collar. One of the wheelchair occupants was rewrapping a leg bandage; Joe glanced at him, and the man suddenly looked up. Another man started choking, but no one seemed concerned. Joe didn't know where to look, so he stared at the front doors. Two veterans left and several more came in. Two of them were much older men who could easily have been veterans of the First World War.

A nurse in a blue cap with a ponytail walked up to him carrying a clipboard.

"Mr. McGrath, Joseph McGrath?" she asked, reading from his chart.

"Yeah, that's me," he answered. She was standing too close for him to get up without bumping into her, so he stayed seated.

"You look fit," she observed, looking him over. "Were you wounded?" Her eyes went back to his chart.

"No, not wounded," he answered. "You got guys here from every war, don'tcha?" he asked.

"We sure do," she said.

Behind Joe an energetic VFW volunteer sporting a cap that proclaimed him to be a veteran of World War II and wearing an Eisenhower jacket covered with medals fussed sympathetically with the afflicted and the bored. When he spoke, his voice penetrated everything that was happening around him.

"Anybody for a drink of water? Scotch?" he called out cheerfully.

The nurse looked briefly, but directly, at the tall VFW volunteer. She spoke quietly, timing her words to occur during the intervals between the veteran's loud pronouncements.

"Your chart says you were in the A-bomb tests in 1962?" she asked.

"That's right," said Joe.

A man sitting three chairs away spat into his hand, earning a disapproving frown from the nurse. The noisy volunteer grabbed up a box of tissues and hurried over to the spitter, and the nurse turned her attention back to Joe.

"Did you ever report anything about your health or injury before?" she asked.

"I called here, and a Doctor Stevenson said to come in and see him," Joe responded.

"How about in 1962, or any time between then and now? Did you report the tests?"

"This is just a big medical experiment, isn't it?"

"Well, no."

"Look ma'am, at first I was in the Army, and we weren't supposed to tell anybody about it. It was top-secret." He stopped for a second, and then grinned. "And then I never have the right form, the one for atomic bombs."

"I'm glad you have a sense of humor about it," she said, smiling. "Okay, I've got what I need. If you'll just wait here, I'll go find out what I can about Doctor Stevenson's schedule."

"Okay. Thanks," said Joe, clasping his hands in his lap. He closed his eyes and settled back to wait. As the time went by Joe was thinking of the questions the nurse asked. When he whispered,

"Theirs not to make reply, theirs not to reason why, theirs but. . .," the nurse returned.

The nurse spoke to him, releasing him from *The Charge of the Light Brigade* spell. "Mr. McGrath," she said, "please go to the elevator and up to Hematology on the fifth floor. We'll run your blood through quickly, and then Doctor Stevenson will examine you."

"Yes, ma'am. Thanks."

On the fifth floor, Joe sat in a booth before two nurses. A pretty Hispanic nurse took his blood pressure. While she was marking the results on his chart, the other nurse drew two samples of his blood. The Hispanic nurse, reading his file, said, "Oh, this is one of the nuclear weapons test cases." Seeming to forget that Joe was sitting right in front of her, she continued, "We're supposed to hold their blood. It needs to be marked 'special' so they'll save the slides."

"They've been waiting for us," Joe whispered to himself.

"I'll take care of it," said the second nurse.

A stricken look crossed the face of the Hispanic nurse, as she had just realized she said more than she should have in Joe's presence.

"You can go back to the waiting room downstairs now," the nurse instructed him. "Someone there will direct you to the doctor."

"Well, I guess I'll find out now. Thanks," said Joe, leaving the booth. He walked down the hall and entered the elevator. *It's like a mass grave: jump in the trench at twenty, die before you're thirty,* he thought as he punched the button, and the elevator began its descent.

When the elevator doors opened and Joe stepped out, he nearly walked into the security guard who had blocked his way at the front door. The nurse in the blue cap strode past, ignoring the guard while she greeted Joe with a friendly wave. As he acknowledged her salutation with a polite nod, Joe noticed another one of those looks of annoyance on the guard's face. "Hey, beautiful, can't say hello?" the man yelled, stretching his neck and rising on his toes to throw his voice over Joe's head.

The nurse pointed Joe to the examination room area. He joined several other patients waiting their turn in the main corridor. Joe leaned against the wall while the professionals slowly received patients. A young man on crutches came up beside Joe.

"There must be a better way, I was here yesterday waiting, and had to come back today," the young man commented, slumping wearily over his supporting crutches.

"Yeah, ya really wait around," Joe replied as two vets hurried past them carrying prescriptions. It was after four o'clock, and Joe was beginning to tire. He and the young man on crutches exchanged thin smiles when another patient hurried out of an examination room with his prescription slip and a satisfied expression on his unshaven face. Joe spotted a nearby stairway and moved over to it, feeling an unexpected equanimity with it all. He couldn't do anything to change his position in line and he was beginning to relax about it, like a guy sitting out a delay in a busy barber shop.

He sat down on one of the lower steps, and the sitting made it easy to recall things again from his years in the Army. Placing his elbow on his knee, he supported his bowed head with the heel of his left hand and allowed his mind to follow his desire to remember.

Unexpectedly, he pictured his buddy Hank Daniels, with his tall, lanky body and dry black hair. He clearly saw the rubbed charcoal appearance of Hank's jaw, freckled face, and well-trimmed mustache. He hadn't thought very often about Hank in the past year or two. The two best friends had fallen out of touch after leaving the military. Hank had spent his Army leaves in Chicago. His family, especially his mother who was a doctor, had made sure Hank felt at home with them there. She, a rare female black surgeon at the time, had a private practice in Chicago.

After they were discharged from the army, Hank and his pretty girlfriend, a Cuban named Charlene, went to the Daniels' family home in Chicago. Hank met Charlene in Portland when Hank and Joe took weekend passes together from Fort Lewis, Washington. Joe had returned to his and Hank's childhood hometown of Philadelphia alone. Except for a few phone calls during the first years, the two great boyhood friends lost contact, each going their separate way. While they had served in the same military outfit, Army life had showed each of them their own path. There are not many roles as self-centering as that of the infantry soldier. Even though you are willing to die for your comrades, you live within yourself. Despite being one soldier in columns of identically dressed men marching in unison, you march alone: the longer the march, the greater the solitude.

Joe saw Hank's gentle brown eyes smiling at him from the past with their usual intelligent and friendly expression as he experienced a sharp longing to see Hank again. His mind suddenly reached out to his old friend. *Hank,* he murmured softly, *how can ya handle all the possibilities? Geez, do they know what they did?* He knew then that when he had more information, he would contact Hank.

Returning momentarily to the present, Joe checked the hallway to determine whether his turn had come any closer. Seeing that nothing had changed, he shifted the bone of his elbow to a new spot on his leg and gave himself over once again to retrospection.

~ ~ ~

"Hey, buddy." Joe felt a nudge on his foot and looked up. The young man on crutches was standing before him, tapping a crutch lightly against Joe's shoe.

"You're next, buddy," the young man said with a smile as he swung away.

"Oh! Ah, okay. Thanks," Joe stammered. *Well, here I go,* he thought, stretching his legs. "Wonder what they'll do if I have leukemia?" He followed a nurse into a small room and climbed onto the examining table. Dr. Stevenson was seated at a wall desk reading a chart, making notes, and turning the pages. As he looked through the papers, he muttered to himself, and Joe heard a stream of words that phonetically sounded like Latin.

Growing a bit irritated at being ignored, Joe blurted out, "I called you this morning, remember? I was exposed to four of 'em. One we just watched. The others, we were right in there."

The doctor kept reading, then closed the file and stood up. "Blood pressures are high today," he said, speaking in a self-absorbed manner. "She's giving everybody higher numbers than they need. Let's see what I get out of it." He wrapped the cuff around Joe's arm and began squeezing the bulb to pump up the pressure. Noting the man's receding hairline and the wrinkles around his eyes, Joe decided Dr. Stevenson must be about forty-five years old. He was small and bony and stood with a slight slouch.

"Just as I thought," the doctor said. "She had you too high. Take off your shirt and lie back and I'll check your glands, liver, and spleen."

Joe did what he was told and tried to relax while the doctor's hands prodded at various organs. When he had finished, the doctor sat down at the desk and opened the file again to jot down new notes. Joe buttoned his shirt, trying not to feel nervous. He noticed posters on the walls with endless print in bold black ink, Joe never reading a word of it.

The doctor lifted a telephone receiver to his ear and began to speak into it softly.

"Is that it? Do I come back?" Joe asked, raising his voice slightly.

Doctor Stevenson answered nonchalantly, moving the receiver away from his mouth but not bothering to cover it. "Your blood is fine . . . and no enlargements," he said, and immediately returned to his conversation. Joe heard his full name spoken, but everything else the doctor said was inaudible. At last the doctor hung up and rolled his chair closer to the table, giving Joe his full attention for the first time. "No follow-up," he said.

"That's all ya have to tell me?" Joe was shocked by the man's indifference.

Dr. Stevenson sighed heavily, then said, enunciating his words carefully as if he were speaking to a child, "You were exposed in 1962. That was years ago. You're a long shot now. You'll probably live a long life. You might get sick, though, and if you do, it's our job to help you cope with it."

Joe stared at the doctor in astonishment, realizing the man was saying almost exactly what he had said earlier that day on the phone, as if it was his prepared routine atomic bomb counseling. Joe's face expressed a myriad of questions until an image of smiling veterans leaving the exam rooms with prescriptions in their hands popped into his head. *So that's it, the V.A. will give me drugs to keep me happy and quiet and to keep me coming back to fill their files. That's what they get out of it—whatever that is.*

"That's it?" he exclaimed aloud. The doctor rolled his chair back to his desk and bowed his head over his paperwork, lips pursed, appearing to suppress any real interest he might have had. Accustomed to obeying the assumed authority exhibited by most nuns and priests and doctors and cops in his childhood world of the forties and fifties, Joe left the room, quietly closing the door. A few minutes later he was walking away from the hospital. As he walked, he imagined that he had slammed that door shut.

Geez, he thought, *the doctor couldn't do any more than that? Guess it wasn't his fault. Whoever he talked to on the phone stopped him; he had limits. They're still collecting data on us, but they don't seem to be doing anything to help us. That's all this was about, collecting data.*

Go to the V.A., sure. That's what they wanted me to do. This'll get me into all kinds of things I'd never expect, never dreamed of. Atomic bombs and me, Hank, and me . . . They just wanted to know my status. What a creepy government. He pushed himself to keep walking toward the parking lot because a part of him wanted to retaliate. With his head down and a determined look on his face, he stopped at a pay phone at the parking lot entrance. He called his boss, Mr. Epperson to explain why he was not in the office all afternoon and to hear himself say aloud what he wanted to believe and remember.

"Hi," he said simply when Epperson answered the phone.

"Hi yourself. You left before lunch. I was looking for you?"

"I came downtown to the V.A. hospital for those tests. I'm just leaving. I got so curious; I couldn't wait."

"Oh," Mr. Epperson said, sounding surprise. "Sorry. I didn't mean to upset you with that article about you soldiers in Nevada, but I thought. . ."

"I'm glad you told me about it. I felt like I had to come down here. My doctor couldn't see me for a couple of weeks, and I needed to find out what I could right away. All kinds of forgotten Army memories are coming to mind now."

"That's okay," Epperson said, "Did you find out anything?"

"Yeah. They checked my blood and liver and spleen and lymph nodes and said they didn't find any problems."

"That's good, Joe. Isn't it?"

"Yeah. It's rush hour on the *Distress-Way*, so it'll take me a while. I still wanna see my own doctor, Dr. Sands. I dunno about all this. It wasn't an impressive exam; it only lasted a few minutes. The government obviously limits what they'll say or do for us guinea pigs. The truth is, now I know we're still part of some damn government medical experiment. They're keeping records on us, almost secretly— but I don't think they ever intended to do anything to help us. Ya shoulda seen how fast the doctor called somebody after he examined me, and how careful he was not to let me hear what he said."

"I don't get it, Joe. Why? Do you think they are keeping a lot of secrets?"

"I dunno. The doctor just says, 'No follow-up.' That's all he says to me. He acts like he isn't allowed to say anything else, even though he could see how curious and worried I was."

"What good is the V.A.?"

"What?"

"That's okay, Joe. We know you're healthy. Besides, you can go to your doctor. At least you know him. Don't let the V.A. get to you. A lot of men have had to distance themselves from V.A. experiences. Listen to your own physician."

Not feeling better even though he had voiced his suspicions aloud, Joe told Epperson thanks coupled loosely to his goodbye. He located his car, not ready to meet the rush hour traffic; he drove the short distance to the river, where he could park along the East River Drive. Outside the car on a bench overlooking the slow-moving waters of the Schuylkill River, he looked back in the direction of the

V.A. hospital. After a moment, and alone on that stretch of riverbank, he spoke aloud, but softly, "What have they done to us? What now? I could really die young from some lousy cancer . . . If I got married, I probably shouldn't have kids … Maybe that's why Salina didn't fight that much against me leaving. She knew about the radiation…" He was remembering the girl he met while he was stationed near Portland, Oregon.

Remembering the V.A. doctor's words and the vets running down the hall with prescriptions, he continued speaking.

"If I get sick, I sure don't want to live on coping drugs. Geez, I can't keep talking to Epperson about this stuff, no, I can't."

Watching the river, its grayness flowing past him, he thought, *I gotta do something to make a difference. They ain't gonna beat me down, the stupid, idiotic bastards. Nobody's accountable. It must be the biggest medical experiment ever. The lousy...*

Somehow the quiet flow of the river lifted him above it all as he connected with its current and his own.

Joe rode home on the expressway, viewing the Philadelphia skyline and the charm of the Schuylkill River with a comfortable sense of belonging. At first, the domed Victorian buildings, jade green and statuesque, like ghosts of the nation's centennial, rose above the trees of Fairmount Park and beckoned him back to his youth. Then an image of the V.A. doctor's face soon filled his mind, and his memories, swirling like an artist's mixture of oils, carried him once again to the period of his life when the nuclear exposures had occurred. He saw the brown/black skin of Sergeant Masters' face, sweaty with fear as the man waited with the others to be decontaminated.

I gotta talk to Hank. Yeah, he'll know what to do. Masters could be anywhere, but Hank . . . We got too far apart. There were guys from New York, too. We gotta find 'em. This is scary. It's us against them.

~ ~ ~

After Joe went to his own doctor to be examined for his radiation exposures, he again became obsessed with the atomic bomb threats. Joe was controlled by the thoughts of his potential for developing cancer coupled with the sense of his country's betrayal. The authoritative voices he had recently heard ran through his mind like a repeating audio tape, repeating their disturbing messages over and over. They were especially loud during quiet mornings in his office at Glen Air when there was little or no work to distract him. At those times, he found it impossible to push them into the background—they buzzed in his head like sprayed bullets in the Laos invasion.

On one such day when the voices had become almost unbearable, Joe felt he had to take a break. As he rose from his desk just before noon, he heard Dr. Sands say, *"I could test you for it now and you wouldn't have it, but that doesn't mean you won't have it in ten years."*

He left the office, telling the receptionist that he would be taking a long lunch. She nodded. As he opened the door of the reception area, he remembered Dr. Stevenson from the V.A. hospital saying, *"You might get sick sometime and worry about it. It's our job to help you cope with it.*" He punched the down button and was relieved to find the elevator empty. *"You're a long shot,"* Dr. Stevenson told him. *"You'll probably live a very long life."*

Joe skirted the entrance doors and walked down the rarely used stairwell that led to the underground parking. *If I got cancer, how long would it take me to die?* He wondered the thought aloud. He visualized himself wasting away in a hospital and this brought on a frightening hallucination like the one he had experienced one night in a state akin to astral flight. He saw himself descending into the trench just before the bomb blast, then watched the desert floor react to the force of the explosion, bucking and rocking like an aviator's horizon level indicator when the airplane is swaying in a violent crosswind. He was being buried alive.

Forcing himself to take long, slow, deep breaths, Joe successfully calmed an impending panic attack as he covered the last few feet to his car. He pulled out of the garage and drove slowly along the two-lane road leading away from the building. The reiterations in his head continued, and when he caught himself driving mechanically, he forced himself to concentrate.

This radiation is like a parasite, he mused. *It's there inside me, and it'll be there 'til I die. They'll be able to detect it in my bone's decades later. How much did I get? What's it doing to my body?*

CHAPTER 5

When he stopped the car at the end of the road, he felt the pull of an old stone church on what the locals called Buckingham Mountain. The old church was built by runaway slaves. Many of those buried in the adjoining graveyard were black veterans of the Grand Army of the Republic in the Civil War.

Making a slow turn onto the highway, he drove a few miles to the seldom-traveled, poorly marked road most motorists would fly past without noticing. Making another turn, he followed the fresh macadam to the snow-packed railroad tracks. The wooded slopes on either side of the road, shaded from the sun by the dense trees, were thickly covered by a vanilla ice cream topping of winter snow that had survived several warm pre-spring days. Beyond the bumps of the rails, running water from the melt-off trickled across a neglected roadbed suffering from poor paving and exposure to extreme weather conditions, a combination that had laid open tire-pounding potholes.

Joe followed the twisting, pock-marked road as it climbed up the small mountain and barely held itself above the little cliff drops that occurred where rock formations jutted through the earth. Finding the widened section which he was seeking, he pulled the car over onto the sparse gravel and shut off the engine. On the opposite side of the road stood the old stone church he had discovered more than a year before when his father was dying.

During the last two months of his father's slow and consuming death, Joe often left work for his father's house to care for him. It was something he wanted to do, something he had to do. He fed his father simple meals, changed his bandages, bathed him, and shaved his stubby whiskers. His father slipped in and out of true alertness but, during his lucid moments, Joe was able to tell him how much he loved him. Joe studied his hands on the steering wheel, remembering his father's once competent but deeply scarred hands and the white and bony things they had become.

Joe knew the war story about his father being wounded in the battle of Okinawa. Both his father's hands were shot by the Japanese when he tried to reach out from his fox hole and pull a wounded American soldier back to safety. He sat back, finding himself experiencing a deepening mood of prayerfulness. He imagined a comforting voice, a woman's voice, addressing him; he heard it as if he were being spoken to by his own mind, the way humans think thoughts within thoughts. She seemed to be off in the distance and speaking very gently of hope and great love. The gentle voice was beckoning. His random-like imaginings created scenes in what seemed to be Japan.

Joe got out of the car and stood in the sunlight in a near trance. The winter snow was deep here and in a white silence around him.

The sunlight, diffused through a white fog, gradually grew brighter. Joe crossed the road and sank to his knees in a snow-cushioned corner of the old graveyard. He reached into the pristine whiteness and clutched some of it in his fingers, then raised it to his mouth and tasted the snow's coolness, its freezing wetness. His lips and mouth felt sanctified by the snow, and in an instant, as if he had tasted and communed with the universe, he was transformed by what he had done.

He was utterly fascinated by the immensity within him. He leaned forward, off balance for just a moment, responding to a presence vague to his newly acute sensitivities, like the feelings experienced during a pleasing song. He closed his eyes, sensing the state of his mind resting just behind the center of his forehead. Like the consumed snow, his fears, his troubled thoughts, and all his imperfections melted away.

He took more snow reverently to his lips, trying to revive the spirit that had visited his being, trying to keep it all within him. It did not return and, when he was unable to extend the experience, he felt a keen disappointment and something else. A period of peace had been conceded to him and he knew he would never forget the moment.

Joe stood and brushed off his slacks, unconcerned about the cold, wet spots on his knees. Turning in a slow circle, he consciously took in the hillside view and the church in the sunlight so he would remember this day. As he drove back to work, he felt relaxed, expanded, and free of all anxiety. Before turning onto the Glen Air's access road, Joe gazed into the side mirror of the car, looking back toward the hillside where the old church was nestled. He was gladdened by the thought of his special place and his new sense of peace.

~ ~ ~

A few days later, Joe decided to drive to Buckingham Mountain again and spend his lunch hour at the old church. He reached the widened road section and climbed out of the car to the stone steps at the front of the old building. He basked in the warm spring air and the sun rays breaking through the trees. He heard a few bird songs but only off in the distance.

A wizened old black man in overalls walked around the corner of the church carrying a long-handled shovel in one hand and two potted tulip plants in the other. The men saw each other at the same time, and the caretaker's face immediately broke into a wide smile of welcome.

"Hello there, stranger!" he greeted Joe cheerfully, setting down his things.

Joe returned his grin wholeheartedly. "Hello, yourself," he said, rising. "This is a beautiful place ya have. I hope ya don't mind my being here."

"No, no, dat's fine, son," the old man assured him. "Ah likes company." He had a deep accent infused with the gentleness of one of the West African linguistics and each time his voice became a bit shrill at the end of a sentence it was a surprise to Joe's ears.

"My name's Joe, Joe McGrath," he said, extending an arm to shake hands, "and I work down in the valley. Nice to meetcha, sir."

"Same here, Joe," the caretaker said, clasping the offered hand warmly. "Name be William Jackson. Dey calls me Old Bill."

"You know, Mr. Jackson, this place is very special to me," Joe said. "Many times, when my father was dying, it brought me peace. A short while ago when I had a big problem, I came up here and seemed to find the solution."

"Lotsa peoples feel dat way about dis place," Old Bill said.

"It's a good place to be," Joe agreed. "It makes you feel a sense of connection, you know, peace."

The caretaker looked at Joe thoughtfully. Finally, he said, "Dey be a service for Memorial Day on May twenty-third. Why don y'all join us? Peoples likes our music."

"Thanks, I'd like that, Mr. Jackson." Joe replied, pleased by the invitation. He nodded toward the front door. "May I take a look inside?"

"Of course, "He'p yo'self. Ah'll jes wait out here. Now calls me Old Bill, no more Mr. Jackson."

The front door was unlocked, and Joe went in alone. He stood before the simple pine altar, painted with thick white enamel like that used on the high baseboards and door moldings of the old Philadelphia home where he grew up. Two pictures of Christ that had probably been cut out of magazines and placed in cheap-looking plastic frames hung on the wall. The windows were draped with plain white sheer curtains and the floor was unfinished red oak.

When Joe finally turned to leave, Old Bill was standing in the doorway, silhouetted by the light outside. The man spoke in a relaxed and friendly tone as Joe passed by him: "This church be a hunnert and forty-three years old."

"Really?" said Joe, stopping at the bottom of the stone steps and looking at the church as if seeing it for the first time.

"Yessuh," said Old Bill. "Reg'lar services stopped more'n fifty years back. Dis was a church for black folk, y'see, an da cemetery was a burial place for former slaves. Many buried dere came up t'roo da Undergroun Railroad. Ah'm one o' the descendants o' the 'riginal folks here."

"Imagine," Joe said, shaking his head. "That's some great history. I'm glad you're taking care of this place. It deserves it."

As Joe was leaving, his new friend waved and called out, "See ya on da twenty-third."

Waving back cheerfully, Joe tuned the car radio to a station playing popular music. He was glad he had met Old Bill Jackson and stored the date for the Memorial Day service carefully in his memory.

He drove down the back of the mountain, enjoying the music from his car radio. His mind connected Memorial Day to the Army and the Army to the A-bombs. *How many guys are sick from it?* he wondered. *What was the purpose? We were really going to nuclear war?* The melodious harmonies swept through him, songs that should be lifting his spirit. Instead, he became somber. *But I'm not sick. Why would I be spared?* He knew emphatically, then and there, that all victims of nuclear weapons would worry about the radiation for the rest of their lives.

They got me and Hank when we were nineteen and they didn't care that we were their own soldiers, not their Japanese enemies. It was all a bunch of bureaucratic excuses for keeping their top-secret atom bomb schemes funded. They are the same poisoned-minded bastards that concocted bogus reasons for killing all those children in Hiroshima and Nagasaki. The wars are the eugenics nut cases tools.

He grabbed the steering wheel extra hard and said, "They killed the kids, the dogs, the old people and every living thing. . ." and with that utterance, he could not continue the thought to its conclusion. He pulled the car over to the roadside and sat shaking when he realized that his thoughts, his conclusions, his experiences, were all based on the evil of his nuclear experiences. In that moment, he knew that the madness in Nevada and Laos could only be explained by madness, a madness that he knew, still prevailed.

No one is safe. I was just one slug in the world, one private soldier once terrified in a trench and out among the Laotian peoples, all used as expendables to advance the nuclear threat, no matter what.

Coming out of his angry thoughts, Joe pulled himself together enough to drive again, faster this time as if he could outrun the madness, the evil of all nuclear explosions. Then slowly he remembered kneeling in the snow and his communion with the cosmos and he said, "Japan." For some reason he could not yet imagine, "It is all connected to Japan."

As he pulled the car into the Glen Air parking lot, he murmured, "Japan. They bombed the Japanese civilians and kids and hospital patients and churches and homes and us, just kids ourselves, me and Hank." His mind flashed back to that day that he and Hank climbed a fence at Jardel Recreation Center in North Philadelphia, and he saw the cop chasing them. With a lurch of his heart, he realized that it had been the same day they had decided to join the Army by pushing up their draft.

I gotta talk to Hank. He folded his arms across his chest and holding himself tightly he closed his eyes again and saw that cop chasing them and how they jumped into the rest of their lives that day in the north end of Philadelphia, when they jumped together off the top of that high fence that stopped the cop from pursuing the two boys.

CHAPTER 6

1968, CHICAGO IL USA

Hank Daniels and his wife, Charlene, were living in Chicago. They were sitting with Hank's mother in the apartment she provided when they eloped after Hank and Joe were discharged out of the army at Fort Lewis. Hank stood up and called the hospital asking for the Chicago University doctor his mother was sending him to see. He was physically weak again and his mother was agitated by his reluctance to continue seeking help. With the next appointment time and place worked out, he sat back down as his mother and Charlene were in the kitchen making tea. His mother, Doctor Murielle Daniels, wanted him to keep seeking support, and whatever medical help she could muster, to help her only son with what she suspected were the consequences of his radiation exposures.

Dr. Murielle Daniels, a black woman determined to beat all barriers, had become one of the very few black women surgeons in 1967. Her son, she was convinced, was the victim of reckless nuclear weapons experimentation and she was seething with rage. Only the boiling kettle in front of her held a likeness to her state of mind.

Three days later at 10:00 AM, Hank Daniels was sitting in the waiting room of Dr. Albert Wade, a black man who went through medical school with Hank's mother. The inner office door opened, and Dr. Wade appeared with warm concern and a faint smile. He did not close the door behind him while stepping into the waiting room where Hank stood up.

"C'mon in, Hank. I want you to meet someone. He'll be here soon."

"Who's that?"

An Asian doctor in his seventies appeared at another door. Dr. Wade, sounding a bit formal said, "Doctor Hito, I want you to meet Hank Daniels, Dr. Daniels's son. He teaches high school history. This is the man I was talking about to your mom, Hank. This is Doctor Hito, and you two have something in common. Come and sit down in my office."

"I teach at the middle school level, not high school, I just started," Hank said with a confident smile as the three men found seats in Dr. Wade's examination office. "Nice to meet you, sir. I mean . . . doctor."

"Mr. Daniels, I am pleased to meet you," Dr. Hito said.

"Hank would like to hear your history," Dr. Wade said to Dr. Hito.

Hank's face showed both heightened interest and caution. "What is your history, Dr. Hito? Your name is Japanese?"

"Yes, Mr. Daniels. I am Japanese; I was born in Hiroshima . . . Let me digress. The government limits what we can know about your exposure, but mine is an open book, a chapter in any history book. First, know please, I am happy I can agree with Dr. Wade, who told me you are responding to the medication."

"I hope so. But, about you, how old were you when the bomb was dropped? I never imagined meeting. . ."

"Meeting the enemy, Mr. Daniels?"

"God, isn't that something to think about?" Hank murmured.

Dr. Hito continued, "I was in high school. My high school was destroyed. Nothing was left but part of the chimney, my friends were gone. I was the only one in my class who survived. I became a doctor; I wonder what would the others have done if they lived? What if my country had only avoided war and its nightmares?"

Dr. Wade interrupted, "Hank, we want you to do something, something you would not expect us to ask."

Dr. Wade looked over at Dr. Hito. The old Asian doctor said, "We want you to let us use your blood samples for further testing in Japan."

"What kind of testing? Why me? You know the Nevada tests were all top secret?" He would never speak to anyone about Laos.

Dr. Wade, speaking to Hank while looking at Dr. Hito, said, "A Tokyo science lab can prove that your blood shows that you were irradiated. Your samples will be used as an evidence exhibit. American nuclear testing is public knowledge. They show documentaries on those atomic tests, Hank. The Army filmed them as part of their nuclear propaganda."

Hank asked, "What do ya you mean by evidence exhibits?"

Dr. Hito said, "The Nuclear Peace Movement in Japan has reason to believe that the UN as well as the international court will rule in favor of banning the use or stockpiling of nuclear weapons in a statute that also makes the possession of nuclear weapons punishable with a mandatory life sentence to any found guilty. The Major Powers will find ways around it but at least a law will exist internationally."

"Well, if that's the case, what would my blood mean to a World Court or the UN?"

Dr. Wade, speaking as if stating notes from a legal brief, said, "It is to establish and enter evidence against the proliferation of nuclear weapons and to make strong sanctions into international law that all those nations that possess nuclear weapons are a threat, and that maybe someday some of its leading authorities will be subject to prosecution as individuals."

Dr. Hito, his Japanese accent now totally controlling his diction, said, "In your case, a friendly government, a major voting nation member of the United Nations, used atomic weapons repeatedly, harming you soldiers and the environments and other human beings, their own law-abiding citizens, many years after Hiroshima and Nagasaki. It is evidence that no one on the planet is safe while nuclear arsenals exist, even if possessed by their own government."

Hank breathed words in an audible combination of forced air and language, "If you got 'em, you're using them against the world just by having them? Is this realistic thinking?"

"Compare not having the nuclear arsenals to what we have now. The Russians alone produced over eighty suitcase-size atomic bombs. Do we even know where they all are?" Dr. Hito asked.

Dr. Wade stood and paced the room, stopping by the open door and speaking while he closed it, "Hank, if you permit the use of your blood, you may have to testify someday before the World Court."

Dr. Hito, with a calm resolve asked, "Are you willing to give your blood? Would you enter a testimony in Japan if necessary? The growing association of us doctors against nuclear weapons may need witnesses such as you and those like you, Hank."

Dr. Hito took a few side steps backward and reached over Dr. Wade's desk and picked up a stack of black-and-white photo enlargements. He handed them to Hank. The one on top showed a child completely burned from head to foot obviously blinded and in a helpless-looking facial position for the cameraman. The second photo, a panoramic shot of a leveled Hiroshima, slipped out of his hand and floated face-up to the floor.

Dr. Wade said, "If your testimony is required, Dr. Hito may want you to travel to Japan and meet a Catholic bishop in Nagasaki in order to proceed more effectively with the mission. We would ask that you to tell the bishop about your nuclear test experiences. You could write an essay on the testing in Nevada from your point of view."

Without thinking Hank offered, "You won't want just me, a bishop would be better off with me and my Catholic friend, Joe…, we were in it together." He stopped himself from saying Joe McGrath's full name. Once again, he was setting up his defenses against all others, no matter what color or nationality or whatever they presented. He would not offer any more but his ears for now.

~   ~   ~

Hank Daniels came to an empty stretch of city sidewalk. He stopped and leaned against a large oak tree with the back of his head pressed on the bark of the tree. As an elevated Chicago train roared by above the other side of the avenue, he pushed himself off the tree and walked away along the long Chicago pavement. With his head down, a somber look formed on his face. He was asked once more when leaving if he would go to Japan and testify. Without answering Dr. Hito directly, he avoided the request and that next step. The idea of such a medical protest he would explore very privately and with the caution that was written on his face. He wondered if he would ever even talk to Joe McGrath about the doctors and their Japan connections.

Hank got on a bus and went to meet his mother at her Calumet office. Hank's mother insisted that Hank contact his old friend Joe and ask him to make an appointment at the Philadelphia V.A. hospital where she also had connections with a head physician. Hank reminded his mother that the atomic bomb testing was classified top secret and that he could not bring Joe McGrath into his dilemma and that she could get them both in big trouble. She cursed the government, but she also knew better than to further broadcast her knowledge of her son's source of sicknesses. "I know, Hank, I know you won't get any justice in a federal prison, son," she concluded bitterly.

~ ~ ~

As it was arranged, Hank and Joe were going to a secret meeting in Chicago. Joe made meeting Hank Daniels part of one of Mr. Epperson's Midwestern business trips. When he was able to break away from Mr. Epperson, he went to the place Hank Daniels picked for their long overdue get together.

Joe saw a tall black man in a light tan windbreaker standing on the curb, looking toward the cab Joe was in. The man stood bent at the waist, supporting the weight of his upper body on the fender of a parked car, and Joe could tell at a glance it was Hank, a much haggard looking Hank. He hurried across the street, scattering into raucous flight the pigeons that had gathered to feed on the bits of food some Chicago street-workers had left on the concrete. Daniels raised his arm in recognition and started for the closest opening in the traffic. They met in the middle of the Fifth and Wells intersection, oblivious to the rain, the puddles, or the traffic.

"Hank!" Joe blurted; his voice filled with joy.

"Hey, Joe, how the hell are ya? You made it!"

They reached out to shake hands, continuing to move forward until they were enfolded in a bear hug. They held fast for a moment and then released each other.

"Geez, it's really you! I can't believe it!" Joe stood swinging his arms in disbelief as he walked off a bit and turned back.

Arms akimbo, Hank stared at him, grinning. "You're looking great, Joe, like a movie star!"

They found the restaurant halfway down the block, their secretly planned meeting place.

In the dimmed golden lighting of the House of Bertine family Italian restaurant, sitting opposite each other in a booth, the long overdue conversation began.

After ordering drinks and their meals, Joe and Hank started to laugh about their changed lives. "Do you believe what we did as kids? It can't be true that all we had to do was hang on a corner, run with a gang of hoodlums, and chase girls," Hank said.

"It was true, Hank. We were having the time of our lives, one laugh after another. If there was no cops or nuns, we woulda been in city-kid heaven," Joe said.

"So that explains why neither you nor I ever became cops or nuns."

"Hold on, man. You'd be a dynamite nun."

"Yeah, now I got a kid, and a wife, a one-bedroom apartment, and leukemia: the whole catastrophe."

"Geez man, how's Charlene? What's your kid's name, Hank?"

"Not even close, it's Sally, but you can call her Hank, just expect Charlene to whoop ya. Maybe she wouldn't mind Hankette. Charlene and I have a great marriage. We're friends."

"What's your dad calling her?" Joe asked smiling and glad they already recognized the leukemia subject. "That worries me. Can you imagine one of his North Philly nicknames on your kid?"

"Ya mean like Nails or Ape?"

"Holy shit, yeah, they'd be among his first choices. Do you think anybody even remembered Ape's real name? Big Sal might be one of his offerings," Joe quipped.

"Remember we all called Albert Kennedy Ears, and my father had to embellish it to Wing-Nut?"

"You'd better hide your daughter from his sight."

"Ya but he'd still call her something totally North Philly. Remember Muscles Dannar and Brute Cavello? They were both girls, and then there was Bonnie Bad Ass."

Joe reached out his hand over toward Hank's side of the table and pounded it a few times.

Hank was doubled over at the waist when the waiter came over and picked up Joe's silverware and napkin from the floor as if it happened all the time.

Four naval officers walked by and the laughter between the two old friends was checked by the somberness of the officers.

Hank pantomimed a salute as they passed and then turned and asked Joe what he would want to accomplish the most now that they were back in touch with each other.

"More than anything else, that you were healed totally. We'll get some help and get some of the guys from the Army to help us. I'd like to see old Sergeant Masters and find out how he's doing." Joe blinked and said, "I've felt I would, 'cause of the old church."

"What's that? You kept talking about that old black church on the phone. I mean it sounded like a special place for you, but you're not trying to talk racial goodness junk, are you?"

"Racial goodness? What's dat? No, Hank, it's just an impressive old church building with a great history. I didn't tell you this part yet, but I went out there again a few days after you and I first talked, and I came across an old headstone for a James Masters. I wondered if Sergeant Masters was related to this guy, who died fighting in the Civil War, and it ended up that there were two graves marked Masters."

"Anything's possible. Two names?" asked Hank.

"Yeah two, problem is, I looked for Masters once, but didn't have any luck. Course, all I knew about him was his last name and that he's from Philly. Do you remember his first name?"

"I'm pretty sure it's Nathaniel and he was from a couple ah places. I don't think he was actually from Philly. He talked about the Carolinas. So, there's grave markers at this old black church with the name Masters on 'em?"

"Strange, isn't it?

"Very strange," Daniels admitted. "It was Masters, you, and then me; the three of us side by side in the trench."

"Yeah. Geez, I wonder where he is."

"James Masters, could be no connection," Hank said. "I don't think many white people know about the origin of black people's names. Some poor bastard was prob'ly called 'the Master's' James,' and when he was emancipated it got changed to James Masters. So, he was free, but still saddled with a reminder that he'd been a slave. It's disgusting, especially when ya realize they were prob'ly stripped of an African name that was really meaningful to the guy's family and ancestors."

"How simple." Joe began to realize that Hank, like a lot of other people, might not be open to the other mysteries of the old black church.

"What do you think we, you and I, should try to accomplish, Joe?"

"You beat the leukemia."

"Did you bring a big freakin stick?"

"Would the elimination of nuclear weapons be asking too much?" asked Joe.

"We have to do something because there is no real accountability laid on all the atomic bomb assholes."

"Yeah, total assholes!"

"Ya think?"

"I guess we're gonna try, aren't we?" said Joe wincing.

"So, where do we begin? I got the leukemia in remission, so now what?"

"Let's go get some help. Let's find some of the guys that were with us in Nevada. How's that sound?" asked Joe.

"I don't have a lot of strength anymore, so you're the main man, Joe. These Chicago doctors want us to do their shit."

"Yeah? So?"

"Well, I can do things like writing. They asked me to write an essay, but traveling to Japan would not be a good idea.

While I can do things, however some stuff is a bit much, like when you were in Cardinal Dougherty High School and Father B told you about an American bishop in Japan who was in Nagasaki when it was creamed. It was too much to deal with when I learned he was the same dude these Chicago doctors want us to meet up with. Ya know, when I was doing some research, I found out that, historically speaking, Japanese trade with the West was mostly confined to Nagasaki. When it was bombed, the city was filled with Koreans and Westerners, lots of 'em Catholics, and Japanese Catholics were treated like aliens or worse. That made me wonder why America picked it as a target," Hank said.

"How come? Was it because there were so many non-Japanese in it?" Joe asked.

Hank said, "I had an Asian history professor once who said that when the Shogun decided to engage in foreign commerce, the only port he opened was Nagasaki, allowing it to be corrupted forever as an offering to the benefits of trade with the barbarians. So, the great Black Ships of the West berthed there, and Nagasaki became defiled in the minds of many Japanese. So, who knows? Maybe the Japanese

Empire had the least to lose with Nagasaki, since much of the population was foreigners and an unusual number of Catholics."

"Yeah, but the Japanese didn't choose the targets," Joe said. In reply, Hank gave him a long, knowing look, during which Joe's eyes widened in astonishment. "What are you saying?" he cried out, coming to a standstill. "They did?"

Hank shrugged. "Dunno for sure but some people think it's a possibility. Not everybody in Japan wanted to follow the emperor or those Shogun holdovers in the Imperial government. They, like Tito in Yugoslavia, were ready for mass suicide, rather than forsake their chosen race mentality."

"So are ya saying some of the Japanese collaborated with us on where we should bomb in their own country, or are ya saying we picked a target that'd be the least offensive to hard liners in Japan?"

"Probably neither, maybe both, but even though it sounds preposterous, the evidence shows there were people desperate to end the war on both sides. Japanese diplomats were talking to the Russians and the British to gain a somewhat conditional peace. It's history, man."

"Geez! That puts a whole different slant on things," Joe said, as if he were stunned. "Helping the enemy to decide which one of your cities to destroy—what a wild thought! War is anti-human, pure madness!"

"Yeah," Hank said. "I always thought Nagasaki was an odd choice of targets but, now that I know the background, it becomes mysterious. I had to try to find the true facts first, though. It's prob'ly not a good idea to believe anything you hear from the authorities about a war, whether you're in it or it's long gone. People are brainwashed to believe what their preachers and governments tell 'em."

"And people get barbecued."

"Yeah, it's something to get sick and tired of, huh? I mean the public knows almost nothing in the end, look what they didn't know about us."

They fell silent, pondering their experiences and the mysteries that lay beneath the actions of world governments. They paid and left the restaurant. That morning they were to meet with the local leaders from the Doctors for Nuclear Disarmament, Doctors Wade and Hito.

To Wade and Hito, it was of great importance that their files on Joe McGrath and Hank Daniels contained information that the two Army veterans were exposed to multiple nuclear bombs in Nevada when they were soldiers in the U.S. Infantry and stationed in their own country. The atomic bomb tests were conducted in secrecy as preparation for a possible nuclear war. As Joe and Hank knew firsthand, it might have been in Laos and southern China.

At the time, that mission was one of the many dramatic, runaway events in the Cold War. It was not too shocking that Hank, while being treated in Chicago University for a related leukemia, was interviewed by doctors who belonged to the Doctors for Nuclear Disarmament. That same university was the site of the first success in their government building a nuclear chain reaction.

The doctors, and Dr. Hito, himself a survivor of Hiroshima, wanted Hank and Joe to participate in evidence-gathering to be presented to the World Court in the Hague. Joe and Hank were invited to attend the Japanese Nuclear Peace Movement's upcoming session in Tokyo. Hank feared U.S. government retaliation against both himself and Joe if they testified about military matters once considered top secret. Hank also feared he would become disabled by his leukemia if he made the long trip to Japan.

The doctors had obviously created background files on Joe and Hank. That became evident when Doctor Wade claimed to know one of Joe's high school teachers and a bishop in Japan that Hank was writing to in order to expand the knowledge he needed to use as a history teacher. This was a great surprise to both Joe and Hank. It was recommended to Joe that he contact the old teacher before going to Japan because the teacher knew the Bishop in Japan that Hank was already in touch with. Somehow that all made sense to the two veterans. Joe recently, he thought privately, visited the teacher, a Father B, his old scholarly priest from high school. After his visit to the V.A. and the office visit to Dr. Sands, Joe had gone back to see the old priest and confided in him: telling him about his concerns and his spiritual experiences at the historic black church. The old priest agreed to be Joe's spiritual director, not that he put it in those words. The old priest simply said,

"I always knew you would need some help, Joe."

Hank arranged the meeting with the retired bishop, His Excellency Dennis Garvin, OSFS, Bishop Emiratis of Nagasaki, himself a victim of the Nagasaki bombing, Bishop Garvin agreed to

Joe visiting when he learned of Joe's upcoming trip traveling to Japan on business.

Doctors Wade and Hito regarded Joe McGrath to be the perfect, strong, anti-nuclear-weapons advocate? Joe, as a promising young executive of Glen Air Company going to Japan to negotiate business contracts, had a scarred history—a health concern of pending cancer and mental health threats he would otherwise never have encountered. All the tasks and shared ambitions were combined as if by some sort of developing destiny, or so it seemed to the old priest who claimed, "A voice and its powerful message may come from where it is least expected. And be sure that many responsible for the testing never wanted any one of you soldiers telling the world what was going on in those trenches."

CHAPTER 7

1968, TOKYO JAPAN

The lights of Tokyo twinkled in the dusk of the far Pacific skies as if beckoning to the three men from Glen Air. Soaring over the great circle route to Japan, they had left New York in the afternoon, refueled in Seattle, and flown over Alaska. They departed the United States on April 13th by their calendar and were now about to arrive on April 13th in Japan.

As Joe studied the glinted sea below, ominous feelings about Japan surfaced and he became afraid that he might find himself in trouble. He grew even more frightened as the plane turned into its landing pattern. *How could this be? How could I even be here?* He wondered. *Those atomic martyrs, the children and the mothers, the old people, and all the centuries—my God, it's about them!* As the plane touched down, Joe wondered if he was mentally ill. A flight attendant smiled at him, and he became more relaxed. She sat down across the aisle during the landing, occasionally glancing at him.

Ken Epperson, along with the president of Glen Air, and Joe checked into the Tokyo Imperial Hotel. They ate dinner together, drawing the attention of the other diners by laughing out loud when Joe's large prawns (*kuruma-ebi*) were served with heads and tentacles still attached. Aware of the quietness of the Japanese hotel guests, Joe hoped the American executives with him hadn't disturbed or offended anyone. Later they toured the city by cab, enjoyed a few drinks and conversation in the Ginza section, and returned to their rooms early. The meeting with Chiyoda Industries would start at eight o'clock the next morning.

The following morning, they met with their Japanese counterparts to iron out the details of the language of a possible cross-license agreement. The negotiations became tedious, involving numerous discussions that lasted two complete days, but they were fruitful for Glen Air.

Epperson said, "Chiyoda wants to host a wrap-up and send-off for us the night before we leave. I'll be booking our return flight for the nineteenth, so we'll all need to be here on the evening of April eighteenth. That gives us almost three days to enjoy Japan."

"You guys'll hafta have fun without me after tonight," Joe said. "I got a schedule I wanna follow, and I prob'ly won't be back til the wrap-up."

"Oh, yeah, I forgot," said Epperson.

"Then we'd better get busy celebrating, fellas," said the president, throwing his arms around the other men's shoulders as if they were all bosom buddies. "C'mon, let's go to the lounge. Drinks are on me, and then we'll hire a cab and paint the town Jap red."

Joe joined them, but his mind had already jumped ahead to the next day. After they ordered their drinks, he excused himself and found a telephone. The bishop himself answered and, after a brief chat, he told Joe he was looking forward to meeting him. He said the train ride would take about two hours and agreed to see Joe mid-morning. After his meeting with the Bishop, Joe hoped he would have enough time to visit both Nagasaki and Hiroshima. In case it happened that he did not, he planned to go to Nagasaki first.

I'm here at last! he thought as he returned to the lounge. He was excited and anxious about the possibilities at the same time. *I wish I knew the language, but I should still be able to find some things out. Hank said they all study English in their schools, so that's a break. The name and address card that Doctor Hito sent me written in Japanese will help people lead me to the Bishop, but I wish I could learn Japanese right now.*

~ ~ ~

Joe's two-hour ride from Tokyo to Kure City had been quite pleasant as he found himself among the courteous Japanese. Contented, he hesitated to watch the train pull out from the center of the little village before he walked down the middle of the main street, gripping a small suitcase. The bishop's town, located on Japan's eastern seacoast, was a quiet place with a steady breeze from the ocean air. From the nearby mountain range, gently sloping fingers of land, like an open palm extended, seemed to offer the tiny city to the sea.

This is very different from Epperson's Tokyo, Joe thought, *with the Nissho Association guiding our every move in a huge metropolis.* He recalled Epperson's choice of Tokyo restaurants with simplified menus for Westerners, where the food selections were displayed as realistic wax models and visitors pointed to what they wanted "Shokudo," he called 'em. Joe wondered if he would find any Western food here. *I'm alone now; it's just me and Japan. I feel like a deaf mute not knowing the language. Man!*

Joe watched a Japanese driver, his face glued to the road ahead, and felt more like a stranger here than he had in Tokyo. Crossing a small intersecting street, Joe noticed the unmistakable stance of a chestnut. Drawn by its beckoning familiarity, he stopped to gaze into the comforting branches, spreading as only the chestnut does. The tree reminded him of the wooded paths of Fairmount Park in urban Philadelphia and for a moment he forgot where he was.

The raucous shouts of a street-wide mob startled him back into his surroundings. Swinging his head around, he saw he was about to be confronted by a horde of crazed-looking black silk–clad Japanese men and boys. They were pouring en masse from a side street, chanting, blowing whistles, and jogging and hopping in a spirited march.

As they came within half a city block, Joe noticed a large tarp-like shape of white silk blotched with red and black floating over the crowd. He heard a bugle calling out a rhythmic blaring jazz sound that disarmed him with its simple tune: happy, festive, and encouraging. When the men and boys drew closer, he saw they all wore white gloves and identical costumes; faces with headbands, determined expressions, flags, and banners began to pass in front of him. Each person had the same red Japanese calligraphy written on the back of his shirt. It reminded Joe of a scene from the Olympic Games. He decided they were a sports team of some kind.

Backing into the shade of the chestnut tree as they went by, Joe discovered that the red-and-black symbol on the huge white silk cloth they carried matched the symbol on their clothing. They bore the giant silk cloth with gusto and pride, and their attitude stirred Joe's emotions and earned his admiration. At last, the entire group had passed, and he could see their heels kicking up as they ran toward the coast shouting and chanting to the beat of the bugle.

Unable to suppress his curiosity, he moved back into the sunlight and the center of the street and followed, feeling like a kid lured into the big top by a circus parade. He soon saw large kites flying in the air over the beach up ahead and realized what the folded white cloth was. *It's a kite!* he thought excitedly. He began to move at a faster pace, wanting to see what was happening but then reminded himself that his appointment with the bishop would have to come first, and he forced his steps to lag.

Hearing an automobile slow behind him, he turned around and walked backward in front of it, waving and nodding to the driver, who returned his greeting. Joe motioned that he wanted to speak, and the driver stopped the car. Looking at Joe with curious expectation, he lowered his window, then motioned quickly with his hand as he shouted, "*Abunai!* [Look out!] " Alerted by the urgency in the man's voice, Joe jumped immediately, following the direction of the hand motion, and felt a rush of air as a car sped over the spot where he had been standing, blaring its horn as if infuriated.

"*Domo, domo* [Thanks, thanks]," said Joe, trying his best to remember what little he knew of the Japanese language.

"*Dozo yoroshiku. Shitsuree shimahsito* [Nice to meet you. I am leaving, Good-bye]," the man replied, and Joe became acutely aware of his problem. The driver's speech was an incomprehensible stream of sounds and Joe knew he would have to try to communicate through body language. Searching for the right method, Joe extended his hands upward, touching his fingertips like a church steeple as if he were praying. "Christian church?" he asked. "Where is Christian church? eh . . . *somima* [excuse] . . . eh . . . *sen* [me] . . . . Catholic?"

"*Sumimasen, Christian hontoo, desu ka*? [Excuse me, you are Christian, is that true?]" the man responded, leaving Joe totally stymied.

Suddenly Joe remembering the card Dr. Hito had sent, reached into his back pocket and pulled out his wallet. Joe remembered the old face of the Japanese American Doctor, Hito while he and another doctor examined Joe for possible radiation effects back at the University Hospital in America. Flipping through the glassine protectors, he stopped at the address card and showed both front and back to the driver. As the man's face lit up with understanding, Joe experienced a flood of relief.

"*Eeto desu nee* [Well, let me see]," the driver muttered as he stepped out of his car. He pointed to a side street and spoke a long stream of Japanese, all the while smiling and nodding to Joe.

His bewilderment showing plainly on his face, Joe slowly spoke the words he thought were Japanese for "I don't understand."

"*Shinpai suruna* [Don't worry]," the helpful man said, opening the passenger's car door and motioning to Joe.

Joe accepted the offer without hesitation. Saying "*Domo, domo*" with a smile and many nods, he climbed into the car and closed the door.

"*Hora are desu* [Look at that one]," the man said, pointing at something beyond the windshield.

"*Domo*," Joe said, not knowing what the man was saying. He shrugged and held up the palms of his hands, hoping he was using a universal gesture.

"*Wakarimasu. Hombun* [I understand]," said the man.

Unenlightened, Joe remembered another Japanese word and said cheerfully, "*Tomodachi* [Friend]," mispronouncing it terribly.

The driver smiled at Joe's attempt and replied, in a very friendly tone, "*Are wa nan desu ka?* [What is that over there?]" They turned a corner, and there before him Joe saw the Catholic church.

"*Domo, domo*," Joe said, smiling and nodding again as he climbed out of the car. Waving, he said, "*Sayonara* [Good-bye]."

In response, the man said the word his way, "*Sayoonara*," and drove away.

Filled with gratitude for his good fortune, Joe approached the rectory. Standing in the large foyer, Joe noticed the movements of people in the store area, just beyond the inner doors. A lovely

Japanese woman wearing a simple cotton A-line dress came to greet him. As she opened the door wider, he said confidently, "*Hajimemashite?* [How do you do?]" He continued in English, speaking slowly. "I am Joseph McGrath from the United States. Bishop Garvin invited me to visit him today."

The woman greeted him with a polite smile. "*Hajimemashite?*" she said agreeably. "*Fumioka desu. Sumimasen McGrath-san desu ka? Hai, soo desu?* [I am Fumioka. Excuse me; you are Mr. McGrath, yes? That is so, no?]" Joe's face fell when he heard the Japanese words. Because Bishop Garvin spoke English, he had assumed the other people at the church would, too. He wondered how he was ever going to get past the language barrier. Noting the expression on his face, the woman stopped speaking for a moment. When she resumed, she said haltingly, "Forgive me, please, McGrath-*san* . . . I forget the bishop instructed me to speak to you in English." Although her speech was clear and her pronunciation excellent, Reiko had not spoken impromptu English for many years, and she found she was much slower at translating her native language into conversational English than into written words.

"Excuse me, please," Reiko said, turning away to serve a pair of elderly customers. She rang up three religious' articles, made change, and exchanged brief pleasantries with the two ladies. When they were leaving, she motioned to Joe to follow and walked a few steps to the reception desk. Gracefully seating herself behind it, she motioned to him again, indicating a nearby chair.

"You are the bishop's secretary?" Joe asked as he sat down.

"*Hai*—I mean, yes, McGrath-*san*."

"The bishop?" he asked, questioning the man's whereabouts with hand and eye gestures.

"We are very sorry," she said, her English becoming smoother as she spoke. "He is not in his office today. He is away. A very important matter occurred last night that required his immediate attention. The bishop was called to Nagasaki. He is very sorry not to meet you today. It was a sudden, change. You understand?"

"Yes. Oh. Well, that's okay. I, eh—" Joe was immediately, deeply annoyed by the absence of the bishop and how far he had traveled to meet him but quickly tried to hide it. He thought the woman might not have noticed because she rarely looked at him directly, keeping her eyes cast down and occasionally glancing at him obliquely. He took advantage of her shyness, or politeness, whichever it was, to study her features and could not help admiring her shining blue-black hair, her large almond eyes, her creamy beige complexion, and her small, even teeth.

Reiko, aware of Joe's scrutiny, pretended to stare at a potted plant standing in front of her, but in truth, she was highly adept at using peripheral vision, and she was studying his face at the same time he was studying hers.

"You have been on the train a long time. Would you like to freshen up and join me for tea?" she asked. "In America, I believe they call it breakfast."

The invitation surprised Joe. "With you?" he blurted. "I mean— I'm sorry, I didn't mean to be rude."

She smiled. "Yes, I would like you to share tea with me."

"Thank you. I would like that very much. Do you have a place where I can wash my hands?"

Reiko nodded and led him into the hallway of the living quarters, where she pointed out the lavatory.

Joe quickly washed his hands and splashed his face. Emerging from the restroom, he walked to the large, sliding, translucent rice paper doors that opened to the grounds behind the Bishop's home. As he looked through the rice paper, he touched the door gently, feeling the outside chill, and sensed the shelter of the Catholic church that had been with him since his boyhood. He slid the door open slightly, staring at the garden plants still in their winter rest, and saw an encysted bud moving in the wind.

Charmed by the scene, he opened the door fully and stepped into the garden, closing the door behind him. He walked up on a small arched wooden bridge that crossed a tiny pond. The sound of his footsteps carried underneath the bridge into the brisk Japanese air. *My God*, he thought, *I'm here, really here, in Japan.* As he returned to the sliding door, he reached up to touch a small late bud, and the twig it was attached to snapped off in his fingers.

The bishop's secretary appeared with trays of food and motioned Joe into an adjoining room. They sat on mats, and she presented a tray to him. Charcoal burned gently in a space in the floor nearby, providing cozy warmth.

The woman's face captivated Joe, noticing again that she never looked directly at him; she did look at the small bud he was holding. Her eyes followed it as he placed it on his tray. Like the sound of his steps on the wooden bridge, something about her cried out to him,

"Japan, Japan. . ." He found her face beautiful, her movements so serene, her existence so modern, yet proceeded by a multitude of his imagined generations. *She epitomizes her country and her culture,* Joe thought, greatly pleased.

They ate in silence, enjoying the simple meal. When they had finished, she poured tea into a miniature cup and served it to him. He smiled a thank you and raised the cup to his lips. As if breaking the silence at that point was a required ritual, she began a conversation. "The garden, you like?" she asked.

"I do, but I wish it were spring so I could see everything in bloom."

"Soon will be spring. You… can you come again?"

"No. Only one time, Japan, your country, is far from my home, too far."

"The bishop explained that you came to learn about my country."

"Yeah, I came on business with others, but mostly I came to learn, maybe just to feel whatever impact Hiroshima and Nagasaki and the people of those cities might have on me."

"May I ask what kind of business you are doing here in Japan?"

"My company manufactures greenhouse controls, ventilation, irrigation, and air handling systems, and we are working out a contract for a new design with a Japanese corporation."

"Greenhouse?"

"Yeah. Glass houses for growing. You know hot house?"

"Agriculture accomplished in glass enclosures, neh?"

"Exactly."

"Too bad the bishop is not here. He would be so excited to learn about you and your occupation."

"I'm sorry I missed him. I was looking forward to our conversation."

"It is unfortunate. Most days he would be here. He lives here, you know. He is officially retired, but every time an important decision must be made, he is called to Nagasaki!" Her gentle laugh tinkled like wind chimes.

"You have a good command of English, and you speak it very well."

"Thank you. The more I speak, the more I seem to enunciate."

"Where didja learn English, if I may ask?"

"When I was a child, I was raised and educated in English by the Sisters until I graduated from the orphanage. I was sponsored by a Christian family, and they spoke English as well. And when I came here, the bishop helped me a great deal."

"What kinda work do you do for the bishop?"

"Typing, translating—with assistance from the university. The bishop is a theologian—he has a doctorate—he is an author."

"Really, what's he written?"

"Many books and many essays, eh, his latest a book called *The History of the West in Nagasak*i."

"Nagasaki?"

"Yes."

"May I see it?"

"Of course."

She left for a short time and returned with a copy of the manuscript. She handed it to Joe, saying, "He has been published in English and Japanese, and four other languages."

"I'm sure it's very interesting," Joe said, flipping through the pages and feeling a rising excitement as individual words and phrases caught his eye. "Thank you."

"You may want to read it on the train. The bishop loves to have his work read. He says the Japanese historians have been remiss about the important presence of outsiders in Nagasaki."

"I'm eager to read it. As the Bishop knows, I'm very interested in both Nagasaki and Hiroshima."

"Yes, he has three chapters on his mission to establish the illegality of nuclear weapons. And that reminds me, the bishop asked me to tell you what my Uncle Shiro related to me about Hiroshima."

"I'm amazed that you can tell me about Hiroshima," said McGrath. "You see, I was in atomic explosions like the ones that destroyed those cities."

"You? Oh, ah. You look too young for those events, but the bishop shared that information with me."

"Not the same 1945 explosions; different ones, years later. Atomic bombs were tested in Nevada—a desert in my country—and I was ordered to be a part of those tests."

"Tests… this I know. Yes."

"You understand?"

"The B-29s carried those bombs, now missiles."

"Well, yeah. I was in two tests, four bombs. Three were carried by missiles. I was a soldier, and I was very close to the bombs when they exploded. D'ya understand?"

"Soldier. *Waa, soo desu nee* (Oh, that's right)," she couldn't believe what he was saying without being so amazed that she reverted to Japanese.

"Hibak'sha, you know?"

The woman frowned and flicked her eyes quickly across his, tacitly questioning.

"Hibak'sha. You know, H-I-B-A-K?" said Joe.

She appeared baffled.

"Hibak'sha," he repeated, "the people who were in Nagasaki and Hiroshima when the bombs exploded and survived." Joe was becoming frustrated by his inability to communicate. "I feel connected to the people in those two cities, and I wanna go to Nagasaki and, if there is time, Hiroshima."

"You wish to see Nagasaki and Hiroshima, yes? What you describe is beyond any Japanese person's understanding."

"Yes," Joe answered, not sure how much of what he said she had understood. "I wish the bishop was here," he said, trying not to show the degree of disappointment he felt. "I had many things to ask about his bomb experience before I went to those places."

"I understand, Joseph."

"You have me at a disadvantage, I'm afraid," Joe said, noting that she addressed him by his first name. "May I ask your name?"

"Oh, please pardon my poor manners!" she exclaimed, her hand flying to her mouth. "I am so sorry! I forgot to introduce myself!" Joe could sense her dismay at her breach of the rules of protocol. "My family name is Fumioka." That is my formal name in Japan, but the bishop always tends to use first names, as you do in America. So please call me Reiko."

"R-A-Y-K-O," Joe said, spelling it out phonetically.

"R-E-I-K-O," she corrected him mildly, with humility in her voice.

Joe bowed his head respectfully, "In the traveler's book," he said, "it tells me to say, '*Dozo yoroshiku* [It is nice to meet you],' correct? Reiko is a proud sound. What does it mean?"

"*Dozo yoroshiku*, McGrath-*san*. Reiko means *gifted*, or *clever*. Does your name have a particular meaning? I should, I suppose, know this from my Catholic education."

"Yes, Joseph means *one who shall add*."

"Ah, yes," she said. "And now," she continued, "If you would care to listen, I would like to tell you about Hiroshima. It is something the Bishop said you would want to know."

"I'm all ears," Joe said, not realizing he was speaking American slang.

A pleasant sound, almost musical and lilting, filled the room as Reiko laughed and said, "I know that saying! 'I'm all ears.' The bishop says that!"

"You admire the bishop, yes?" Joe asked.

"*Hai, soo desu* [Yes, that is true]," she said. "He is a holy man."

"He certainly struck us as such," Joe agreed.

"Now let me refresh your tea, and I will relate to you the story about Hiroshima my uncle told me."

Joe felt a strange excitement. *Who would have thought the bishop's secretary would be connected to Hiroshima, too? But in what way?* he wondered, impatient to hear. He moved his legs into a more comfortable position and prepared himself to listen carefully.

"It was the day I left the orphanage where I was raised," Reiko said, handing him a full teacup. "My Uncle Shiro, at that time a Shinto priest, was summoned to escort me here to work for the bishop. Before he brought me to this place, he took me to Hiroshima to tell me about my family history. My mother and father died there when I was a year old. They were killed by the atomic bomb."

"And you survived?"

"I was even more fortunate than that; I was with my grandparents in the country and knew nothing of what had happened."

"I am so sorry about your parents," Joe said, feeling a lump in his throat. He imagined their horrible death, and then the feebleness of his apology mortified his spirit.

Reiko began to recount where Shiro had taken her and what he had said. Joe didn't need to hear much before he knew he would want to have a permanent record of her story, and after she had spoken a few sentences, he interrupted and asked her permission to turn on a recorder. She was puzzled by his request but agreed willingly. He removed a small tape recorder from his suitcase, and when he was ready, she began again.

As Reiko spoke, Joe was enchanted by her tone and the tenderness of her words. As his mind pictured her descriptions, his eyes lost their focus, and the mauve forms on her clothing at which he was gazing metamorphosed into nebulous patches of color. He was immensely pleased to be with her and to be listening to her, in spite of the basis of her story. *This would not have happened*, he thought happily, *if the bishop had been here. She would've been different. I guess I should be thankful for whatever emergency called him away. She is lovely.*

~ ~ ~

As Reiko was nearing the end of her story, a yellow car with a black insignia on each door parked alongside the church building in front of the bishop's residence. Two well-dressed Japanese men, one carrying an expensive-looking camera, got out of the car and knocked on the rectory door. Hearing the knocks, Reiko concluded her tale quickly. She handed Joe an old black-and-white photograph of her parents that had been her uncle's, then bowed and left the room hurriedly to answer the door. Joe was still studying the old photograph when she returned with the two men.

"These men are from the newspaper," she announced.

The man without the camera spoke up in a friendly voice. "Hello. Mr. McGrath, is it not?"

"Yeah," Joe answered.

"Welcome to Japan! I am a reporter. My name is Toson, Natsume Toson. And this is my cameraman, Kanagaki-*san*."

Joe bowed at the names. The Japanese men did not, and Joe was confused about how to act. The men's presence made him uncomfortable, and he wondered what they wanted.

Reiko began to explain. "These men have heard about you and your visit, and they—"

"What?" he interrupted in utter amazement.

"They were informed of your visit here and, as they put it, the controversial nature of your interest in Hiroshima and Nagasaki."

"Controversial nature?" Joe repeated. "Did the Bishop arrange this with them?"

"*Iie* (No)," she said emphatically. "Surely not!"

Joe was incredulous. He noticed his heart rate increasing rapidly. *Is this the danger I've been sensing,* he wondered? He crossed his arms over his chest defensively. "Whadd'ya want?" he asked, facing the two men. He had taken care to enunciate his words carefully when speaking with Reiko, but for these men he felt no such obligation and lapsed into his full urban Philadelphia accent.

"We are covering the days of this town's *Toku-age* [Kite War]," the man who called himself Natsume Toson answered.

"It's what?" Joe asked.

"Kite War," said the reporter. "Also called *Hato-age*," he added.

"Kite—oh, yeah, I saw part of that. A bunch of Japanese guys were running down the street with a really big kite, but what's that got to do with me?" Joe was totally confused.

"Are you familiar with Japanese Kite Wars?"

"No, just what I saw coming here."

"My cameraman is famous for his filming of Kite Wars."

"Is that right?" Joe didn't get the connection. He was beginning to think maybe there wasn't any, and his suspicions were confirmed when the reporter abruptly changed the subject.

"May I ask you three questions?" the man asked, stepping forward.

"I guess," Joe said, picturing Doctor Hito, while suspecting him to be behind this surprise.

"You were in the radiation from nuclear tests, right? Was that in the United States?"

"I was in four A-bomb tests there, yeah," Joe answered, frowning as he did so.

"Do you think Japan should listen to you?"

"I haven't said anything to Japan."

"Are you on a spiritual mission?"

"You'd like to make a fool outta me, wouldn't ya?"

"What do you mean?"

"That's question number five, Mr.—sorry, I can't remember."

"Toson, Natsume Toson. Please call me Natsume, or Nate, if you prefer. Many people called me Nate when I was studying in the States."

"What paper are ya from?"

"We are from *Tookyuoo*—excuse me, I mean Tokyo."

"Ya mean ya wanna write me up in a Tokyo newspaper? Ya can't be serious!"

"That's our assignment. We'll turn in the results, but whether it gets printed isn't up to us."

"Ya sure speak good English."

"I studied journalism at Southern Cal."

"No kidding. That sounds like something from an old war movie."

"It does, doesn't it? It's so Hollywood, but it's true."

"Look, I don't wanna be in a newspaper. Why don'tcha just forget it?"

"You are our assignment, Mr. McGrath, and we must follow our orders. You can treat it as you wish, but we have to turn in a story of some kind. I believe using your answers will be better than making something up."

"Why would ya do that?" Joe asked, alarmed by the thought.

"So, we'd have something to turn in, of course," Toson said indifferently.

"Geez!" Joe exclaimed. Giving up, he dropped his arms to his sides. "Okay," he said. "What else d'ya wanna know?" The photographer advanced toward him, snapped two photos, and stepped back. Reiko stood quietly aside, a look of puzzlement on her face.

"Are you going to both Hiroshima and Nagasaki?" Toson asked.

"Nagasaki, definitely," Joe answered. "Hiroshima, too, if I can stay on schedule. I don't have much time."

"You're taking the train to Fukuoka Station and Nagasaki?" Without waiting for an answer, Natsume asked, "Did your government send you?"

"No, of course not!" said Joe in a raw voice.

"Are you taking the trains alone?"

"Yeah, I'm taking the trains, and I'll be by myself."

"Thank you, Mr. McGrath," Toson said. "I think that gives us enough."

Reiko spoke up then, asking in Japanese how the men knew where to find Joe. Kanagaki took her picture, and then answered, "*Tookyuoo.*"

Turning to the reporter, Reiko asked him what was going on. "*Ii desu ka? McGrath-san, wa? Daijoobu desuka?* [Is everything all right? How about Mr. McGrath? Is he safe (okay)?]"

"*Anoo, ee karma kara Tookyoo* [Well, his friends or enemies created this, starting in Tokyo], Karma." Toson said, uttering the words carefully. "*Wa zannen desu ne* [Certainly that is too bad]."

"*Hontoo desu ka?* [Is that the truth?]" Reiko asked, wanting to know if there was another explanation.

"Hai," said Toson, nodding his head vigorously, his eyes studying Reiko.

The man looked sincere, and Reiko believed he was telling her all he knew. Feeling she had learned all she could and that she was being rude by continuing to speak in Japanese, she turned to Joe and said in a low voice only he could hear, "These men really don't know—or they won't say clearly—why the Tokyo newspaper is interested in you. They were sent here, you understand?"

Copying her undertone, Joe said, "He's concerned, isn't he? Did he say it won't be good? That's what it looked like he was saying."

"*Hai.* He sympathizes with your situation but is unable to explain it."

Toson removed a business card from his wallet and handed it to Joe with a degree of trained formality, holding it in both hands and adding a slight bow. "Here is my contact information," he said. "If you have difficulty of any kind during your travels, call me, and I'll do what I can to help. *Ja mato* [I'll be seeing you]." The two men bowed to Reiko and turned toward the door.

"Sayonara," Joe called after them as they departed.

When she heard the front door close, Reiko turned to Joe and looked at him compassionately. "Maybe he is right; maybe whatever is happening to you is your fate," she said.

"Karma?" Joe asked.

"Yes, karma," she replied with a sigh. "I asked Toson what was happening, and he said your friends or enemies, or your karma created this.

"That's the only word I understood. Whadd'ya s'pose he meant by that?"

"In part, it means he doesn't know, since each person's karma is private. Buddhists and others believe that every thought, word, and action send energy into the world that, in time, is returned to the sender through other people."

"Send out bad energy and get bad energy back?"

"Yes—or the opposite. Karma forces people to face the consequences of their actions and thus improve and refine their behavior or suffer if they do not."

"What else did you ask him?"

"If you would be safe."

"Will I?"

"I hope so," Reiko whispered, her eyes downcast, "but I cannot be certain."

Joe was shocked. He put his hands into his pockets and touched the undeveloped flower he had found in the garden. Drawing it into the open, he considered the withered bud lying across his palm. "Sorry," he said. "I didn't mean to break this off. It's like me, out of season and in a stranger's hands."

"The bud is from the past," Reiko replied. "You are the here and now."

"I sensed danger in coming to Japan and now here it is."

"Danger in Japan?"

"Yeah. Shouldn't I be concerned? Wouldn't you be if a Tokyo newspaper had ya on its radar for nuclear issues? I dunno what's going on, but I feel threatened by something."

"Perhaps. You should not be in the newspaper, especially not the Tokyo paper."

"It wasn't my idea."

"I know. It is bad they came."

"It might help if I knew where the danger was coming from, but I got no idea."

Hesitantly, Reiko offered her opinion. "It could be from a secret organization. Surely from time to time you have heard about such things. In Japan, these groups never really seem to go away. They get pressured from time to time enough to make them remove themselves from public view but are never totally eradicated."

"Secret organizations?" Joe asked, blinking his eyes. Contrary to what Reiko was thinking, Joe knew nothing about such factions in Japan, except what Hank had said about them. Once again, the involvement with that Doctor Hito came to mind, but he couldn't connect it with any certainty.

Reiko nodded; her expression serious. "There is one gang in this country that still carries much hatred for Americans and anything nuclear. So, you do not want it set against you. Coming to Japan to see and become informed about Nagasaki and Hiroshima is something you should do very privately. There is much bitterness and bitter memories that should not be awakened."

"But all I wanna do—all I ever wanted to do—is visit the cities," he protested. "And my trip over here was for legitimate business. Where would anybody get the idea, I've got a nuclear agenda, or I'm in cahoots with the government?"

"This is good that you are warned," Reiko said. "I do not know why they would think such things, but if they are watching you, you should know that these thugs are fanatical about their beliefs, and you must be very careful what you say in public."

"Geez! This is Japanese eccentricity!"

Reiko waved a hand through her hair and said, 'I don't recall the meaning of the word you just used."

Oh, I'm sorry. What is that word?"

"Sorry, what did you say, eccent, something?"

"Eccentricity?"

"Yes, what does it mean?"

"Strange, that it is strange."

"Thank you, sorry to interrupt. I was warning you to be careful what happens when you are dealing with the public in Japan."

"I'm sure you're right, Reiko. I'll be careful what I say, but I'm here, gangster fanatics or not. I can't change that, and I can't just leave, I got my job to think about, and not when I'm so close to seeing these cities. I hafta see it through. After your description of Hiroshima, I feel like I've already been there, but I still want to see it. I just hope I have time. Today's the sixteenth, and I gotta be back in Tokyo by the evening of the eighteenth. By the time I leave Nagasaki, Hiroshima may not fit in, but I'm gonna try for it."

"That, of course, is up to you," Reiko acquiesced with a slight bow. "May I please see your train ticket?"

Joe removed his ticket from his wallet and handed it to her. She looked it over carefully. "You are leaving today at 3:30?" she asked.

"That's the plan," Joe said.

"Please forgive my intrusion, I may go with you?"

"To Nagasaki?" Joe was shocked by her words. He had not envisioned having company—certainly none as comely as Reiko— and he felt his heart rate accelerating.

"*Hai*," she said, "and farther, if necessary. You have not been in Japan before, and the bishop instructed me to guide you personally in your travels. I know the language and the country, and I can help make your trip easier. The bishop would be doing the same if he were here."

"I'd like that very much," Joe stammered. "It's very nice of you."

"It is our pleasure," she responded. "Now come with me to the train station and we will exchange this ticket for two seats together. You may leave your suitcase here."

They went to the train station, where Joe hung back as Reiko conversed with the ticket seller and concluded the exchange in minutes. She gave the tickets to Joe to put in his wallet for safekeeping, and they returned to the rectory by way of the beach.

Standing off at a distance, he and Reiko watched the spectacle of the Kite War. The din of whistles, drums, bugles, and human noise, though muffled by the winds, was constant and frantic. The sky was filled with the large kites, and the beach was alive with moving crowds in a frenzied swirl of color. Spirited shoving contests alternated with quiet interludes, and now and then small children could hold the kite wires with their teammates. Old men gazed into the air with patient endurance. There was no letup in the efforts of the teams. Many flag bearers bravely led their teams in charges against the wind and the other teams. A few kites fell slowly, with inspiring humility. Some triumphantly returned to the sky amid great applause and the singing of metal pulleys turning fast.

They returned to the rectory, where Joe packaged up the recording of Reiko's story and addressed it to Hank. After he had added a brief explanatory note, Reiko added what she knew would be enough air mail postage and placed the envelope in the rectory's outgoing mail. By two o'clock they were eating lunch and by three o'clock they were headed to the train station, Joe carrying their luggage.

"I'm glad you're going with me, Reiko," Joe said as they walked toward the train station. "If I seem nervous, please understand that this has been an upsetting day. I can't believe that reporter came to interview me. It doesn't make sense. I'm nobody."

"It is odd," Reiko agreed. "I have been thinking about it and I have concluded that the bishop must have told him about your coming to our village. I cannot imagine any other way they could have known you were here. If this is so, you have nothing to worry about. The bishop would never endanger you or expose you to unwanted publicity."

"I wish the reporter had told me. If I knew it was Bishop Garvin, it would make all the difference."

"You must ask the bishop about it when we see him in Nagasaki."

"We're gonna see him?"

"Oh, yes. He is there at the cathedral. I called him, and he wants me to bring you to him as soon as we arrive tomorrow afternoon. He is looking forward to meeting you."

"I'm glad I'll get to see him," Joe said with the trace of a smile.

CHAPTER 8

I t was early April in Japan, and in the offices of the largest newspaper in Tokyo, a neatly dressed reporter of increasing public fame took a folded memo out of a notepad he always carried and opened it on his desk and read it again:

To: Natsume Toson

Tokyo: In Osaka and Tokyo today, there is a reaction to media contact from an anonymous source in the USA. The Nuclear Radiation Victims' networks are interested in an upcoming visit by an American survivor of excessive radiation exposure from experimental nuclear maneuvers in Nevada and/or on a Pacific Island. The source says this man claims to have a mission in Japan and to be connected somehow to Nagasaki and Hiroshima. We suspect an association with a new or unknown anti-nuclear organization. The man is otherwise described as a sales agent for a small American manufacturer. His name is Joseph R. McGrath.

We know that he will be arriving on April 13th. He will be staying at the Imperial Hotel in Tokyo, and he will attend meetings with

Chiyoda Industries there beginning April 14th. The source says that after the business meetings have concluded McGrath plans to visit Bishop David Garvin and then Nagasaki and Hiroshiima but did not provide the dates.

Other reporters may have been dispatched to intercept the visitor and cover this story, but they will most likely look for him in Tokyo. Since you and your photographer are already scheduled to be in the bishop's town to cover the Kite Wars, we believe this may be the best place for you to obtain an interview.

~ ~ ~

Reiko and Joe arrived at the station platform, which was beginning to fill with its daily passengers. Joe felt hemmed in by the growing crowd and looked around apprehensively.

"Here we are." Reiko said.

"I gotta admit," he said, trying to calm down, "I'm feeling uneasy. I can't explain my attraction to Japan or my fear of it. I just know I'm scared way down inside, scared of being in your country. Maybe it's a premonition, maybe it's nothing—but that reporter got me spooked. I didn't expect those newspaper guys to track me down like that. Why would they wanna talk to me, anyway? That reporter asked if I had a spiritual mission. Maybe his question was connected to the bishop, but I don't think so."

Reiko looked up with a puzzled and sympathetic expression.

'That guy was after me. He wanted to know what I had to say; he didn't care about anybody else. Asking about the tests like he did—I was a nuclear issue to him. I dunno what he was after, but it sure didn't have anything to do with kites."

Beyond Joe's shoulder, Reiko was studying a paper prayer hanging in the window of a sidetracked train engine. "I am not you," she said, "but your concerns are easy to understand."

"I can't believe I'm gonna be written up in a Tokyo newspaper. I'm in a weird predicament, and I dunno why. I don't get it."

"Perhaps the Bishop will be able to enlighten us on this matter," Reiko said.

"I sure hope so." He reached for his wallet to get the tickets. "Strange, isn't it?" he muttered. "Some things in life come to us the way hailstorms or earthquakes do. No wonder we ask *why*."

"I hope that you will like this ride. Southern Japan is much warmer than here, and the countryside retains much of its ancient beauty."

"I read in a travel brochure that I will see a country in a timeless response to its own beauty."

"That is so," Reiko replied. "Do you hear the train?" She steered him to the end of the station platform so that when they boarded, they would be in the first car. She knew he would have a more panoramic view from one of the front seats.

The train pulled up to the platform with a loud grinding of wheels that swallowed up all other sounds. Abandoning any attempt to speak, they climbed into the first car and claimed seats in the very front row. They continued to sit in silence for quite some time after the train pulled out, content to gaze out the windows at the passing scenery.

Joe spoke first. "What crop is that all covered with straw?" he asked, pointing out the window at the fields.

"It is what you would call indigo, a major source of blue dye for clothing and paint pigments."

"Oh, yeah, indigo plants."

"You know about them?"

"Yeah, a little bit. It's the pink flowered knotweed, correct? Too bad I didn't get here in the spring or summer."

"Ah, yes, it is first pink. The springtime is best, yes? Summer is grand, but it is very hot in the summer." Reiko was gladdened by the small talk. Despite all his awkwardness and oddities, there was something about this man—a gentle innocence—that she liked a great deal. "The train will bring us into spring in the south. It will be warmer there."

"I'll look for signs of spring as we go."

Reiko nodded amiably and made herself more comfortable. Their conversations touched on many different topics as the train sped south. As if discovering her all over again, Joe sensed her unusual open-mindedness. Even though he knew she had probably read or was told about Hank's account of the nuclear tests, he felt the urge to share his own reactions with her. He told her about the trench and the atomic bombs, and then, unexpectedly, he related his final experience at the old Black church on Buckingham Mountain.

She listened patiently and, when he concluded his strange account, she looked up at the ceiling of the train for a while before she responded.

"Maybe you realize that if you tell others about this, you might be ridiculed."

"I know," he said. "You're only the second person I've told. I'm Just remembering how it makes me exhausted." Joe murmured as he propped his head up by placing his palm on his forehead and his elbow on the armrest, and within minutes he had fallen asleep.

Reiko sympathetically decided against pointing out one of the oldest Shinto shrines on Honshu. It was 7:30, they were already over two hundred miles south and as she had promised, spring had made its arrival.

Waking, he will see the blossoms of Japan like a land in renewal, the happiness of the cherry trees, Reiko thought. *Strangeness always travels with everything nuclear, even him. The nightmares never cease to stalk.*

Joe dozed fitfully as images of Reiko, the reporter, and the cameraman flooded his imagination. He would open his eyes for a few minutes, look over the landscape and comment on its beauty, and then succumb to sleep once again, still aware that he was fighting personal demons,

Reiko did not disturb him until they approached the small town where she planned for them to stop over. She gently nudged him awake, and they descended the train steps and walked the short distance to a small hotel. Alone in his tiny but extremely clean room, Joe placed his wallet, his comb, and the withered bud on the dresser and stretched out on the bed. When Reiko tapped on his door just before six in the morning to rouse him for the remainder of their journey, he was still sleeping soundly.

Reiko purchased rice wafers and fruit earlier from local vendors at the train platform which allowed them to eat a light breakfast while sitting on a wooden bench.

"This is a crowded country," Joe remarked as he bit into a fresh peach. "Ya said this is a small town, but it's teeming with people—and so early in the morning."

"Ah, yes!" Reiko replied. "But the population is decreasing."

"I think I'll have to take your word for it," Joe said, astounded by the number of people who walked past. "I sure can't tell by looking."

Reiko smiled.

"How much longer will we be on the train?" Joe asked.

"Another six hours on this one," Reiko answered. "We will transfer to a different train at Fukuoka and ride it for another two hours to Nagasaki."

"I'm glad ya chose this stopover," Joe said, stretching his arms above his head. "I feel rested and relaxed now, thanks to you. If I'd done this my way, I'd be very tired by now. Thanks."

"You are welcome," Reiko said automatically as she peered down the track. "Our train is coming. We should get ready to board."

Joe picked up the suitcases and followed her to a spot from which they could enter the first car. They leaned away when the engine squealed past, then climbed the steps and took the front seats again. They passed the time reading, conversing, gazing out the windows, and napping, as they had before.

Joe spent a great deal of time trying to study the landscape. At one point, after dozing, he opened his eyes halfway and looked out the tinted window at a wide expanse of rolling grasslands. He was able to distinguish bright yellow mustard rows surrounding fields of barley sprouts.

A spring rain was falling, and dancing droplets found their routes in the curvature of the train's sleek glass windshield panels. Farther south, Joe watched the work of the wind in blossoming trees. He closed his eyes momentarily, remembering the withered chamomiles, the trellis covered with barren wisteria in its seemingly agonized twisting, and the *sado* rocks in the bishop's garden.

Reiko, waking from a half-sleep, noticed Joe still slumbering. She reached for the bishop's book, tucked into the seat pouch. She opened the book where a piece of paper was folded between pages. Joe's writing was on the paper. She read it quickly at first and then paused realizing that it was about the war with the West. Within seconds her eyes were tearing as she read the scribbling about the lasting horrors of the American war a second time. Embarrassed by her invasion of Joe's privacy, she put the book back into the seat pouch.

As the train slowed and thumped over cross tracks and they went through the undersea tunnel, she recovered her composure and realized it was almost time to transfer to a different train. She nudged Joe gently and was surprised to find him awake.

"We have reached Fukuoka and will now take, *eeto* (well) eh, the Japan National Railroad to Nagasaki," she informed him.

"Are you upset, Reiko?" Joe asked, looking at her intently. "Your eyes are tearful."

Reiko bent her head low in obvious embarrassment, and Joe, realizing his lack of sensitivity, said, "Please forgive me."

She nodded as they gathered their things and walked in an uncomfortable silence from one train platform to the other. As they neared their transfer spot, the mellow tones of a bell tolled ceremoniously through the station.

"Listen to that," Joe said, relieved by the music of the bells. He knew that the deep ringing was not connected with mass transit.

"The bell is lovely, especially in the city, where peaceful sounds are needed," said Reiko.

"It has a mystical and ancient quality."

"In Buddhism, the bell is the voice of the Buddha. It, like the Buddha, represents a faith that tries not to trouble the soul."

While Joe wondered what Reiko meant, he dismissed questioning her amid the bustle of switching trains. On the national train they settled in for the last leg of their journey passing the fishing villages on Omura Bay and the rice paddies until they were replaced by the suburbs of Nagasaki.

~ ~ ~

The Nagasaki train station was crowded with travelers, and Reiko and Joe made slow progress. Reiko heard Joe's name being announced repeatedly on a bullhorn by a voice with a heavy Japanese accent. Swiveling her head to locate the caller, she spotted a news van with a mounted television camera at the curb outside and an overweight, neatly dressed man standing a few feet beyond the exit doors, a portable microphone in one hand and a megaphone in the other.

Reiko tapped Joe on the arm finally gripping it tightly. As she did, Joe realized what was happening.

Joe froze still and watched as the reporter raised the megaphone to his lips and called out "Joseph McGrath," looking around at the streaming passengers to see if anyone was responding. Joe's spirits fell when he saw the newsman's eyes light up; an obvious foreigner in Japan, Joe was easily recognized among the sea of Japanese.

"McGrath San?" the man shouted excitedly. "Are you Joseph McGrath?" He charged through the crowd, rudely pushing people out of his way, as he headed directly toward Joe. Catching the reporter's excitement, many followed him, forming a tight ring around the two men from which Joe saw no means of escape. The rush of strangers heading toward him was unnerving and Joe frantically searched the crowd for Reiko. He was relieved to find that she was only a few steps away. He hoped she would not go any farther away; he was afraid she would become part of the crowd and they would be separated.

"What does an American nuclear test victim expect to discover in Nagasaki?" the would-be interviewer asked, holding the

JOHN A MCCABE

microphone a few inches from Joe's mouth. The question, amplified by the bullhorn, resounded throughout the waiting room area of the station, and more people began to drift over to discover the source of the commotion. Joe stared at the concrete floor.

Looking back at the television camera to make sure its view was unobstructed, the newsman tried again. "Will you answer our questions, Mr. McGrath?" It appeared most of the people in the station had no idea what the English words meant, but some understood and stopped to listen. The eyes of the crowd darted back and forth between the two men as their owners tried to understand who Joe was and why he was being videotaped for television.

Joe's eyes followed a crack in the concrete until they reached pant legs and sneakers, and he wondered idly if the fissure was from 1945 or some previous quake. His gaze fixed, he listened to the murmurings of the crowd. Finally, he raised his head to eye the faraway camera lens and took a long, quiet, deep breath. He gazed into the faces in the crowd, and they suddenly all looked the same, like a formation of foreign soldiers, all staring at him.

When the microphone impatiently dropped away, Joe muttered, "*Tomo dashi* (friend)," remembering his brief and cordial encounter with the Japanese man who gave him a ride to the Bishop's church. Seeming almost alive, the microphone jerked back to his chin.

"What did you say, sir?" The man was motioning insistently to a man with a portable television camera to get him to move in closer to the interview.

"Eh... Friend, I hope. Geez! How'd ya know I'd be here? How'd ya know anything about me?"

"Why, you're front-page news, friend! In Tokyo, Osaka, Hiroshima—many places—with pictures, too."

Joe was terrified. Reiko had said his visits to Nagasaki and Hiroshima should be undertaken privately so as not to trigger the gangs that hated Americans and anything nuclear. Joe thought, *And apparently that Toson guy had splashed his picture all over Japan. Talk about making yourself a target! And now this Nagasaki reporter wants to do the same thing in Nagasaki. Now this is about her safety,* he hoped Toson hadn't published Reiko's picture, too.

"Let's move over here, shall we?" the man asked, sidestepping through the crowd as he cleared a path for Joe to follow.

"Why?" Joe asked, even as he trailed behind.

"It is just a better background, Mr. McGrath." They stopped in an area with a bench backed against a wall, inviting the crowd to reassemble into a semicircle. Some of the group had begun to drift away, but new onlookers were still arriving.

"I don't—I didn't come here to be on television. I'm not looking for publicity."

"But, Mr. McGrath, you're here, and people want to know why your government sent you to Japan."

"But they didn't—I have nothing to do with the government," Joe protested. "I'm not here to be in the news. I'm afraid I might say something wrong."

To attract a larger audience, the newsman tried another tactic, first asking McGrath a question in English and then repeating it in Japanese. "The people ask simple, easy questions: Why are you in

Japan? What happened to you? What is it you want here? Has your government adopted a different stance on the nuclear issue?"

Before Joe could formulate any answers, he noticed that the man's eyes were focused on the crowd of curious onlookers, and Joe watched the plump face sag with dismay as his scheme backfired. Instead of drawing more observers in, his questions had caused many of them to depart—a behavior typical of the Japanese, who tended to shy away from open, direct confrontations and who might even be more skittish at a public gathering, especially one where anything to do with atomic bombs is presented.

He's not lis'nin, Joe thought with alarm. *My God! What do I say now?*

"Why don't we sit down?" the reporter asked, gesturing toward the bench. As Joe automatically sat down, he glanced over at Reiko, who frowned a warning at him, and he immediately popped back up again.

"The newspapers have dubbed you 'The Curious American in Japan,'" the reporter persisted, standing with him. "Do you agree with that description?"

"Curious?" Joe murmured. "In this country ya can see where human beings, our brothers and sisters on this planet and their children, were subjected to the terrible death and poison of the atomic bomb."

"Are you going to Hiroshima?"

"I dunno if I'll have time for Hiroshima," Joe answered, forgetting that Reiko had taken care of that problem. "I got a deadline for returning to Tokyo."

"Mr. McGrath, you were in nuclear tests performed by your government in your country, or in the Pacific, correct?"

"In my country, yeah. It seems that's what started all this—part of it, anyway."

"What do you mean, part of it?"

Joe sighed. "Look," he said, "If I knew what to say to you—what I should say—I would, but I don't. I just came here to think and feel. Sometimes we just have to feel. I wanna see this place. Forgive me, but I'm uncomfortable with all this." He turned away from the microphone and began to make his way between the remaining Japanese people. "Please excuse me," he said to the people in his path. He had already stopped himself from trying to say Japanese words a few times, but finally stumbled through, "*Sum im... a... sen*. Excuse me." He stopped near Reiko.

"What do you think of Nagasaki?" the reporter challenged him.

Joe's eyes traveled to Reiko's face. "Geez, we've only gone fifty feet into the city," he pointed out. "We're still in the train station. So, I dunno."

"You're together?" the newsman interrupted, snapping his fingers to order his cameraman to get a shot of Reiko.

"Yes," Joe said in a breath of regret. Instinctively concerned for Reiko's privacy, Joe had hoped to conceal any further information about their connection.

As the video camera swung toward her, Reiko quickly lowered her head and stepped out of range. She turned her back and moved slowly through the crowd, advancing steadily toward the exit. Joe kept his eyes on her, walking fast through the throngs in the station as politely as he could, and finally caught up. Outside the station, Reiko also set a fast pace as she led him into the city, leaving the onlookers and the television crew behind.

Joe began to take in Nagasaki with its heavy industry and surrounding mountain hillsides. The two travelers stopped on a bridge. *I'm in Nagasaki! Oh, my God! This place is—it really exists.* He felt his emotions surging.

"Ashes, Reiko! Ashes!" he breathed, remembering vividly what he had experienced in the old black churchyard. "The red was bright, but that hideous lightning-colored blue, a strange flash of blue-white brightness." He saw the scene in the Nevada desert of the first bomb, its shock wave plowing across the ground with unearthly speed. Studying Nagasaki before him, he cried out, "Oh, God! There was nothing left in places but a death carpet of gray-white ashes. Mothers and babies burned to death in destroyed homes." He moaned in sympathetic agony.

Reiko enclosed Joe's hand within her own. "Are you saying you have been here before? I don't understand you, McGrath-*san*."

"I know, Reiko, it's confusing," he said. "In Nevada, when I was in the bombing, I ran over smoldering patches of atomic ash, spots of blackened earth, ashes, and bright red floating embers that seemed to be boiling. Every one of us there—and everybody here—expected to live full lives, to have children and grandchildren, to be a part of normal human history. But that's not the way it happened." For some time, he stood in silence looking at a large persimmon tree standing along the river. His body was twitching, and he had a strong desire to go over to the tree and sit in its shade.

Reiko broke the silence, saying, "Atomic disease is still found here."

"Yeah, from atomic insanity. Like some fierce beast separated from God, the Second World War was a mysterious nightmare of every race of people killing people, fathers and sons killing, killing, and killing."

His eyes scanned the wooded hills with a somber intensity. "Reiko, it's a mistake for me to be in the news," he said. "I can't take that. I feel like another bomb is falling on me right now."

"Shall we go to the cathedral, Joseph?" Reiko suggested. "The bishop will be there."

"Yeah, but first I'd like to go to the site of the martyrdom— Saints Hill, at Nishiza, or something like that," said Joe, remembering the historic crucifixions. "I need to be there. I gotta find out what my connection is."

"We can walk to the place of the martyrdom," Reiko offered. She was puzzled by his knowledge and apparent deep association with the Twenty-Six Martyr's Monument on Nishizaka Hill overlooking Nagasaki Bay, the shrine that marked the Shogun's historic decree of Christian expulsion and the interruption of Western influences on the main islands of Japan.

At Saints Hill they found a large limestone monument with full-size figures of the twenty Japanese and six Europeans, all of them Christians, who had been crucified four centuries earlier. Joe stared at the crosses formed in the shrine and then at the large cross at the top. He studied the Japanese calligraphy a long time, until its configurations seemed to match his own tangled sense of purpose. He touched the pink flowers on a bush nearby and remembered the agonized whimpers and cries of the crucified in his experience at the black church.

Turning toward the inner city, Joe said, "Seventy-five thousand dead the day they dropped that bomb, and all of humanity threatened. Jesus."

"You are pacing?" Reiko asked sympathetically. "That is how I felt in Hiroshima, at the place of my parent's death—and my Uncle Shiro, too, I believe we both were reduced to pacing."

"I wonder what I'm doing here," Joe said. "I don't really know. I believe a great change is coming; I dunno how. God! I feel what happened here, and I just know—I know the devastation, I know how these people died, I know how they felt. And where are the survivors now? Am I s'posed to learn more about it? Or should I—I dunno—I can't explain it. And I'm shaking. Look at me!"

"Let us go to the cathedral." Reiko's calm voice had a soothing effect on Joe's jangled nerves.

"Yeah. Okay."

They walked through the Urakami region to the large salmon-colored brick cathedral. Reiko, anxious to find the bishop, quickened

THE GIRL IN JAPAN

her pace. Realizing Joe was no longer by her side, she looked back and saw him sitting at the base of the white statue of an angel. He seemed like an old man who had walked too far and needed to rest, so she left him and went on to find Bishop Garvin.

She returned after a few minutes accompanied by a kind-looking man whose face was all smiles. "Joseph, this is Bishop Garvin," she said. "Your Excellency, I am honored to introduce Joseph McGrath, the American." Joe stood up and walked toward the bishop, who extended his hand in greeting.

"Thank you, Reiko," the bishop said, shaking Joe's hand. "How do you do, Mr. McGrath? No one has ever been so happy to see me as Reiko. Hah! I feel important. Mr. McGrath, we are truly honored to meet you. Reiko, unlike herself, exploded with emotion about your visit. Perhaps it is no accident that my meeting was moved to Nagasaki. Let's go into the cathedral."

"Thank you for seeing me, Your Excellency. We make an unusual group, the three of us." He was thinking of their connection by nuclear experiences.

"Unusual? I've been called that before. My mother always said I had big ears. Is that what you mean?" The bishop guffawed with pleasure, holding a hand across his stomach. "Just joking, Joe," he smiled as he clapped his free hand on Joe's shoulder. "Your friend Hank Daniels wrote about you, and we have learned much from his letters. He's a descriptive narrator and an effective writer, and I'd bet he's a good schoolteacher, too. His use of those simple declarative sentences is awakening. His tapes were compelling. He understands the flaws of governments and the checks and balances that can't be neglected if we're ever going to eliminate war.

I was astounded by your experiences. You should have never been asked to undergo those tests in Nevada—and now you two are out to change the world, huh?"

The more Bishop Garvin talked, the more Joe liked him; he was especially drawn to the man's verbosity and jocularity. *Why couldn't more of the hierarchy be like this?* he wondered briefly, remembering from childhood, the pomposity of a Philadelphia cardinal riding in the Mainline area in a long black limousine, and approving his name being engraved on plaques on the walls of buildings while he was still alive.

Suddenly the rotund man in the natty business suit appeared in the distance, and Joe's eyes widened in anger and alarm. "It's that guy from the news!"

"Who?" the bishop asked as the man cautiously approached.

Reiko looked at Joe, who was vigorously waving the reporter off. "He was waiting for us at the train station with television cameras," she answered. "He must have followed us here."

"Mmm-hmm," the bishop responded.

"Are you aware of the news media's interest in Joseph McGrath?" Reiko asked.

"No, I've been sequestered here and haven't seen the news. What in blazes is going on, Reiko?"

"Did you talk to the news media about the Americans' meeting or McGrath-*san*'s visit?" Reiko asked, answering the bishop's question with one of her own. "The reporters following Joseph have upset him very much."

"No, of course not. Someone—I have no idea who—delivered a letter to me asking when I expected him, but I never replied."

Joe, watching the reporter retreat, asked the bishop, "So you didn't somehow alert the news media to my being in Japan?"

"Not a chance, Joe, I assure you," the bishop answered.

"I wonder who did, then," Joe said, screwing his forehead into a puzzled frown.

"How very strange all this is!" Reiko exclaimed. "What do you think is happening?"

"I'm sure I don't know," said the bishop. "Oh, I almost forgot! Reiko, your Uncle Shiro called today. He said he was concerned about your safety, and now I know why. He wants you to call him right away."

"I will, Your Excellency," Reiko said. Lowering her voice so Joe could not hear, she added, "Please have a talk with Joseph. You must hear what he says about—I cannot explain. You will have to hear for yourself."

"I will, my dear. Now go call Uncle Shiro so he will stop worrying."

"Of course." Reiko headed for the rectory.

"Let's go to the cathedral, Joe," said the bishop. "I think we have a lot of talking and praying to do."

"I could use some time there, Your Excellency," Joe replied

CHAPTER 9

That evening the conversation among the three was sparse, especially after dinner. The Bishop and Reiko stole glances during the meal that conveyed complete bafflement about the news media's involvement and Joe McGrath. Nonplussed by their visitor's publicity, both Reiko and the Bishop began to retreat within themselves. As the evening progressed only Reiko truly came around to Joe, while the bishop became more and more engrossed in conversation with the other residents of the rectory. Bishop Garvin, with occasional studied observations of Joe, covered his concerns with thin smiles when their eyes met, or he found Joe looking at him. Later it was only Reiko who spoke to Joe at all.

It was dark when Reiko and Joe left the bishop, and Reiko took him to a traditional Japanese-style Nagasaki hotel located in a residential section on a hillside overlooking the reclaimed Dejima Island in the Bay of Nagasaki. The fact that their lodging was both out of the way and traditional promised a night of sound sleep with no interruptions, but Joe spent restless hours on a tatami mat. Giving up at about 4:00 AM, he walked out to the garden area that overlooked the bay, where he found Reiko seated on a garden bench under palm branches. She scooted to one end of the bench so he could join her, and they spoke quietly for a while.

A light drizzle began to fall, and the area where they were sitting suddenly became an isolated, cozy little nook sheltered by the palms. The solitude, the darkness, and the patter of the raindrops on the leaves imparted a sense of being alone in the world and within this sanctuary that was so conducive to confidences.

"The bishop is worried, isn't he?" Joe asked.

"He is a good bishop. You were supposed to meet, and Nagasaki was the place for your meeting. We can only wait and see now. At least you know he had nothing to do with the news people."

"Karma again?" Joe asked, and he could sense Reiko nodding her head. "Yeah, it seems obvious now, doesn't it? Rieko, I know your home was Hiroshima, but does Nagasaki evoke the same feelings and questions?"

"No. To me, nothing is like Hiroshima. I never told anyone this, but an unexpected mental, arctic mindfulness, a deep chill, came over me when I was seventeen, while my uncle was describing the morning of the bombing. I felt hypnotized, and I even stopped hearing what he was saying and began to experience a living nightmare. I began to imagine things around me from other worlds and murmuring from the pit of evil."

She stood and turned facing toward Joe, where the palm fronds above were separated just enough for an errant moonbeam to dart between their tapered fingers and illuminate her whitened face with its concerned expression and the glistening black hair that framed it like a hood.

She whispered, "The imagined or real voices soothed my senses at that time, as if I had not imagined them. I also thought I heard words reaching out to me from somewhere over the Oto River, but I could not understand them."

Joe felt no need to respond other than to give her a knowing glance, as Reiko sat down beside him again. Joe's mind flashed back to the Nevada desert and the music and voices he imagined and then how the Sergeant came up on him and questioned him after the blast. The images faded with only E7 Fogey's concerned face outlined and the spent scene of the ruined desert in a fog of memories.

Joe and Reiko sat silently, wrapped in a sense of unexpected ease that made the night inviolable. The thin, almost undetectable mist that had been filtering through the palms and keeping them cool was so fine they remained almost dry, and eventually they told more of their stories to each other. The depth of their new friendship was a wonder to both, and both were surprised by how comfortable and relaxed they were with each other. The ingrained barriers of their cultures all but vanished as Reiko rested against Joe's chest and shoulder seeking comfort.

When the rainfall increased and large drops dripped through their tropical canopy, they moved hurriedly to another bench in a dry place under saga and camphor trees. It was darker and cooler there, with only the light from the walkways. Joe sat first and invited Reiko to sit close to him wrapped in the warmth of his arm. She held his arm against her breast as she sat beside him. An excitement within each of them kept them from speaking. Neither of them wished to move from the embrace until the sun lit the horizon.

The morning was overcast with easy lighting, and all seemed peaceful. To avoid detection by the media, they took a cab to a different Nagasaki station. At this time Reiko was so mystified by the depth of their understanding of each other that she felt shyness about going with him. At the station she whispered to him, "The Bishop will need my help now, Joseph, so I must stay in Nagasaki and return home with the bishop. I know he would want me to do that."

She handed him her notes on what she wanted him to do in Hiroshima.

Joe took the 5:00 train alone.

~   ~   ~

Joe made it to Hiroshima, where no reporters bothered him. Like Nagasaki, the city clawed at his emotions as he went about his tour following Reiko's instructions. He stayed for just over two hours, until it was time to catch the outgoing train to Tokyo. He arrived at the Imperial late that afternoon and, when he checked at the front desk, the clerk handed him a scalding message from the Glen Air president:

Joseph, we want to see you right-away. Your atomic publicity stunts here have embarrassed our Japanese friends and Glen Air. Perhaps you should have come here on your own time. You must discourage those news people. The Japanese executives are curious about you traveling un-chaperoned with a Japanese woman, too. None of this makes sense to us.

Irritated by the message and its haughty tone, Joe stuffed it into his pocket. As he withdrew his hand, another piece of paper dropped onto the carpeted floor. Joe bent to pick it up, recognizing it as the second folded paper Reiko had given him just before he boarded his train. Wanting to postpone his discovery of what it might say, he put it back into his pocket and went to his room.

As he entered, he was impressed once again by the understated elegance of the Japanese décor. "Less is enough," he thought, looking around the spacious room with the overstuffed chairs and large desk that had been provided for Western guests. He closed the heavy drapes, noticing that their color blended seamlessly into the orange walls, making the room a one-color experience.

Feeling increasingly melancholy, he paced slowly around the room on the plush carpet. He hadn't yet been able to detach himself from his trip, Reiko and the Bishop, or Nagasaki, and Hiroshima and thoughts of them floated through his mind in bits and pieces. Finally, remembering Reiko's note, he pulled it out and sat on one of the comfortable chairs to read it. Her fine script jumped out at him as he opened it:

Now with the wind here in this gentle time—and our time here— like looking into that mist we knew—we see the past moving through the world . . . and know that peace on earth is due.

Joe's melancholy was replaced by a feeling of well-being and the satisfaction of knowing he had accomplished more than what he had come for. *It was worth it*, he thought just before he heard a knock on his door. Looking through the peephole, he saw a familiar face. "Oh!

It's you," he said, hoping he did not seem rude as he tried to remember his Japanese visitor's name.

~   ~   ~

"Hello, Mr. McGrath. How was your trip to Nagasaki?" his visitor asked as soon as Joe opened the door.

"Well, it was… very impressive. Eh… I couldn't really begin to explain."

"You didn't call me, so I assumed you didn't have any problems."

"That's correct. Besides, I had a guide."

"Ah, yes, Reiko-*sama* was with you. You were fortunate, as she is an intelligent and very beautiful lady," Natsume said, putting his hands together with a thoughtful expression on his face.

"She most certainly is," Joe agreed. "Why don'tcha come in?"

"Thank you. I appreciate that." The Tokyo reporter settled himself in one of the Western chairs and waited for Joe to do the same, then blurted, "Why did you not plan to go to Hiroshima?"

"But I did!" said a startled Joe.

"You did? You went to Hiroshima?"

"Yeah," Joe said, "the day after I arrived in Nagasaki. I could only spend a few hours there, but I did manage to fit it in. Why are ya so surprised?"

"Why did you tell the television people you didn't have time to go to Hiroshima?"

"That's not what I said—did they report that I...? I don't understand any of this. Why d'ya ask?"

"Mr. McGrath, you really have no idea what is going on, do you?"

As Joe studied the man's facial expressions, he saw interest rather than hostility and decided this was a reporter he might trust. "Name's Joe," he said cordially. "Your name just came back to me, I'm happy to say. You're Natsume Toson, right?"

"Correct."

"So, why didja come here, Natsume?"

"As I said before, I am willing to help you in any way I can, and I think one way I can do that is to inform you about the problem you have here in Japan."

"Problem? Ya mean the news reports?"

"Partially, but it's more than that. May I explain?"

"G'won ahead. I'm all ears." Joe remembered using that expression with Reiko. *There's trouble*, he thought, and he wished she were with him.

"If you did go to Hiroshima—" Natsume began.

"Whadd'ya mean?" Joe interrupted. "I just told ya I did go to Hiroshima."

"As you certainly should have. I believe you." Natsume looked quite sincere.

"Then why would ya question me about it?"

"I'm sorry," Natsume apologized. "Before I try to explain, perhaps you should tell me about your visit to Hiroshima and what you did there while I take notes."

"Okay, but this'll hafta be off the record unless I give ya permission to print it."

"Fair enough," Natsume agreed, reaching for his notebook and pen.

"Well, I was alone, which made navigation difficult." He rummaged in his suitcase and pulled out a city map. "All I had was this map," he said, handing it to Natsume. "I could've ridden the tram Reiko told me about, but somehow that didn't seem right— don't ask me why—so I left the train station and walked, even though with every move I felt like the weight of the world was on me. I can't explain that, either."

"Is it true you are working for the United States government and that you have a mission to fulfill?"

"Geez, you can't imagine how crazy that sounds to me! My boss left a message for me about all this; I guess they read the same thing in the paper and it sounds like they've had enough. But to answer your questions: No, I most definitely do *not* work for the U.S. government. And yes, I *do* have a mission but it's my own personal mission and has nothing to do with anyone else."

"That's straightforward. Thank you."

"Are you Christian, Natsume?"

"No."

"Oh. Okay, then." Joe grabbed the hair over his forehead and sighed.

"Must I be Christian to understand what you tell me?"

"I dunno. Maybe, and maybe not."

"Why don't you tell me, and we can decide afterward? I think it's important that I know everything about your visit there."

"Okay. I need to tell somebody, I think, and this is off the record?"

"Til you say otherwise," Natsume assured him.

Reassured, Joe continued his account. "As I walked down the street, Heiwa I think, Peace Street or Peace Boulevard—I kept thinking of the past and the bombs and God—or, I guess, Christ. Well, you look 'round Hiroshima and ya can't tell anything happened. Then I saw the Atomic Dome and all and—Oh, God. I kept hearing, all the way down the street, the words 'I am, I am, I am.' I didn't understand what was happening, but it got me stirred up. I turned my back to the Dome and stood staring at the front of a department store, seeing the reflection of the Dome in the front window, for about fifteen minutes, trying to understand my feelings."

"Did you go inside the Dome and see the exhibits?"

"I couldn't. They were right across the street, and I was so upset my legs wouldn't move. I kept seeing what I saw on the desert in Nevada—the explosion, and then that mass destruction coming at us like an immense asteroid crashed onto the surface of the earth and was rolling into us—and I was afraid. I never before dreamed of feeling bad because I was an American."

"You left Hiroshima then?"

"No. When I decided not to enter the Dome, it seemed like a spell had been broken and I was able to walk away. I went to a shrine Reiko told me about and asked to see a monk there, her uncle Shiro, who had witnessed the destruction in Hiroshima. Reiko had already told me his story but thought it'd be good for us to meet. I was mentally lost, like somewhere in a dream. I felt guilt. I think I lived some of the guilt because it was the guilt of all humanity. I imagined, in a crazy way, men in khaki shirts—soldiers, I guess. I dunno. And a woman crying for her children, facing away from me—not real, ya know, just imaginary."

"Yes. Please go on."

"I was there a long time, it seemed. Like in a dream, I was praying—I guess it was praying—and even if it wasn't—well, I felt like God was with me there. I even lit some incense. The monk, Shiro, came out finally with a very tall monk who spoke perfect English. Shiro never spoke any English. They talked to me about Reiko telling Shiro how I was in the tests. I asked the tall monk to explain to Shiro how I felt being in Hiroshima and when I was in Nagasaki.

"I told him I felt tormented 'cause of what I saw in the desert. They both looked at me very sympathetically and said they don't usually speak to visitors, but that they understood. I wondered if Shiro could believe me seeing it all happening like it did in 1945. He said he would ask the monks to pray for me. He kept saying a Japanese word, "*Eeto* [let me think]," over and over. I believe he appreciated what I was contemplating and what I was trying to tell him. Maybe he originally only arranged to speak to me because of Reiko, but I think he knew why I went there."

"Possibly," Natsume agreed. "Family is very important to the Japanese."

"Yeah, I know. He gave me a little card, a good wish or prayer thing, and the tall monk said to keep it with me. I told him I didn't understand what it said—it was written in calligraphy, ya know, Japanese letters, and I dunno anything about them. I asked him to explain, but I don't remember much of what he said about the card. I do remember that he prefaced his remarks again with 'Because we usually do not speak to visitors,' and he said something about me blessing myself."

"Do you still have that card?" Natsume asked.

"Sure," said Joe, reaching into his shirt pocket. "He said to keep it with me, so I will, just in case—at least as long as I'm in Japan." He handed the business-size card to the reporter. "What does it say?"

"It says something about you, perhaps," Natsume replied, looking at the card intently. "Basically, it says you must be open to what happens in your life."

"Be open to what happens in my life?" Joe repeated. "What's that s'posed to mean?"

"Sounds as if it would mean different things to different people," Natsume said.

"Ya mean like karma?" Joe asked.

"Yes, something like that, I think. You should continue to keep this on your person."

"I will," Joe promised, accepting the card from Natsume's outstretched fingers and sliding it back into his breast pocket.

"Did you experience anything else while you were in Hiroshima?" Natsume asked.

"No, because when I left the temple, I had just enough time to catch the train for Tokyo."

"Okay." Natsume flipped over the cover of his notebook and tucked it into his pocket along with his pen. "Thank you for being so forthright, Joe. Now it's my turn to be just as straight with you," he said, his face holding an expression of concern and warning.

"Yeah, whadd'ya wanna tell me?" Joe asked, thinking, *here comes trouble.*

"You told them in Nagasaki you didn't have enough time to go to Hiroshima."

"Who'd I tell that to?"

"The television interview."

"Oh, that! They got it wrong! What I said was I didn't *know* if I'd have time to go."

"Unfortunately, that's not the meaning they heard—or reported."

"Uh-oh. I shouldn't have said it, should I?" Joe remembered Reiko's cautionary advice about vengeful gangs in Japan and was afraid he was going to hear the same from Natsume. Having both people whose intelligence he respected telling him the same thing would only make the danger more real - and that was a situation he did not relish.

"I'm afraid it was a big mistake even to mention Hiroshima," Natsume said. "You told me the same thing and, I must tell you, I also reported that you said you might not have time to go to Hiroshima. Like you, I qualified my statement, but I regret even mentioning it because too often people, sometimes even most readers, see and hear what they want to, not what is really there."

"And didja report that I was goin' to Nagasaki, too?"

"No, nor did I tell the television people that. Someone else did; I don't know who."

"Okay, but I don't get it. Even if I did say I didn't have time to go to Hiroshima, what's wrong with that? What've I done?"

"I know it was the TV reporter's fault, but you are being blamed for offending at least one gang of seriously dangerous fanatics."

"I have offended fanatics?"

"Yes. It's easy to do that in my country, especially when the matter of the atomic bomb is brought up."

"Geez! How did I offend them?"

"By going to Nagasaki and then implying that going to Hiroshima was unimportant. It's happened before. Once Americans comment on or become publicly involved in Hiroshima, they had best spend equal time with Nagasaki, and vice versa. At least they must not publicly announce that one is not as important as the other."

"That's balance. Yeah, it could be a big issue. Geez."

"Absolutely. You have triggered a threat to yourself from those who will be satisfied only by full Japanese military retaliation for Nagasaki and Hiroshima. As a nuclear victim yourself, your sympathy for the victims is too much counterbalance, even though you're only one person. These are extreme fanatics who want the Japanese to hate all Americans forever. In their minds, your chances of stirring public sentiment—no matter how slight—as your story becomes public could alter or delay what history has always shown about mankind's avenging spirit."

"You mean to tell me ya know of Japanese plans to retaliate militarily?"

"Joe, we are all part of the same universe. We all study history. When tribes or nations suffer certain defeats, such as the enslavement or brutal murdering of their children and women, disgrace of their soldier-sons, and their deities, well, they retaliate, oftentimes even many generations later, depending on the magnitude of the offenses. Mankind is infected with the lust for revenge."

"And I fit into that madness?" Joe asked.

"You have touched it, for sure," Natsume replied.

"I can't imagine someone… or anyone…" Joe's voice trailed off.

"We know how these people think. We did a story on one of those nuclear fanatic people about ten years ago, and you would be quite amazed by what we learned."

"I'm amazed now," said Joe.

"Your country was able to satisfy its desire for revenge multiple times by warring with the British twice and the Indian nations and the Mexicans and the Germans in two world wars," Natsume declared.

"So, because she hasn't had her revenge, someday Japan strikes again?"

"The fanatics are not Japan; they are individuals or small groups. But history runs backward and forward in time, and these fanatics date back to the turn of the century, when the militaristic aims of the country followed their most evil, insidious plans."

"Ya mean like Pearl Harbor?"

"Yes. Pearl Harbor happened in the forties, much later, of course, but it, too, was a result of these people finally influencing the military. These imperialistic-type plans were mapped out by those with a hatred for other Asians and the white race. They wanted the complete domination of Manchuria and, subsequently, China. They wanted control, vengeance, power—all the nasty ambitions. They were Japan's Nazis. They wanted what they called Pan-Asialism through military conquest, assassination, and espionage. They invaded China before the Nazis invaded Poland."

"Geez!"

"For some, the *Enola Gay* has never landed, Joe."

"I was always afraid to come to Japan, even though I wanted to and now I know why! Sounds like I pissed off everybody without even trying. I've pissed off the fanatics, my boss—and who else, I wonder? Who told everybody I was coming here and where I was going?"

"I'm beginning to wonder," Natsume said with a deepening frown. "I think somebody set you up; it's the only thing that fits. Probably someone you know or a different group of fanatics. The lead we got came from your country."

CHAPTER 10

S till in his room at the Imperial Hotel in Tokyo, Joe began to open the drapes so he could continue to watch the rain. As he tugged on the orange curtains, three men in business suits crossed the patio: one of them appeared to be an American; the others were Japanese. Filled with curiosity, Joe opened the door as they approached.

One of the Japanese men, speaking perfect unaccented English, told Joe they were agents of the Pacific Office of American Affairs in Tokyo who had been sent to assist him and to give him their names. The only name Joe caught was the American's: Reginald Teach. Tall and thin with rain soaked, flattened black hair that curled up over his ears, Agent Teach looked stressed and excitable.

As Joe looked at him, the man repeatedly opened and closed his palm against the wall beside Joe's door and leaned forward in a menacing manner, then retreated a few steps. Opening his eyes wide, he rocked his head back and demanded in a challenging voice, "What are you trying to accomplish in Japan, Mr. McGrath?"

Quickly deciding he did not want to be alone in his room with these men, Joe stepped out of his room onto the patio, leaving the door slightly ajar in case he needed to retreat in. "Whadd'ya mean?" he asked.

"You got something wrong with you, pal? This ain't Philadelphia."

The man's belligerent attitude made Joe scared and confirmed the wisdom of not inviting them in. "Look, *pal*," Joe answered testily. "Ya need to explain what you're doing here."

"Don't call me *pal*, buddy," the man growled.

The man who had spoken first spoke a few words of Japanese and whispered in English to Teach. Then he waved his arms in a circling gesture as if to control his companions, his pursed lips commanding attention. He sounded upset. The American, obviously ignoring the others, spun around and stood with his back to Joe while the three of them held a whispered conference. The American fumbled through some papers, and Joe heard him say in disgust, "They copied the wrong freaking papers, the freaking morons!"

"Got a problem?" Joe asked nonchalantly.

"You're the problem," Teach replied, "and you got us in your face unless we get you out of Japan fast."

"Why do I think I'm not gonna like any of this?" said Joe, leaning back against the door jamb and trying to contain his mounting annoyance.

"What are your plans? When will you be leaving Japan? Will you be flying back to the United States right away?" the first man asked. His hands flew as he punctuated his questions with gestures.

"You guys are being slightly invasive, don'tcha think?" Joe asked. "It's no secret, though. If ya must know, we're going back home tomorrow. Is that soon enough for ya?"

"Good," said the third man, who had not previously spoken. "If for any reason you change that itinerary, Mr. McGrath, please call us." He extended his arm to give Joe a business card.

Brushing the man's arm aside, Reginald Teach pointed threateningly at Joe and hissed, "People like you don't deserve your citizenship! Who did the setup work for you? Somebody did, because the media knew you were coming to Japan before you landed. What organization are you with? What do you call yourselves?"

"What's this all about?" Joe asked, directing his question at the American. It was no longer a matter of being just annoyed; he was becoming angry. "Ya think ya know something about me?"

"I know you ought to be arrested for revealing United States government secrets and embarrassing your own country in a former enemy nation," Teach retorted. "How do you think we look to the world, using our own troops for those tests—?"

"Hey, you're talking about human guinea pigs!" Joe interrupted.

"You shouldn't be talking at all, McGrath. It's complainers like you that jeopardize our position in this world, even our nuclear defenses. I was a naval officer, I served my country, and I don't like what you're doing one bit."

"What'd ya say your name was?" Joe broke in.

"Agent Reginald Teach; Agent Teach, to you."

"Well, Reggie," Joe said, taunting Teach with the nickname, "Ya got any idea what happens when governments experiment on human beings?" Getting no answer, he continued. "Ya ever imagine six hundred American infantrymen, six hundred of your own guys, your friends, having a damn A-bomb blown up in their laps?"

"I was in the Navy," Teach said, as if that somehow made it unnecessary for him to take heed of what Joe was saying.

"Ya think they didn't use our Navy guys as guinea pigs, too? Well, lemme tell ya, I wasn't surprised when a friend of mine found out some of the things they did to our guys on ships at sea. Horrible things, just so they'd know how to fight a nuclear naval war."

"What do you think you know, know-it-all?"

"Guys were on the deck of a British ship as an atomic bomb test was exploded at sea. The force field broke their arms and legs. Did you know some of our guys out on the desert were buried alive?"

"But—"

"But nothing!" Joe interrupted in a loud voice, wondering when people would ever accept the truth. He grasped the door handle and took a few steps back. "Never mind," he continued. "I think you'd better leave now. It's raining and you guys are already all wet."

~ ~ ~

While Joe sat alone in his room that evening failing to convince himself that attending the send-off dinner was unimportant, Agent Reginald Teach was in his Tokyo office sifting through Joseph R. McGrath's file. He found the weapon effects group report as well as an NTPR (Nuclear Test Personnel Review) file for radiation-exposed atomic veterans. He began to whisper audibly as he read, "Ionizing radiation—Electromagnetic pulse effects—five hundred fifty maneuver troops plus approximately fifty rear support troops—two hundred thirty-five tests—4th Infantry, troops in trenches—troops entered their vehicles and moved into shot area—Approximately fifty minutes in shot area."

He continued to study the paperwork and McGrath's film badge data from his Nevada exposures. *This is what keeps the Chinese from starting a war on us*, he thought. *They don't have the money to match our nuclear arsenal.*

As he read and whispered, Teach became increasingly outraged at McGrath and whatever group had sent him to Japan. "McGrath, Joseph, Operation Joey Boy—that's ironic, ain't it? Gamma, Rem, 0.000 total operation dosage: zero." Teach's face registered surprise. "What? No radiation; nothing?" he exclaimed under his breath. "What a joke! The guy wasn't even irradiated, so where's he get the right to complain? I was right about him; he's just another one of them peace nuts."

He studied the report again, and then hissed, "That jerk is anti-American! Somebody's gotta get him outta Japan!" With a kind of reverence born from his version of patriotism, he read aloud the names of the atmospheric tests: "Buster Tangle, Red Wing, Plumb Bob, Hard Rock, Hard Rock II, Dominic II, Plow Share. . . "

Going back to McGrath's exposure incident report, Teach found a current list of men exposed with McGrath who had died since the A-bomb tests. He read down the twenty-six names, noting that many of them had succumbed to some type of cancer. "Not even thirty outta six hundred?" he murmured. "That ain't so bad." He stopped in surprise at the name, "Garcia, Louis S." and starred at it for a moment. *Huh!* he thought. *I never knew men could get breast cancer.* He searched Garcia's file for his weapons effect datum in the group report. It had, "Gamma, Rem, 0.000 total operation dosage: zero."

~ ~ ~

When Joe entered the lobby of the Imperial Hotel the next morning, he stopped at the front desk to leave his bags while he went for breakfast. Joe asked the clerk if he had any messages. The clerk checked the cubby holes above a panel with little red lights and found one note above Joseph McGrath's room number. Opening the message, Joe found it to be a curt summons from Agent Teach ordering him to be in the main lobby at 8:30. It was already 8:57.

Joe looked around and saw Teach standing in the center of the lobby beside a column enclosed by a circular bench. An American man whom Joe judged to be approximately thirty-five years old lounged on the bench. He was dressed in an old Army field jacket, faded jeans, and moccasins, and with his long hair and silver steel-rimmed glasses, he reminded Joe of John Lennon of the Beatles.

Teach motioned Joe onto the bench beside the American. "I'm glad you're both here," he said, facing them. "I know you don't know each other, and this may be awkward, but having you here together helps me do what I need to."

The seated men glanced at each other, shrugged, and turned back to the POAA agent, keeping each other in their peripheral sight to pick up anything of interest.

"You two have one thing in common and you're both here right now for the same reason," the agent stated with confidence. "We need you out of Japan and we want your guarantee that you'll leave within 48 hours."

The other man objected. "Whatcha talking about, Teach? I don't care if you *are* the head agent at Tokyo's Office of American Affairs, you can't order me outta Japan. I live here."

"You're not listening, Gould," Teach said. "You're a convicted felon. The slightest hint of renewed criminal activity on your part and either we move in or the Japanese get you again."

"I haven't done anything wrong," Gould protested.

"That remains to be seen," Teach warned him.

"So, what am I doing here?" Joe asked with a deep frown.

"We are requesting," Teach said with exaggerated politeness, "your departure."

"Oh, yeah, and just why is that?" Joe asked. "I haven't done anything wrong, either." He glanced at Gould and then back at Teach and said, "You, Reginald, Reggie—whatever your name is—

you must be nuts. I dunno what authority you're assuming but I find it offensive. If you represent the U.S.A. in any way, we need more help in the State Department than I ever imagined."

Joe held the man with his gaze as he continued. "I'm not in any organization and I got no idea why or how I attracted all this attention. I sure as hell didn't ask for it and I sure as hell don't want it! What's going on? Are ya conducting a trial here?"

"That's a good speech, McGrath," Teach said sarcastically, "and I hope it made you feel better—but the fact is, you're a danger to yourself here, and you'd be smart to leave."

Fear registered on Joe's face, especially in his eyes.

"We saved you more embarrassment by getting your company to un-invite you from that Japanese business dinner last night. The Japanese didn't want you there—and, by the way, McGrath, unlike you, your bosses didn't put up any resistance when we told them what we needed. So instead of stirring up more trouble, you'll hafta leave Japan within forty-eight hours. Ain't that right, Gould?"

"What would this guy know about it?" Joe burst out. "I told ya yesterday, Teach, I'm leaving today on the noon flight." He jumped to his feet; his fists doubled. "Now don't bother me anymore. Ya got that?"

"You're going to want to get home so you can start looking for a new job, McGrath."

"You probably cost me my job, you bastard!"

Teach, his face wizened into a satisfied smile, stood very still.

Then, raising his palms in the age-old sign of surrender, Teach moved out of Joe's path. Outraged and dumbfounded, Joe stalked off, talking loudly to no one in particular and disturbing the gentle Japanese he passed. "This is ridiculous! There can't be anybody among the heads of government endorsing these antics. I don't need this guy. Geez!" A middle-aged Japanese couple froze in place as he passed close by and everyone nearby watched with alarm.

CHAPTER 11

J oe walked heavily through the Tokyo hotel and down the largest hallway, headed for the breakfast buffet. At first his rage blocked any sensitivity to his surroundings but, as he calmed down, he noticed several Japanese men walking near him. They were very close, almost hemming him in, and this made him uncomfortable.

Joe sensed something dangerous about them and slowed his pace. Alarmed by his suspicions, he stopped walking, and, acting like he forgot something, turned around to walk back the way he had come—but one of the men approached him directly in his path.

Joe jerked to the left to avoid the man but suddenly found himself surrounded by eight Japanese men who merged into a tight circle around him. One of them slipped a gag over his mouth while another grabbed his arm and, with a quick twist, expertly dislocated his shoulder. Muffled but groaning through the gag in agony, Joe slumped forward. All the while, Joe realized that he was effectively hidden from sight and hearing in case anyone else happened to use the same hallway.

Overpowered by the pressure of his attackers' bodies, he was half-pushed, half-lifted a short distance to an empty conference room, where the men stopped abruptly and shoved him through the doorway. He plummeted to the floor, the impact of his body on the thinly carpeted concrete knocking him breathless. Someone kicked him in the ribs and, when Joe scooted out of the way, the same person kicked him again. The foot continued to herd him until Joe was backed up to a wall, at which point the owner of the foot grunted with satisfaction and stopped kicking.

Joe knew that his eyes were tearing and felt his face contorted in disbelief. He leaned into the wall in a vain attempt to alleviate the painful throbbing of his midsection and shoulder and saw that the hand he was using to hold his dislocated arm was shaking. Even more frightening than the pain was the fact that he did not know what was happening or who was behind it. At first the men had said very little.

Speaking in hissing and guttural sounding Japanese, the kicker said, 'Jōshi ga kite imasu,' (Boss man is coming).

'Kono kirainahito wa junbi ga dekite imasu,' (This asshole is ready), said another.

"Yowai o shiri Amerika," (Weak ass American), the kicker said.

After the attack, the door to the meeting room opened and a very short, slender man approached Joe. In a high, reedy voice, the man proclaimed in perfect English that Joe was a prisoner of the Neo-Imperial Japanese Empire. His thin frame partially concealed by his suit; the man was like a walking nightmare-one of those near-human skeletal creatures archaeologists discover.

The man's words about *Japanese Imperialists* repeated in Joe's mind in the imagery that Joe's childhood knowledge of the history of wartime Japan brought forth until the word, "neo" registered fearfully in Joe's awareness and terror. He found himself thinking, *"It's the Japanese madness all over again... and I'm in it... What the... Geezus."*

Joe spotted several tattoos of menacing dragons on the man's arms. While he was staring at the sinister symbols, the thin man gave orders in Japanese to another dark-skinned man who approached Joe who tried to flatten himself against the wall.

The dark man lifted one leg, and with surprising power, pushed his foot against the pit of Joe's injured arm, forcing him on his side. Taking Joe's arm and wrist in both hands, the man placed one shoe into Joe's armpit and yanked forcefully until he heard a mechanical yet fleshy "Snap!" Having reset Joe's arm and shoulder, he abruptly released his victim, who remained on his side, stunned and curled in acute pain. The thin man grunted appreciatively.

In an instinctive attempt to withdraw himself from the situation, Joe deliberately blocked out the words that passed between the thin man and his henchmen and channeled his field of vision to the floor, seeing only the carpet in front of him. He was unconsciously limiting the visual impact of his abduction; he did not want to see anything— no dragons, no Japanese faces, nothing to confirm that what was happening was real.

As a group, his kidnappers seemed to have doused themselves in pungent colognes and shaving lotions which mixed with breath that broadcast the Asian foreignness of their last meals, created a sickening odor that virtually assaulted Joe. Like trapped beasts they paced the room restlessly, peeking out of doors and windows and closing drapes, then adjusting the latter to prevent the smallest sliver of light from coming through; any curtains that fell out of place and allowed the light in were tweaked again and again.

The Japanese conversations were brief, their language a harsh, hammering staccato. Each man had his identifying facial expression, and the taut muscle movements of their faces were angry and hostile. Their eyes were never still, filled with unrelenting menace, the black, bird-like orbs shot threatening darts whenever they turned his way. Without a chance of escape, Joe felt overwhelming fear.

Long moments passed. as the acute pain in his shoulder subsided to a dull throbbing, Joe righted himself and sat with his back against the wall, his mind incapable of believing what was happening. The drawn curtains had plunged the room into almost total darkness, the exception being a vertical slit of blinding sunlight where two drapes refused to touch ends. That sliver of menacing whiteness, like a molten extrusion of aluminum, stood rigidly fixed, as if not light at all. It appeared unreal and might have served well as the torch of a satanic warrior on guard at the entrance of hell.

In the minimal lighting, the skin of Joe's enemies turned so pale that the jaws and teeth in their banefully malignant faces no longer looked distinctly human. The ogres stood menacingly around him, maintaining nearly constant angry debates in the hissing, and grunting that Japanese becomes when rage barbs that inflected language.

With his legs stretched outward on the carpet and his face giving off a frosted appearance, Joe closed his eyes and silently prayed the Catholic prayer he had repeated thousands of times during his childhood, *Saint Michael the Archangel, defend us in the battle—"* He stopped, finding himself forming uncontrollable tears of fear and fighting against great confusion.

The dragons he had seen on the thin Japanese man's hands came to mind, and he began again. *Defend us in battle—be our protection against the wickedness and snares of the devil.* As he prayed, he began to breathe more deeply, holding inhalations for a few seconds then exhaling slowly. After years of suffering from panic attacks after Nevada, he knew how to cope with panic anxiety. He placed both hands against his face and pressed his head into them, slowing the cadence of his words as he continued to repeat the centuries-old prayer to the archangel.

In what seemed like an hour, but was only about fifteen minutes, the criminals removed Joe from the conference room by way of an outside door. After binding his hands, they formed a phalanx around him again and hustled him into an innocuous-looking white heating and air-conditioning service van. Three climbed in with him, and a fourth, the tallest and darkest of them, locked the doors from the outside. While the other four looked on from the motel walkway, the dark one climbed into the driver's seat and pulled the van into traffic.

After a short drive, Joe was quartered in a storage room on what he perceived to be the estate of some rich person, judging by the expensive landscaping he had glimpsed while being unloaded from the van. His gag had been removed, but he stayed silent, knowing that crying out for help would be useless and dangerous. He knew that he was truly a prisoner for the rest of that day and night.

~ ~ ~

It was Ken Epperson who reported Joe McGrath's absence to the Tokyo police. At first, the new president of the company was unconcerned when Joe didn't meet them in the hotel lobby at the appointed hour or show up later at the airport. Imbuing Joe with his own personality, the president was sure Joe was sulking about not being allowed to attend the send-off dinner and guessed that he had probably exchanged his ticket for a different flight.

Epperson, after quite some time, finally asked the hotel management to call the local police as soon as he realized Joe wasn't going to appear. Filled with a sense of foreboding, he wanted to stay and help but was told by the authorities there was nothing more he could do and that he should go home as planned. Reluctantly, Epperson boarded the plane and flew back to the U.S., all the while deeply confused and wondering what had become of Joe McGrath.

Meanwhile, the police launched a city-wide search, tracking Joseph McGrath's movements as best they could with what little information they had. By the end of the day, having found no sign of him, they decided to enlist the help of the news media.

Their first action was to subpoena media entities for access to the source material they had used for their stories on McGrath in hopes that one of those sources would supply a fruitful lead. At the same time, the police informed the media that Joseph McGrath had disappeared, gave them what information they had, and asked them to announce the missing person news in their next editions.

They called Natsume Toson and asked him to send copies of the photo he had published earlier to the other papers and the television news stations, to which he readily agreed. "Karma for the worst? Or just bad luck?" Natsume breathed as he hurriedly jotted down all the information the policeman could give him. His mind was racing as he tried to think of ways to help. First, he decided, he had to get the story of Joe's disappearance onto the front pages; he would call the editors and try to persuade them. Next, he would send out not only the photo, but a finished article ready to be in print and read, which would practically guarantee the story would appear in other newspapers and on television. He only wished the news could break that day, but it was so late it would have to wait until the next day.

~ ~ ~

American agent Reginald Teach of the Pacific Office knew exactly when and where Joe had gone missing. The night before he had ordered his agents to carry out a twenty-four-hour stakeout, but they had lost sight of McGrath in the Imperial Hotel that morning. The first report on Joseph McGrath by Teach's cover agents was that McGrath had caught on to them and evaded them by sheer ingenuity. A second report gave evidence that McGrath had been abducted in a white van, witnessed by a landscape worker employee of the hotel.

Teach knew he should have reported McGrath's disappearance immediately to the authorities but instead he contacted the POAA

Director, and his Assistant Director and they called staff and reached out to a representative of the United States 97th Congress who was on assignment in Japan at that time. The next morning, the earliest he could get them all together, they held a closed-door meeting at which Teach briefed everyone on the status of the Joseph McGrath situation.

A consensus was reached to initiate damage control by immediately, downplaying McGrath and his safety no matter what. During the ensuing discussion, no one seemed to care much about McGrath's plight but the possibility of his becoming a big news item was a matter of great concern.

~ ~ ~

That same day, Joe was transported to a warehouse on the west side of Tokyo, owned by the thin man. His captors confiscated his shoes, belt, and wristwatch and the contents of his pockets. Recognizing his gold medal and chain as a religious object, they allowed him to keep the medal, but not the chain. They shoved him into a windowless basement where a fluorescent light was left on in a small lavatory, casting a dim light over the rest of the basement.

Fortunately, they had untied him, and he was able to navigate his way around the room. He walked the perimeter, running his hands over the walls and poking his stocking feet into dark corners, but found nothing except a few sheet-metal screws. He absentmindedly pocketed the screws as he stood in the center of the room and surveyed his surroundings where his captors had left two folded blankets.

Geez! he thought. *There's nothing here 'cept a toilet and sink, not even a window!* He stacked the folded blankets against the wall and lowered himself onto them, his legs crossed as if he were practicing yoga. *Who the hell are these guys? A gang?* he wondered. *Who d'they think I am, and whadda they want? I don't get it. Geez.*

Frightened and bewildered, Joe leaned back against the wall and tried unsuccessfully to relax. "How long're they gonna keep me here?" he asked as he dozed fitfully. *God, I sure hope someone's looking for me. Epperson will be. I've been gone a while now. How long . . .? Oh, yeah, they'll be looking for me. . .*

Joe stood up and went to the steps thinking, *the best time to escape is immediately after being captured.* It was his infantry training being recalled. The first steps were silent to his climb, but two of the steps higher up creaked. Joe stopped for a few seconds. When he crept to the door and, even though he was in his stocking feet, and reaching for the doorknob, a dog barked loud and mean and scratched wildly at the door. As he quickly descended the stairs, someone was unbolting the door and a shaft of fluorescent light covered him before he reached the bottom of the staircase. "*So much for that plan,*" he thought.

~ ~ ~

The day after the kidnapping, the thin man studied the newspapers and watched the television newscasts to find out how much was being said about the disappearance of the troublesome American. He was pleased to see that Joseph McGrath was the lead story on all the television networks. As for the papers, apparently

Natsume Toson had been convincing because Joe's disappearance was splashed across every front page, complete with bold headlines, his photograph, and a story that was a composite of what had been written earlier and the new missing person's information.

Also, on the front page was a POAA news release. The thin man nodded his head in satisfaction when he saw how fast the U.S. government had distanced itself from McGrath. Contrary to its intended effect, the statement strengthened the fanatic's belief that McGrath had been collaborating with the U.S. government in a conspiracy against Japan. He reminded himself to tell his fellow Japanese patriots they had done the right thing.

But now, he thought, it was time for more pressure. He picked up the telephone and dialed the residence of Bishop David Garvin. Disguising his voice by wrapping a cloth around the mouthpiece, he informed the bishop that his Brown Dragons had kidnapped Joseph McGrath and were taking full responsibility for the exploit. They had the American in custody, and what happened to him would depend on how the U.S. government responded to the situation.

Calling Joe, a "Western propagandist," the thin man demanded a public admission of guilt for the insults he said Joe's mission and deceptions had brought down upon Japan. He reviled Joe McGrath as "Another American nuclear impurity in my country" and declared that if they didn't get a satisfactory apology McGrath would be left to rot on "the soiled ground of Japan." Finally, to the bishop's horror, the thin man said they knew Reiko was the woman who had traveled with McGrath and suspected she was a traitor to her country. He insinuated they were thinking about abducting her as well, especially if the bishop did not follow his orders and relay everything, he had just said to the Japanese news media.

Warning the bishop not to think he could trust the newspapers and the reporter Toson to save Reiko and McGrath the thin man abruptly broke the connection, and the shaken Bishop acted immediately. First, he called Reiko into his office and told her what had happened. Next, he called her uncle Shiro and alerted him to the thin man's threats. Then he sent identical telegrams to Hank Daniels's address in Chicago to be sure to apprise him of the situation. Finally, the Bishop called Natsume Toson. He also called the police, although all he could tell either of them was that a group of fanatics had claimed to be holding Joseph McGrath and threatened to abduct the bishop's assistant.

From a reporter's viewpoint, Natsume was gratified to receive even the smallest amount of new information about Joe, but he shared the bishop's alarm when he heard of the Brown Dragons and their threats against Reiko. He was slightly comforted to hear that Shiro had left the monastery and was in route to the rectory, where he would stay until the danger had passed. Shiro, the Bishop told him, had declared that he would stay close to his niece as necessary to prevent a similar abduction.

The monk's long-ago promise to her mother to always be the priest of their family had been fulfilled, but he had also promised his protection. This was the first time Reiko had been in real danger, and he would keep his vow to be there for her. Known to many, the monasteries had always trained their monks in self-defense for centuries.

Asking pointed questions until he was satisfied Reiko would be carefully defended, Natsume cautioned the bishop to warn Shiro never to let his guard down, reminding him that the fanatics were devious devils who would go to any lengths to get their way. Only after the Bishop had promised to do that did the concerned Natsume release him from the conversation.

CHAPTER 12

D espite the health threat and his wife and mother complaining frantically, Hank Daniels flew all night and all day—some twenty-two hours, with three connections—to Tokyo. When awake, he repeatedly read a copy of the pamphlet he had brought that was printed as a language educational services aid that offered English-to-Japanese translations. He also spent hours listening to an accompanying Japanese vocabulary and pronunciation audio tape. His plane landed in a stiff Tokyo crosswind with the skidding sound of soft, hot rubber as he viewed rapidly passing window scenes of Japan. He felt eeriness as the aircraft came to a stop.

When he stepped out of the airport van, Hank was amazed by the spectacular landscape that welcomed him to Japan and the Imperial Hotel. Like a regular tourist, he gawked at the huge, bowled fountains with their majestic waterspouts, each like a posed ballerina dancing to the theme of the architect's vision. Walking in the stride common to ex-soldiers, his scant luggage held in one hand and the language book in the other, he passed by flags and plants in decorative gardens and trees, all of which moved constantly in the Tokyo wind. He gazed upward at the staggered, towering geometry of the proud, floodlight illuminated structure of the Imperial Hotel.

Hank checked in, ate dinner at the hotel restaurant, and retired immediately afterward so he could get a good night's rest. He awoke refreshed and re-energized, and after a Western breakfast, he went to the lobby to wait for Bishop Garvin. Seating himself in a plush easy chair, he opened his language pamphlet again and studied it as he also watched the front door traffic. He soon forgot the folder, becoming fascinated by the people who came and went. Despite the serious situation that had brought him there, the uniqueness of some of the guests lifted his spirits. Distracted, he began to quietly whistle a song through his closed teeth, a melody remembered from an old Hollywood movie, title and lyrics forgotten. He stopped abruptly when he saw a Catholic Bishop and a Japanese woman enter the hotel lobby.

Hank stood and approached the couple. "*Ohayo gozai mase* [Good morning)]," he said with a friendly smile. Before leaving Chicago, he had arranged a meeting with Reiko and Bishop Garvin. They had agreed to travel from Kure City to Tokyo and meet Hank at the Imperial Hotel when he arrived, and he was pleased to see they had honored their commitment.

Reiko nervously patted her hands on her thighs as she bowed her head slightly so that her eyes could continue studying Hank, the first American black man she ever met. She apparently did not notice his Japanese greeting. The bishop, shaking Hank's hand, said, "Good morning to you as well, Hank Daniels. This is Miss Reiko Fumioka, whom I am pleased to introduce to you. And I am Bishop Garvin."

"Thanks. You've been very kind to read and answer my correspondence. How d'ya do, Miss Reiko?"

"Fine, thank you. It is an honor to meet you, Mr. Hank Daniels," Reiko replied as she bowed again, her fingertips touching the black-sheen of her simply styled but unmistakably Asian hair as she let her hands conceal her eyes and face. She was trying to hide her interest in the black American.

"Hank, I read everything you sent us more than once," the bishop said. "So did Reiko."

"That was really nice of you both. Thanks." Hank was surprised the woman spoke and understood English and was grateful he would not need an interpreter. He forced himself to speak in a measured tone to suppress the raw energy of his curiosity, even as he asked what was uppermost in his mind. "Any news?"

"Nothing significant is yet known," Reiko answered with a sigh.

"Unfortunately, we are still in the dark," the bishop added. "There has been no sign of him, and the police have reported to us every day now."

"How did they snatch him here, in such a fancy place, with all this security?" Hank asked, looking around the lobby and waving a hand to reference the abundance of guards and cameras.

"The police said the kidnappers held him out of sight in one of the meeting rooms on the first floor," Reiko said, her words full of tension. "The security then was not as it is now, and the kidnappers moved quickly, right in front of everyone."

"Is the police investigation getting anywhere? Can we find out anything about it?"

"How she does it is a mystery," the bishop replied, "but Reiko probably knows everything there is to know. I know people come to the rectory to discreetly inform her of anything they know." He smiled at Reiko. "People in Japan love to trade secrets," he continued. "Some have relatives on the police force, and one woman in our church has a son working at this very hotel. Stories get around."

Reiko nodded her head in assent. "I wish we could tell you more," she said.

"Just the same, I'm glad you have sources of information," Hank said. "Who did it? Do they know?"

"If we can believe what we have been told," the bishop answered. "Mr. McGrath was abducted two days ago, on the nineteenth. Yesterday a person called me to claim their foul responsibility for the act. He or she—I could not tell, as the voice was disguised—spoke only in Japanese and told me the group that did this is the Brown Dragons, a so-called secret society, an organization from the war times."

"It was predictable," Reiko interjected. "The newspapers exposed Joseph McGrath as if he was expendable information, a headline for a day in the news world, and this placed him in danger of aggression from nuclear fanatics like the Brown Dragons. Natsume Toson, a reporter for the Tokyo newspaper, says someone sent an anonymous press release to the news media, TV and newspapers alike, which they accepted as authentic, and this is how the Browns became aware of Joseph's presence in Japan."

A flicker of fear ran through Hank, quickly reminding him that there was good reason to believe the press release could be traced back to his cooperation with Dr. Hito. He tried to push that knowledge away, determined not to speak of it.

"D'ya know anything else about the actual kidnapping?" he asked as his soul filled with guilt.

"Yes," Reiko answered. "He was taken away in a white work van with '*Nishi*' written on its sides."

"What does '*Nishi*' mean?"

"West," the bishop said. "There was more lettering on the van, but no one remembers what it was," he added. "The van was for commercial use, probably a company vehicle from some business in West Tokyo. Perhaps it was stolen."

"So, the cops don't have much to go on, do they?" Daniels said, scowling. Knowing Reiko and the Bishop wanted to help, but having gained no sense of comfort from them, he became mentally distanced from them. "It's April 21st here in Japan," he murmured in a slow, deep tone, "so this is the third day he's been missing—and that's all the cops've got? Unbelievable!" he declared. He had no idea what to think or do.

When she was not speaking, Reiko's face became expressionless and Daniels felt seized by Japan and what it shielded from outsiders and what if anything, it reluctantly held out to him. He was beginning to wonder why he thought he could help Joe at all in Japan.

After eating a requisite lunch together in the Imperial Hotel, the trio separated, and Hank saw Reiko and the Bishop off at the hotel entrance. Before they left, Bishop Garvin extended an invitation to Hank to stay with them in their hometown but knew he would not accept. They parted on friendly terms, promising to contact each other if they learned anything else about Joe's situation.

Hank, somewhat irritated by the name Imperial, decided to find other lodging. It was important, he thought, to retrace Joe's steps by starting in the place of his abduction, but he saw no point in staying any longer. His traveler's checks and small number of Japanese yen would not last long. He packed up his belongings, and as he was making a last-minute check of the room, the phone rang. Hoping it was his wife, Charlene, he lifted the receiver quickly. *It would be good to hear her voice in this place*, he thought. He missed his wife, and he needed to tell someone he trusted about Hito and what price was being paid by him and Joe. His thinking concluded with a sigh, and "God, Joe, I'm sorry."

"Hello there!" He greeted the caller cheerfully.

"Mr. Daniels?"

Disappointed to hear a male voice, Hank was curious, nonetheless. "Yeah," he answered cautiously.

"I am Natsume Toson. I met your friend Joseph, and I just left Reiko and Bishop Garvin."

"Oh, are you Japanese?"

"Um . . . Yes." Natsume was thrown off by the question for what seemed like obvious reasons to him.

"You say you know Joe McGrath? How is that?"

"I am a press reporter here in Tokyo, and I was assigned to cover him while he was in Japan. Your friend Joseph and I had a few meetings and talks. He is an ingenuous person. You two must be very good friends, Mr. Daniels."

The words "press reporter" triggered an alarm in Hank. "We're good friends, all right," he said, "Whatcha reporting about?"

"Please don't take me wrong. I have only your friend's well-being in mind. I think Mr. McGrath would want us to talk. I know a few things you should be aware of. Please believe me."

"Things such as what?"

"How you and others can help to some degree."

"Why should I believe ya? I dunno who ya are."

"Let's meet. I am here in the hotel, at the So Desuka Restaurant. Please come down and allow me to buy you some coffee or tea. I am wearing a black suit and red tie, and I will be looking for you."

"Well, I'm wearing black skin, and I can get red as hell if you're up to any reporter tricks, Mr. Toson."

"Please trust me. Will you come down?"

"Okay, I'm on my way." He carried his suitcase down to the front desk and checked out, then looked around and saw Toson standing by the small cafe off the main lobby. He walked over to the well-dressed reporter.

"*Konnichiwa* [good afternoon]," Hank said with almost perfect pronunciation, bowing slightly.

"*Hajimemashite Toson desu* [Pleased to meet you, I'm Toson]. *Konnichiwa, Daniels-san,*" Toson said. "*Kore wa watoshi no meishi desu* [Here is my business card]," he said respectfully, formally handing Hank his business card. It was a politeness for Natsume to act as if Hank was efficient in his language.

Daniels glanced at the business card and then at Natsume. "Sorry," he explained, "I don't speak Japanese. All I know is some words from a tourist book."

"*Domo arigato goziaimasu* [Thank you very much]; that is, thank you for meeting me."

"Sorry about the language."

"Don't worry, please. I am happy to speak in English. Shall we go inside for some coffee or tea? By the way, everyone in the States calls me Natsume. It is unusual in Japan to use your first name with new people, but I got used to it during my college days in the United States."

"Okay, Natsume. Please call me Hank." He felt at ease with the man and was relieved to find another involved person with whom he would be able to speak English.

They ordered coffee and a Japanese version of cinnamon buns. As they waited, Natsume asked, "did you come to find Joe by yourself?'

"Yeah. I just had to pack up and go. He woulda done the same for me. We've been friends for a long time, since we were kids."

"That's impressive. We have those kinds of friendships in Japan, too, but they are rare."

Hank nodded. Their buns and coffee arrived, and Hank waited until the server was gone before asking what was uppermost on his mind. "What's going on? Do ya know? And what didja mean when you said ya knew how I could help?"

"Yes, I do know what's going on, and I do know how you can help—but you're in for some unexpected advice from me, and I'm asking you not to do anything more about this til you think about what I'm going to say."

"Okay. What is it ya hafta say?"

Natsume leaned forward and spoke earnestly. "Joe and I had two talks, a brief one when we met at the bishop's house with Reiko, and another meeting in his room at this hotel. I warned him he had provoked some dangerous factions here in Japan and that he should be careful. The truth of the matter is someone set him up."

"Whadd'ya mean, set him up?"

"Somebody, probably an American with a Japanese connection, got the news media in Japan interested in him by sending out medical press releases. By the way Joe acted when I told him about that, I could tell he wasn't shocked. Whoever did this must have known how dangerous such publicity would be for Joe. Somebody wanted all this to happen to him. He was deliberately set up."

Daniels thought of his involvement with the Doctors for Nuclear Disarmament and felt a gripping sensation in his throat, but he said nothing.

Natsume's face was serious as he stared intently at Daniels. "They kidnapped him right here, just down the hall, and held him in the *Yoi hi* meeting room.

"*Yoi hi?*"

"Yes. It means '*Have a nice day.*'"

"Huh! Not a nice day for Joe!"

"True. Unfortunately, they probably hurt him to get him in there."

"Hurt him? How did they hurt him? Why?"

"There's no info on that. We just know from experience with these thugs that they move fast to eliminate resistance if they want to take you alive."

"God!" Daniels said, sucking in an audible breath through clenched teeth. His imagination began to work overtime, flipping quickly through different scenarios as it churned out one gruesome image after the other of ruthless gangsters hurting his friend.

"How d'ya know this?" he finally asked.

"We read police reports when they let us, plus we have reliable sources inside the police department. We get bits and pieces and put them together. It's just like in the movies; the information gradually forms a complete picture."

"Except in this case," said Hank.

"I admit it's been slow going and I'm sorry. The good news is that the Brown Dragons wanted him alive, so they'll probably keep him that way. It's a tragedy this happened, but there is hope he'll come out of it okay. I like your friend. He's a truly nice guy who didn't want trouble; I could tell that right off. I thought I could help him, but my warnings came too late. They were already coming after him."

"You're right about his being a nice guy. He wouldn't hurt anybody and never in Japan."

Hank felt worse than ever for Joe and bitter about Hito's cruel disregard for his best friend. What made things even worse was that he felt so helpless. "You said ya know how I can help?" he asked, ready to take whatever action Natsume recommended if it would help bring Joe home in one piece.

"Go home, Hank," Natsume advised.

"W-what?" Hank was shocked and dismayed. "Whadd'ya mean, go home? I thought ya said I could help!"

Natsume looked at him with understanding and compassion. "The best thing you can do for your friend right now, Hank, is to go home," he repeated. "Come back when they release him. If you and the others drop the matter, he'll be yesterday's news in a short time, and the Browns, unable to use him to advance their cause, will release him. There might be a bit of fanfare on their part, but that would be for show. That's how they operate. But," Natsume said emphatically, tapping his finger on the table to underscore his words, "if you raise a big fuss about his abduction, you'll arouse public interest because the Japanese people love a sense of sacrifice, and the Browns may feel they have to respond in a radical way to defend their actions. And you also have to worry about what the Americans would do about him."

Hank, thinking about how making a bigger deal out of it all would hurt Joe, also imagined how the Japanese police would treat him and Hito. He thought, *if they put the doctor's involvement together with what happened, it might even seem criminal. Hito's like a conspirator in this. I dunno what to think. It's crazy. Good thing mom is not aware of this.* He looked at Natsume and restated the issue: "So what you're saying is, these Brown Dragons prob'ly made a tactical mistake when they kidnapped Joe."

"Yes," Natsume confirmed, "If they make a big issue out of somebody who is not, and if they kill him, he becomes somebody's martyr and a big issue. The Browns would prefer not to do that, especially when releasing him will be to their advantage by showing their control of matters. The public will know those that are kidnapped can be abducted and released with impunity."

Hank nodded his head in understanding. "Right."

"Although he probably would die a martyr if I have him figured out correctly," Natsume guessed.

"Maybe," said Hank, surprised by the validity of Natsume's many opinions.

"There is another issue you should consider, Mr. Daniels," Natsume continued, "and that is the language problem. You say *good afternoon* very well, but that, by your own admission, is almost the extent of your ability. What can you do here without a working knowledge of Japanese? Tokyo is the most confusing city in the world, especially if you are from the West. For example, if you go to look for a place, we don't necessarily number our home addresses in the sequence patterns as you do. A number on a home might indicate in what order the homes were built in that locale. Strangers become totally lost driving around Tokyo, even when they know the language."

"Thanks for all your advice, Natsume," said Hank. "You've given me lots to think about. I'd like to talk about Joe now. D'ya know where he is?"

"No, but the police probably do. A Chinese hotel worker saw him being put in a white van."

"Yeah, I heard about that."

"From the Bishop?"

"Reiko."

"She cares about him and probably has conducted an amateur investigation."

"So, if they know where Joe is, why don't the cops get him back?"

"There are probably some delicate negotiations involved. The Brown Dragons have claimed responsibility for the crime, and they're a powerful organization the police can't treat lightly. Corruption spins many webs."

"One small-time guy in a big-time game?"

"Yes, Hank. It's like a Mafia kidnapping, or worse."

"Worse?"

"Yes, there is worse—very bad, and worse."

"Go home, you say. Well, I have to go soon anyway. I don't have much money, and I already know I'm powerless. Right now, I'm a smaller guy than Joseph McGrath."

"Just think about what I've told you. I'm sure you'll do the right thing. Are you not going to be staying here, at the Imperial?" Natsume said as he eyed Hank's small suitcase.

"Nah, I already checked out. Can't afford another night. I need something with lower rates," Daniels admitted.

"There's a nice, clean, economic hotel on the river. It's owned by an American, a guy who stayed here after the Korean American war, but you probably won't see him because he stays in the background. He named it *Jinrikisha*, after the rickshaw carts. Do you know what I mean? It's one of the *Ryokans*, or Japanese inns, simple and small with tatami mats and no shoes allowed. I stayed there when I first came back from college. It turned me back into a Japanese."

~ ~ ~

Before going to the *Jinrikisha*, Hank decided to get what information he could from the Tokyo police. His cab ride to the Tokyo Central Police Station was nearly one hundred dollars, and he gave Natsume a mental nod. A uniformed policewoman escorted him to the overcrowded area of the detectives' offices and asked him to sit and wait. Forty-five minutes later he met a pair of young, impeccably dressed men who worked in the International Investigation Department of Tokyo's massive police force.

"I speak only English and a little Cuban Spanish," Hank told them.

"That's okay. We speak English, Mr. Daniels," said one of the detectives.

"I'm a friend of Joseph McGrath, the American man who went missing from the Imperial Hotel on April nineteenth. Do you know where he is?" Hank spoke slowly thinking of the English language and his enunciations. He thought about himself being two races, and them a third, hearing him as both black and white; he wondered how different he would sound to them if he were all white or all black. The Japanese men appeared to be deciding who would reply by exchanging glances, until the one who had addressed Hank first said, "Before we discuss the case, Mr. Daniels, we'll need you to fill in some forms with us and answer some questions."

"Can't we skip the bureaucratic approach?" Hank asked somewhat testily.

The other detective said, "It's tiresome, we know, Daniels-*san*, but it's important. Nothing about an investigation ever comes easy."

By the time the forms were completed, and the interview had ended, the skillful Japanese investigators knew everything Hank knew, including Doctor Hito's probable role in the matter. In the middle of the interview, one detective had asked, "What do you think of the evidence that someone from your country anonymously created an interest in Mr. McGrath in Japan?" The issue struck Hank as a serious part of the case, and he felt compelled to help them separate the kidnapping from his mother's doctor friends' desperate attempts to foster sympathetic publicity for their anti-nuclear crusade. Convinced that only his full assistance would help find his friend, Hank became completely cooperative. He also produced a picture of Joe for the investigators, unknowingly adding to what Natsume had already provided. Finished at last, the detectives left the room.

About an hour later both detectives returned and asked Hank to go with them to the Pacific Office of American Affairs. Thoroughly alarmed by this suggestion which sounded much too governmental, Hank rejected their plan repeatedly. The two investigators finally conceded, shook his hand, and told him they would be in touch.

The police dropped Hank off in front of the *Jinrikisha* late in the afternoon. As his eyes scanned the surrounding marshlands, he was met by a courteous staff member and welcomed to the hotel. He removed his shoes without being told, and a chambermaid bowed and escorted him through a sliding paper-paneled wall to a spartan accommodation with only a small low table, a water pitcher, and a tatami mat with a futon folded on it. A long scroll depicting barren tree limbs decorated the wall. The woman brought a meal to his room, and Hank wolfed it down. Not long afterward, the maid returned, discreetly removed the dishes, and laid out his futon bedding.

With everything in twilight, sleep descended upon Hank. He imagined the marshlands outside that framed the Somida River scene. All he saw was gradually darkening. Distracted by the grandeur in the simplicity of traditional Japan, Hank succumbed to his rest and a night without the otherwise constant anxieties about his friend.

~ ~ ~

After that night of simplicity and refreshing sleep, Hank set out on the streets of the west side of Tokyo, looking for a white van marked "*Nishi*." Surrounded by heavy traffic and confusion, he drove up one street and down another in a rented car. Sometimes he parked the car and watched for the van as the traffic passed by, but he was too restless to sit for long. When the gas in the tank got low, he bought more and continued his search. By early afternoon, he was tired and hungry and feeling car sick. Discouraged and angry with himself for thinking he could accomplish something the entire police force could not, he had just decided to go back to the inn when a white van passed him, its side panel emblazoned with the word "*Nasai*."

Startled into action and sure he had found what he was looking for, Hank pounded the car horn again and again as he tried to keep up with the white van, convinced it was speeding to get away. When it moved into a turning lane and Hank passed it, he slammed on the brakes and jumped out of the car. Leaving it with the door open in the middle of heavy traffic, he stepped across the lane divider and waited for the slow-moving white van to pull forward. When it was beside him, Hank put his hands out to signal the driver to stop. The Japanese man driving the van rolled down his window and stared at Hank, his face displaying a mixture of surprise and curiosity.

Placing one hand on the door panel and waving the other in the driver's face, Hank shouted, "Stop, stop! I've been looking for ya! Have ya got an American?" He raised his palms and gestured for the driver to wait, then ran back to the rental car and quickly pulled a picture of Joe out of his suitcase's side pouch. He ran back to the van, which was inching along, and waved the picture in the driver's face. "Here, look at this," he demanded. "Have ya seen this guy?"

The Japanese man looked intently at the photo, then at Hank. *"Nani-oshite imasuka?* [What is it?]" he asked, expressing sudden alarm. Horns began to blow as people realized Hank and his car were causing an obstruction, and vehicles veered angrily as their owners tried to find ways around the rental car.

Unheeding, Hank continued to wave the picture, shouting, "Where is this man? Where is he?"

The Japanese man tried to understand. *"Moichido. Itte kudasai* [Please say again]," he said with a puzzled expression.

Hank's eyes bulged as he interpreted the man's expressions as a guilt-ridden demeanor. He grabbed the door handle of the white van. "Where's McGrath?" he demanded again, rattling the door. "I'll rip this off, you little bastard," he yelled.

The Japanese man's hands were shaking uncontrollably as he hastily rolled up his window. While Hank pounded on the van and shouted threats, the man signaled to the driver of a delivery truck, *"Keisatsu-sho!* [Call the police!]" he said, pointing past Hank. The truck driver nodded vigorously, assuring the driver of the white van he would get the police. Apparently, however, someone else had reported the tall angry black man brandishing his fists at a delivery van in the middle of traffic on a six-lane bridge-feeder street. A moment later the Tokyo police appeared on the scene. Forced to restrain Hank physically, they wrestled him away from the van and sent it on its way, much to the driver's relief.

Hank once again found himself in the Tokyo Central Police Station. Since they recognized him from his earlier visit, they did not lock him in a cell but held him in an interrogation room. After three hours of sitting quietly, he was joined by one of the International Affairs police with whom he had met previously.

"Mr. Daniels," the man said sternly, "you made a grave mistake. The word on the van that took your friend was *'Nishi,'* spelled n-i-s-h-i, which means 'west,' and the word on the white van whose driver you intimidated was *'Nasai,'* spelled n-a-s-a-i, which means 'night.' You terrified an innocent man who works for Oyasumi Nasai, the 'Good Night' bedroom furniture store."

"Damn!" Hank exclaimed. "I'm sorry. I thought—"

"We're well aware of what you thought, Mr. Daniels. Now here is something else for you to think about: If it *had* been the van in which McGrath was abducted, the attack you made probably would have gotten you and your friend killed."

Struck to the core by what he could have done to Joe, Hank threw back his head and ran his hands through his hair. "Shit! I just wanted to help."

"You have noble motives, but you don't know what you are doing. You need to leave this matter to professionals, as you could ruin our attempts to get him released safely."

"You're right, of course," Hank agreed.

"Mr. McGrath would be missed back home, correct?"

"Yeah."

"Go home, then, Mr. Daniels, and hopefully his family will see him again."

The next morning, Hank was on a plane for Chicago.

CHAPTER 13

Without a window to follow the sun's daily patterns, Joe had to rely on sound to keep track of the days. He noticed the sounds of vehicles, especially motorcycles, outside his confinement area and began to separate days from nights by the differences in volume. Mornings were the most clearly defined and recognizable -- when a new day started, he heard a raucous bustle of car horns and motorcycles, mixed with the louder diesel engines of trucks and buses. By what he judged to be the middle of the night, these sounds diminished to almost nothing.

He was fed only twice between the morning and night sounds, usually by the big, dark man from the van. On other days two smaller men would be at the door. They did not come down the basement steps but were content to place Joe's meal at the top of the stairs. They chattered between themselves in rapid Japanese that, of course, Joe did not understand but they never spoke to him, even when he persisted with questions. The big man brought Joe's food in silence but each day he came down the steps to inspect Joe and his surroundings.

The man's physical proximity had a remarkable effect on Joe's abilities to keep his sanity. Joe received the dark man's presence as social contact and the inspections as being cared about. He felt he recognized partiality in their simple exchange of nods and this perceived benefit was made more credible when the dark man bowed to Joe as he left, the depth of his bow indicating that he respected his prisoner. The gesture bespoke something far less threatening than the circumstances of Joe's capture. At each of these encounters Joe gradually felt less threatened by his confinement than he had during his abduction.

The cellar door creaked open twice every day, first with the obvious remains of a breakfast meal, and then, to the best of Joe's judgment, about seven hours later, with leftovers from an exotic array of dinner foods. Served on a tray with tea in a simple pot, the scanty meals consisted of scraps from those in the building above him and there was never enough to make him feel full. His starving body took nourishment from what little body fat he had, and he began to lose weight at an alarming rate.

Water was also in short supply. Some days the men didn't bring the pot of tea and, even though there was water in the bathroom, it tasted sour and gave him stomach aches. Without realizing he was becoming dehydrated; he drank as much of the murky liquid as he could tolerate.

Time passing was maddening. At times he found no important differences in the outside traffic sounds and became confused and, subsequently, more apprehensive than his acquired daily state of anxiety. When deep, truly nocturnal sleep failed to happen and long, drawn-out nights passed, he became more distressed as each day slipped away and he hadn't been found. The scratch marks on the floor became patterned so that he almost wished he had never found the screw to mark his time. There would be six groups of seven and two loose vertical lines on the floor calendar before the writing on cement would cease.

~ ~ ~

Most of the time during his confinement, Joe was left completely alone. When he had been in the basement for five weeks, the thin man surprised him by coming in and speaking to him brusquely.

"You are a small-time issue," the man said, his high, reedy voice once again projecting perfect English, "and it is likely you will soon be released to eradicate any attention still being generated toward you. If we do release you, remember we can retrieve you anytime, anywhere. When you get your freedom, you had better disappear. We could look at this very differently in the future." He held out his hand and gave Joe the card that the tall monk gave Joe in Shiro's monastery.

As much as he longed for conversation, Joe was disinclined to give the tiny tyrant the satisfaction of a reply as he stared stubbornly at the monk's card in his hands, refusing to speak. Illuminated by the dim light of the open bathroom door, his hands had a skeletal look, and he was reminded of the X-ray effects of the exploding atom bombs years ago. The thought came to him that if he had been able to foresee his current predicament, he might have allowed the radiation he underwent with his fellow soldiers to remain a hidden crime among many in the plans for war. Even though he tried to stay fit by exercising, he knew he was losing weight drastically to the point where his health was failing due to a lack of fresh air, sunshine, and proper nutrition.

While his captor waited for a response, Joe wondered whether he would last until the release the thin man had almost promised came to pass. He wondered, too, what the man had meant by "attention still being generated." Could it be that someone was still actively searching for him? Was this nightmare going to end? He felt a rush of thankfulness as he clung to that shred of hope.

~   ~   ~

Bishop Garvin sat in his rectory office. It was early morning, and the telephone rang. Reiko was shopping in the Kure City marketplaces, so the bishop was the only one there to answer. He was tempted to unplug it until Reiko returned but his intuition told him he should not ignore this call. He lifted the receiver and answered in Japanese but was startled when the male voice began to speak in perfect English.

It was the kidnapper. Bishop Garvin knew the voice immediately, even though it was no longer masked. His grip grew vise-like as he pressed the phone to his ear and made the caller repeat himself. "What did you say, sir?" he asked artlessly. "Who is this, please?"

"You know who I am," the voice rasped. "I'm calling to do you a favor, so quit playing games. Listen closely. McGrath is of no use to us anymore, and we have decided to let him go. In three days,

Friday, we will leave him in Nagasaki—near the Monument of the Twenty-Six Christian traitors. You know the place?"

"Yes, the martyrs, yes, I do," the bishop answered breathlessly. "Is he all right?"

"That depends on you. If you tell anyone else of this, anyone at all, my associates will kill him, and you will find a corpse."

"I need Reiko to know and help me. Please! I am an old man," the bishop begged. The man was silent while the bishop held his breath as he prayed for the right answer.

"The orphan girl, then—but no one else," the kidnapper finally said. "Understand?"

"I do. But…"

The phone clicked and the connection was gone. Bishop Garvin cradled the receiver, walked briskly to the chapel, and briefly gave thanks for God's care and intervention. He found the housemaid and told her he was taking Reiko to Nagasaki and would be leaving right away, allowing her to assume they were needed at Oura Cathedral again. He told her he did not know when they would return and that he would call beforehand. "And please," he said, "I need a fit young man to run to the markets as fast as he can to find Reiko and bring her back."

"I know just such a fellow, Your Excellency," the woman replied.

"Wonderful," he said.

The housekeeper hesitated in case he had any more instructions.

"Well, go then!" he cried, surprising her. "This is an emergency!" Scurrying like a frightened rabbit, she rushed out of the room to get the runner.

The bishop hurried to his chambers to pack. *We must leave as soon as Reiko returns if we are to be there in time*, he thought. *We will travel straight through and sleep afterward.* He carried his suitcase to the entrance and set it down. All he could do after that was pace the floor and wait.

Minutes later, Reiko rushed into the rectory. She had run all the way back, gasping for breath, when the bishop hustled her into her room and urged her to start packing. When she looked at him questioningly, he told her about the phone call. As soon as she knew the purpose of their trip, there was no need to tell her to hurry. She pulled out a suitcase, started to fill it, and within a few minutes she was ready. They left for the train station, prepared to board the first available southbound train.

They arrived in Nagasaki the day before McGrath's scheduled release. After apprising the Oura Cathedral Prelate, the Bishop's successor, of why they were there and the need for secrecy, they ate supper and retired for the night, with assurances from the Prelate that he would wake them the moment anything happened.

~ ~ ~

Early Friday morning, amid torrential rains, a white van raced toward the hill of Nishizaka. As it drew opposite Oura Cathedral and the sanctuary of the Twenty-Six Martyrs, its doors opened and a man's body jettisoned out, landing face up on the manicured grass of the hillside. The white vehicle careened down the street, back doors flapping, and disappeared. At the same time, a black car squealed to a stop in front of the statues of the Twenty-Six Martyrs. A man leapt out and ran to the monument, found a somewhat sheltered spot, and wrote something on the wall with red paint. Running back toward the car, he stopped on the steps, pulled out a knife, and scratched something into the concrete. He jumped back into the car and sped off in the same direction as the white van.

Joe McGrath lay spread-eagle in the driving rain, unconscious and mercifully unaware of his battered condition. The rainstorm slowly abated, and the sun rose in clear skies, beating down on Joe's sodden clothing, creating a steamy mist. The Christian worshipers who discovered his body were horrified by the number of cuts and bruises on his head, face, and hands. Blood oozed slowly from his wounds as he lay unmoving, with not even a twitch of his fingers or a flicker of his lashes. He did not appear to be breathing. Convinced they had stumbled upon a dead man; the panicky worshipers stopped the Sacristan on his way to the Oura Cathedral and asked for his help.

A short, sullen-looking man, wide-backed with muscular shoulders and thin legs, the Sacristan's limp and poor posture painted a grotesquely misshapen figure. Bending over the inert form, the Sacristan clucked sympathetically at the carcass spotlighted by the brilliant sunlight now streaming through the trees. Without hesitation, he scooped Joe up, cradling him in his arms as a father would a small child and carried the drooping body into the rectory. The Sacristan laid Joe gently on a couch in the reception area solarium and went to fetch the Prelate.

The Prelate immediately rushed to inform the Bishop and Reiko who were at breakfast and then he called the police. Lights at flash and sirens screaming, two police cars appeared in less than five minutes, followed closely by an ambulance. A short while later, a conspicuously American-made black car pulled up, and two FBI operatives plus Agent Teach from the Office of American Affairs parked in front of the rectory. The reporter Natsume Toson and his photographer also arrived and hastily set up their equipment to capture unfolding events.

The rectory bustled with activity. Surprised that the police, emergency crew, American agents, and media had converged at the scene within such a short time, Reiko shot a questioning glance at the bishop. "Is this rapid response the result of the call you made from Kure City?" she asked.

"Yes," he answered. "I felt I could trust Natsume, so I asked him to discreetly use his influence with those he deals with in the police force and other people he knows in high places to make sure all involved in Joe's case would be on alert today. The reporter, the agents, and everyone else have been stationed within a few blocks of the cathedral, well out of sight, since early morning and were ready to sit there all day, if necessary, until they received word Joe had been found. This plan decreased their response time enormously, plus having a reporter present with a photographer will ensure an accurate record."

"That was wise," Reiko replied, certain that having a reporter at the site had been the bishop's idea. She stepped back from the couch to allow the medics more room. Her eyes welled in tears.

Joe lay limp and unmoving. His skin had a death-like pallor, and his muscles were beginning to show the first signs of rigor. Though they had been told their patient was no longer alive, the emergency medical technicians treated him as they did all seriously injured victims until a doctor declared them dead. After taking his temperature, they stripped off his wet clothes and wrapped him in heated blankets, murmuring among themselves about the excessive bruising on his torso. They moved him onto a stretcher and cleaned his head wounds, which were still oozing slightly, and wrapped his head in a gauze bandage.

As the medics were working on Joe, Agent Teach entered the rectory. The FBI men followed, stationing themselves beside the couch and beginning to make radio calls.

"What do you think you're doing?" Teach shouted at the EMTs. Uncomprehending, they looked at the angry man, then at each other, shrugged, and turned back to Joe. One of them was adjusting an oxygen mask while the other began to fill a hypodermic needle from a small bottle.

"Stop!" Teach shouted frantically, waving his hands in the air. "You're tampering with evidence! We want him officially pronounced dead by a physician at the hospital before anyone touches the body anymore. *Wakari masu?* [Do you understand?]"

"Hey, Teach," one of the FBI agents interjected. "Can you identify this guy?"

"What? Oh, yeah," said Teach, "It's Joe McGrath, all right."

"Mr. Joseph R. McGrath, Army veteran, from America," Bishop Garvin stated, giving the name all the dignity, he could muster.

"Whatever," Teach said.

The Japanese medical technician tugged on the agent's sleeve and pointed to Joe's bandaged head. "*Li desu ne?* [This is good, isn't it?]" she asked. Gently pressing the oxygen mask again and asking permission through gestures to continue treating Joe.

Teach wagged his head violently. Lowering his voice and slowing his speech, he struggled to communicate his meaning. In all the years he had been stationed in Tokyo, Teach had not bothered to master Japanese, relying instead on his Japanese subordinates. When he did try to speak the language, his pronunciation sounding so garbled that only a skilled translator paying close attention could decipher what he was trying to say.

"*Matte* [Wait]," he intoned. "*Moo ichido onegai shi masu* [One more time, please]. *Wakari mashito ne?* [You understood, didn't you?] *Chigai masu* [It is not correct]." Unsure whether they understood, he pointed at the oxygen mask and the hypodermic and waved his hands in a dismissive gesture. "*Jya mato ne* [See you later]." When the EMTs continued to look at him vacantly and made no move to put away the equipment, Teach turned to the room at large. "Can anybody here translate?" he asked, clearly frustrated.

"Reiko, will you please?" Bishop Garvin requested.

"Yes," said Reiko, moving closer to the stretcher.

"Good," Teach said. He asked Reiko if she understood what he had been trying to say and, when she answered in the affirmative, he asked her to repeat it in proper Japanese. When she had finished, one of the technicians gave her a long answer which Reiko translated into English for Agent Teach.

"This person believes Joseph McGrath may not be dead, as he is still bleeding slightly, and she can find no lividity. She wants to continue to administer oxygen and give him what she called, inotropic therapy. She said it was for his heart," Reiko spoke in a matter-of-fact manner.

Teach snorted derisively. "These people are only technicians," he sneered. "Of course, he's dead. Just look at him."

Reiko opened her mouth to object but Teach overrode her with another request. "Ask where they put his clothes, will you?"

Despite the agent's rudeness, Reiko did as he asked. After he had bagged the soggy garments, Teach turned to her and said testily, more as a demand than a request, "Will you please tell your people not to corrupt my evidence or my crime scene? Bad enough that dunce brought McGrath's body all the way over here from the actual crime scene, without people handling everything and tramping over the grass. Damned rain didn't help, either probably destroyed all kinds of clues."

Reiko nodded politely but said nothing. She listened to the FBI agents and realized they would be calling the U.S. soon to give the terrible news. Her heart was filled not only with her own personal sorrow but also with deep sympathy for Joe McGrath. She followed the medical technicians as they carried Joe to the waiting ambulance. Her concern showed on her face as she stood aside to watch, unconsciously stretching out her arm when the litter threatened to tip over. She wanted to go with him in the ambulance but did not have the authority. She would have to ride to the hospital with the bishop.

Ignoring Agent Teach, who was watching to ensure the technicians did nothing else to revive the man, Reiko called out to the emergency techs in Japanese. "*Matte, kudasai* [Wait, please]," she pleaded. Seeing her delay the EMTs, Teach started yelling from the church steps, but Reiko paid him no attention. She fixed her eyes on the medics and begged silently, the intense emotion in her face making it clear that she wanted their maximum help for Joe. As Teach ranted, she blinked rapidly to quell her rising tears.

The medic who wanted to give Joe oxygen and the heart medicine stopped in mid-action and held the rear door open. She investigated Reiko's tear-filled face for a long moment. Throwing a contemptuous glance in Teach's direction, she gave a deep nod and said, "*Sumi masen. Hai, lie daijyubu desu* [I'm sorry. Yes, don't worry about it]." She locked eyes with Reiko before pulling the door shut. Reiko said, "Hontoo desu ka? [Is that true?]"

"Hai," the emergency medic assured her, while staring defiantly at the rude man still watching their every move as she pulled the ambulance's door shut.

CHAPTER 14
NAGASAKI JAPAN

When Joe awoke from his corpselike state, he was in a hospital bed surrounded by a nurse and doctor, Reiko, the Bishop, and Natsume Toson.

"Where am I?" he mumbled.

"You are in a Nagasaki hospital, my son," the bishop replied, "surrounded by friends."

"They let me go! Thank God! I'm out!" Joe breathed.

"Yes," the bishop said in a reverent whisper, "and by the grace of God, you are alive!"

Joe's body visibly relaxed and he fell into a deep sleep. The doctor assured the visitors it would be normal for Joe to sleep for a long time and suggested they take a lunch break. They politely refused, stating that everyone wanted to be there when Joe woke up again.

An hour or so later, Joe opened his eyes. He looked around the room and saw his friends. "So, it wasn't a dream," he said weakly. He began to sit up, but the bishop restrained him with a gentle yet definitive hand motion near Joe's shoulder.

"No, son," the bishop cautioned, "lie back. You've been severely injured. Don't even move your head."

Joe smiled at the bishop wincing as his lips pulled on a cut. He gingerly fingered the bandaged wounds on his head and remembered the vicious beating he had received from the two men who had fed him without ever talking to him. They had attacked while loading him into the van and had rained blows from their pointed shoes and hard leather heels onto his head and torso so swiftly he had been unable to fight back. He wondered why they had assaulted him and guessed it was because they resented the thin man's decision to let him go.

"But I wanna see everybody," he protested mildly. "I'll be careful." Using the bedside rails for support, he raised himself to a sitting position while doing his best to stifle involuntary groans. Reiko and the Bishop showed deep concern when Joe disregarded the latter's advice but became calm when a nurse who had been assigned to check on Joe every fifteen minutes entered the room and, apparently undisturbed by his desire to sit upright, adjusted his bed so he could lean back comfortably.

"Are you with us now, Joe?" the bishop asked. Reiko remained silent, searching Joe's eyes and noticing how the overhead lighting reflected in them.

"I'm here," Joe said. He looked around the room and came back to Reiko, whom he acknowledged with a long look and a smile. "It's good to see all of ya again. I wasn't sure that was gonna happen."

"We weren't either," said Natsume Toson. "The police think the kidnappers left you for dead. They used bright red paint spray to write 'Ayamachi [Mistake]' on the sculpture of the Twenty-Six Martyrs, and they scratched the symbol 'Cm,' for 'Critical Mass,' into the steps. You were found on the hill of Nishizaka, across from Oura Cathedral."

"Geez!" Joe responded.

"They drugged you, you know," Natsume continued.

Just then the doctor, who had been informed that Joe was awake, entered the room.

"Tell him about the drug, will you, please, Doctor?" Natsume requested.

"I talk Japanese, you say what I say?" the doctor asked.

"It would be my honor," Natsume answered respectfully in Japanese.

Joe listened carefully while the physician, using Natsume as his interpreter, explained that the people who found Joe thought he was dead because the thugs had injected him with an ancient Samaria-era potion often used for nefarious purposes in historic Japan. The drug reduced the body to a state in which the muscles tightened, mimicking rigor mortis, and making movement impossible, decreasing the rate of all bodily functions to such a low level they were virtually undetectable. "To the untrained eye, you seemed dead," the doctor declared, "and your body was sent here so a physician could sign your death certificate."

"Then a miracle happened, Joseph," the bishop interjected. The doctor looked at him with a puzzled frown as Natsume translated the Bishop's English to him. "Reiko and the emergency medical technicians saved your life."

Startled, Joe looked at Reiko, who modestly lowered her head. The doctor spoke again. "Yes, the EMTs saw that your head wounds continued to bleed—very slowly, but bleeding, which does not happen if you are dead. They also saw no lividity, a darkness caused by the pooling of internal blood in the lowest part of a dead body."

The bishop interrupted again. "But when they told the agent from American Affairs about these possible signs of life and that they wanted to give you oxygen and administer a shot to stimulate your heart, he denied them permission to do anything else for you and ordered them to transport your body to the hospital. I was there, and I heard all this—and so did Reiko."

"Who was the agent? Teach?" Joe asked.

"Yes, that was the man's name," Reiko said quietly, nodding her head.

"And you saved my life?" Joe asked, staring at her.

"Indeed," the bishop affirmed. "Before the ambulance left, she begged the EMTs to help you, and—as they told the FBI later—they interpreted that as permission to do whatever they felt was necessary to bring you around—and sure enough, you showed signs of life for the first time just as the ambulance arrived here."

"Your eyelids, we were told, flickered ever so slightly," Reiko said softly.

"Yes. So, they took you to the emergency room instead of the hospital morgue," the bishop added.

"Geez! Thank you, Reiko! Thank God!" Joe exclaimed gratefully. He leaned back and closed his eyes while he considered the enormity of what had happened and how blessed he was. "I could be dead right now," he whispered. "Thank you, Reiko and everybody, *thank* you."

The doctor, for whom Natsume had continued to translate, smiled and pushed a pitcher of water toward Joe. "I leave now," he said. "You drink. Good for you."

Joe's eyes flew open as the doctor departed.

"Relax, Joseph," said the bishop.

"Yes, Joe," Natsume chimed in.

"Okay," said Joe, "But I want to know more."

"That's understandable," said Natsume.

"Thanks."

"You're welcome. Now let's get your head back down. You've been through quite an ordeal, and you need to heal."

"I know. I was lucky, though."

"Lucky? How so?" Natsume asked but Joe was fast asleep'

After a few awkward moments all the visitors filed quietly out of the room and gathered in the hallway. They left the hospital in a group and agreeing to meet again in the morning.

~   ~   ~

That same evening Joe awoke after Natsume came back by himself and was talking to the nurse in Japanese outside Joe's door. Joe was having a nightmare and yelling incoherent words when Natsume arrived, and the nurse asked the inquisitive reporter to let Joe sleep.

~   ~   ~

The following morning about ten o'clock Joe's visitors were all back in his hospital room again and waiting. The nurse said that Joe had been taken to have more X Rays and that he would return soon.

The nurses, doctors and patients and visitors all speaking Japanese, and the beeping and electronic noises of different devices along with phones filled the senses of Joe's visitors, and the odor of coffee and cleaning chemicals and medications captured them all consciously and unconsciously. Reiko seemed most affected. She was standing near the door motionless when Joe was wheeled into the room. Reiko almost collapsed into a chair and crossed her legs with her folded hands on her knee. She appeared exhausted.

The bishop was obviously in prayer when Natsume spoke to Joe, Hello Joseph, it is good for us all to see you again."

Joe nodded and said, "Good morning, and thank you all for being here again."

The bishop blessed Joe and all in the room with a sign of the Cross, muttering something in Latin. He was holding a small bottle of Holy Water with his arm extended and sprinkling its contents over Joe's bed. The Japanese nurse seemed to accept the bishop's ritualistic actions perhaps as not unlike Japanese practitioners of thaumaturgy.

Natsume was sitting against the wall farthest from Joe when he asked, "Joe yesterday you said that you were lucky about something. I can't tell you how curious I am to know what that lucky something was?"

"Yeah, I was thinking that, well, it coulda been a lot worse. The only time they hurt me was when they first grabbed me and when they were getting ready to get rid of me. They didn't do me any other harm—'cept for feeding me swill and stale water, just enough to keep me alive. The rest of the time they left me alone, day and night, and I had lots of time for thinking and praying."

Reiko said, "We are glad you are free now, Joseph, and that you found a way to survive."

"I was afraid at first, really scared," Joe admitted. "Then I started to feel detached." He looked earnestly at Bishop Garvin. "Ya know," he said, "I've known something about these things for a long time, and it consoles me." He filled his glass with water and drank it all down. "Ya won't believe me." He refilled the glass and took a few swallows.

"What is it?" the bishop urged.

"If you're interested and you really want to know…"

"Go ahead, what is it?"

"Well, okay, here goes nothing," Joe began, taking a deep breath. "I think we're about to see a real miracle, cause—well, first, something's really wrong with the whole world, ya know what I mean? People go on killing each other in the name of religions, drugs are still ruining people's lives, children are abducted and enslaved, governments are screwed up, entire nations are in financial shambles, and scholars-turned-scientists think they're gonna develop great things but end up making horrible weapons instead—worse than their predecessors. Chemical companies sell poison as if it wasn't poison. The whole mess. The world remains crazy."

He drank a few more swallows of water as his audience waited patiently. He looked at the bishop. "Does the Church know what's going on? I mean, if there isn't something ultimate going on, what is it? Maybe I'm gonna need heavy medication, but I think even time is different. If God isn't in charge, we're all gonna go nuts. Otherwise…" He expelled a long breath through his nostrils and put his hand to his forehead. "No earthly plan to correct our lives seems convincing. The global economy and governments depend on chance and strategies that are nothing more than gambling. I believe everybody—the whole planet—is in something cosmic, a totally new relationship with time and time's changes."

The bishop quickly looked down but in a way that stole some of Joe's confidence. Joe stopped talking and leaned back, closing his eyes, and holding his head with both hands.

"You should rest now, Joseph," the bishop said.

"Maybe I'm too simple," Joe persisted. "I'm not a theologian, like you, Your Excellency. I realize theologian types are prob'ly more sophisticated. Simple things. Oh, well, I guess I thought you'd understand." His listeners exchanged concerned glances as Joe spoke more of things they didn't fully comprehend. "Listen—I—eh— the whole reality of my being in Japan would be for nothing, and I can't believe that. Listen, please, this is important. We're in the time of our lives. Doesn't the Church know that? Geez, my head hurts."

"What do you want to say, Joe? What is it? What is so important?" asked Natsume.

Joe held his hand to his mouth and bent his head down as if unsure of himself, but the bishop said, "Go ahead tell us, Joe."

When he spoke again his obvious pain distressed everyone in the room.

"Something will happen, just happen one day. No one will earn it, but somehow everyone will see themselves as God sees them. That's it. That's what I know—in my basement prison, I called it the transformation."

The room fell into a curious silence, as if everyone expected someone else to speak. No one did, and the muffled sounds from someplace outside the room were absorbing enough to satisfy the possible awkwardness.

Reiko left and returned with a nurse, who gave Joe a shot of painkiller. "Thank you," Joe mumbled gratefully. The drug took effect almost immediately. Joe smiled as the nurse cranked his bed down, putting him into a flat position. He opened his eyelids halfway and glanced drowsily at Reiko and the others, then closed them again, his body relaxing as he fell asleep.

Reiko insisted that she would stay and that he should have someone recognizable when he woke again. Natsume and the Bishop left the room quietly, leaving Reiko and the nurse behind. The nurse stayed to adjust Joe's covers and monitor his life supporters. Reiko, feeling comforted by Joe's rest sat listening to his gentle breathing.

~   ~   ~

Hank Daniels, with his leukemia nagging at his concerns for endurance, returned to Japan. When his plane touched down in Nagasaki early Saturday afternoon, Hank quickly gathered his luggage and hailed a taxicab. Even though he was very tired from both the flight and his increased doses of medications, he intended to visit Joe McGrath as his first stop. In the hospital he rode the elevator to Joe's floor and was told his friend was in the solarium.

Looking like the weary traveler he was, he walked into the solarium with his suitcase and carry-on. Joe was the only person in the room. He was sitting in a wheelchair between two large potted plants, looking out the window, his back to the door. Hank set his baggage against the wall and hooked his thumbs into his belt. "Hey, good buddy!" he said quietly. "What's up?"

Joe's head jerked around as he fumbled with the wheels. "Hank?" he cried out excitedly. "Hank?" He managed to get the chair turned around by the time Hank reached him. Clasping arms, they voiced the code words their North Philly teenage friends used when seeking each other out in the dark. Their eyes filled and they both looked away as they surreptitiously wiped them dry.

Joe's heart flooded with joy. "You came all the way to Japan?" A very full grin spread across his face.

"Ya want me to say I was in the neighborhood or something?" Hank shot back, but his face quickly became serious. "Heck, I can't kid around." He looked Joe over thoroughly, noting the amount of weight he had lost and his cuts, bruises, and bandaged head. *He looks like hell,* he thought, and said, "Ya look kinda rough, like you lost an alley fight in South Philly. Are ya okay, man?"

"Yeah, I'm good," Joe said. "Still a bit weak in the knees, so they're making me use this chair. I'll look better once I get some meat on my bones. Ya didn't happen to bring an Italian hoagie with ya, did ya?"

Smiling, Hank pictured the big Philadelphia sandwiches while he pulled up a chair opposite Joe. Then filled with guilt, he figured the police had told Joe about Dr. Hito's publicity stunt. He began his apology. "That Japanese doctor—well, I guess ya know—eh—" he faltered. "Hito, Doctor Kiesha Hito, is his full name. He churned up the attention that got you in trouble. He gave your name and your mission, he called it a mission, and he gave it to the Japanese news media."

"Was he trying to get me in trouble?" Joe asked, his eyes widening in surprise.

"I couldn't say, I guess not. I guess he was being the activist that he is."

"Whatcha talking about?"

THE GIRL IN JAPAN

"What Hito did," Hank repeated. "He sent out a news release all about you being in Japan over the nuclear issues and about you and me being atomic bomb veterans."

"No, I didn't know that. Was he against us?" asked Joe, completely bewildered.

"He made all kinds of contacts with the Japanese press about us—about *you*—and the bombs in Nevada!"

"Oh, wow! He's the one who set me up? I'll be darned! The reporter *said* it was prob'ly somebody I knew. Geez!"

"I'm sorry, Joe. Ya know I'd never do anything to hurt ya." Hank hung his head, his shame for getting them involved preventing him from connecting with Joe's eyes.

Joe pondered all the new information about the doctor and his group for a moment before he spoke. "I know how bad ya feel, Hank," he finally said, "but what Hito did ain't important now. Things happen, one way or another. You could never convince me that this wasn't all gonna happen to me somehow, no matter what. There's something going on that surpasses all we know or do. We're messengers, nuclear war messengers, you and me. Nobody will listen, but we are."

Hank was astonished by Joe's tranquility. Relief rushed into his mind and nervous system, prompted by the forgiving tone of Joe's voice, while at the same time, he was mystified that Joe seemed so composed. It set his heart at ease and Hank made a mental note to ask more about it later. "I'm impressed that you can forgive Hito and the others," he said.

"Well, ya know ya can't let people drop a freakin atomic bomb on ya and not do something about it," Joe replied. "Doctor Hito just got things started.

"Okay, man. Guess so, good buddy."

"Natsume," Hank said, "he told me the U.S. government put out an official statement that there's basically no evidence of large-scale health risks in their human nuclear guinea pig stunts. They compared the radiation exposure we got to the amount a person acquires in a normal life span. They said it's about the same and based their claim on that. Oh, and while you were kidnapped, that's when I got in touch with our old buddies, Hutton and Perkins."

"Really?"

"Yeah, I'll tell you about that. Hutton is a lawyer in Chicago and Perkins is a New York cop, a detective in Manhattan. It's unreal! Hutton and Perkins thought the government made the statement to discredit all of us 'participants.' But guess what—I found out they approved medical compensation for American servicemen who were within one hundred fifty miles of Hiroshima or seventy-five miles of Nagasaki during the 1945 occupation. Now what does that say about our exposure?"

"That trench was mighty close, man. Hutton and Perkins, wow, you've been busy, man!"

"Yeah, it was all about you," Hank said.

Joe nodded absently. His mind had been somewhere else since Hank had spoken the reporter's name. "How d'ya know Natsume?" he asked. "Didja meet him here today?"

"Nah, on my first trip over here. He found me and kept me from causing more trouble for ya. Ya got a few Japanese allies, and he's one of em."

"Your *first* trip? Ya mean ya came over before when they grabbed me?"

"Like a fool, yeah. Didn't know Japan, didn't know Japanese but I flew in as soon as I heard. I was looking all over for you."

"Geez! Thanks!"

"You'da done the same for me. 'Course, I almost made things worse for ya, stomping all 'round Tokyo. I scared the shit out of a guy driving a white van and the cops hauled me in. It was North Philly all over again."

"Oh, man!" Joe laughed as he pictured Hank and the Japanese cops. "I wanna hear about that!"

"You will," snorted Hank, adding his own guffaws. "They prob'ly got my picture up in all the Japanese post offices."

A nurse looked in on them and held a finger to her lips to quiet their boisterous laughter, but her smile showed that she was pleased to see Joe in good spirits. So, the two of them covered their mouths and spluttered as they fought for control, feeling like kids again. Joe thought it was the best medicine anyone could ever give him.

"When I get home," he said, "ya gotta come back to North Philly so we can visit the old neighborhood. Then ya can tell me the whole story—all the stories."

"Sounds good to me. I can hear that juke box at Jo Jo's right now."

"The place is about the same, I guess, but not all the music is the same."

"Are the marks still on the ceiling from guys squeezing those plastic ketchup bottles into the air?"

"Prob'ly. They wouldn't wanna destroy that -- it's a work of art," Joe said.

"Sure is." Hank leaned back, a smile on his face.

"I gotta ask ya," Joe said. "What's your attorney say about all this jazz? Is Hutton really a lawyer? And Perkins a cop?"

"Yeah, they are. I haven't talked to my lawyer since way before you were abducted but he'd say there are more lawyers who will support the government than there are ones who'd take our case."

"Do you know what? There's this government agent in Tokyo who's got it in for me for some reason. He's with the Office of American Affairs and, if he had his way, I'd be dead by now. He acts like I'm a scab on our country's nose."

Hank ran a hand over his hair. "I dunno what that guy's job description is but the government knows all about our exposures. They've catalogued a dozen or so cancers that've popped up among us and forms of leukemia are at the top of the list. My Army disease issue sounds like some supply sergeant handed it out: 'Daniels, H. Sergeant E5, one each, men's O.D. (olive drab) pistol belt, helmet liner, socks men's, deadly leukemia one each—move on, soldier!'"

"Hey, ya know a lot about what they've done regarding our Nevada days, don'tcha?"

"Well, like I told you back home, I've done piles of reading and research. There's a large amount of data now, and it's all public information. You can even view the films the Army took."

"It's never gonna be a big issue, though, is it?"

"I don't think so. People are desensitized to these kinds of things. I'm surprised you stirred up anything at all. Must be different in Japan."

Feeling guilty again about Hito's role in it all despite Joe's acceptance, Hank said, "I sure wish this hadn't happened, especially to you, Joe."

"Don't worry about it. I think the bad part is over now."

"I hope you're right."

"Hey, remember those fifty-mile withdrawal marches we did at Fort Lewis during the Cuban missile crisis?" Joe asked.

"Yeah, I remember three of 'em -- one time at the Star, then over in Yakima, and in the rain at Fort Lewis. The last time they took us down to that river crossing where that guy drowned right up ahead of us."

"If ya slip off a wet, steel pontoon bridge with your backpack and steel helmet and rifle on ya, ya sink. It's in the manual."

"We got by, man. Missed dying in Laos by a hair, and the whole Vietnam War opened up in front of us and we didn't hafta go. We were lucky. Think of Eddy Drake, and Sloane, Big D, and the other guys on the corner who died in Vietnam." Hank stared solemnly out the window.

"They were training us for that invasion of Laos and the beginning of Vietnam," said Joe. "They knew what was coming."

"Ya wonder what they were really training us for, some kinda nuclear nightmare."

"Like ya said, we were lucky it never happened. Ya'd think it was in case of a war, like a Third World War," said Joe.

"Or the insertion of the whole Chinese army into someplace in Southeast Asia," Hank offered.

"Who knows?"

"Who knows? The Middle East, or Pakistan and India, or splintered nations in Africa could blow the socks off it all, and any of the nuclear power." Joe nodded in agreement and the two fell silent.

Joe finally raised his head to ask, "Ya love that teaching job ya got, don'tcha?"

"Yeah, I do."

Joe started rubbing his shoulder. "I remember you taking my B.A.R. (Browning Automatic Rifle) off me just when I felt my arm was coming out of the socket from carrying the damn thing?"

"Yeah, good buddy, I felt bad for ya. The Browning weighed nineteen-point-four pounds gets to be five hundred point four pounds when ya march fifty miles. God! That was drudgery, total drudgery."

"I remember ya strolling up and taking that weight off me. Your M.I. felt like a feather duster compared to that thing. Anyway, thanks for carrying my B.A.R., Mr. Daniels. Those shitbirds, the guys who snatched me, pulled my arm out of the socket on purpose when they grabbed me, and it made me remember carrying that weapon fifty miles."

"The cops told me the kidnappers prob'ly hurt ya, Joe. It killed me to hear that when I was over here looking for ya. You're welcome about the B.A.R., but I prob'ly did it cause I sometimes feel guilty as hell. I'm the one got us into this. I'm the one said we should join the fuckin' Army when we were kids back in Philly. And now I got you into this activist jazz, in Japan no less. God, man we gotta stop listening to me!"

"Don't blame yourself, Hank. Back then when we were growing up, ya went in the service. Everybody did."

"Yeah."

"They were gonna use us and we were gonna go. The bad part is, cause of political and corporate corruption, they started sending us to other people's wars to make money or protect money."

"Yeah," Hank uttered, "fuckin' American aristocracy nuts playing with people's lives. I remember. You're right. But ya know, after the Second World War, we shouldn't have sent young Americans to die or be wounded anywhere. None of the wars since have been worthy of that. What's the United States doing getting involved in other countries' civil wars? Can you imagine Koreans or Vietnamese armies fighting alongside the Confederate states in our Civil War?"

"Maybe if the communists and capitalists didn't engage in wars, they wouldn't have generated paths for psychopaths like Hitler, Stalin and Mao Zedong," said Joe.

The two men continued to discuss all sorts of issues, large and small, just as they had as kids in Philadelphia. Joe accompanied Hank to the cafeteria and Hank bought a carry-out dinner so they could eat together in Joe's room. They resumed their conversation after that— it seemed they would never run out of things to talk about—until Hank showed signs of exhaustion. Persuaded by his friend not to bother with a hotel that night, Joe asked the nurse for an extra blanket and Hank slept in Joe's room on the reclining chair.

CHAPTER 15

The next morning as the elevator doors opened for the first time, they revealed Reiko and the Bishop. "I thought you were returning to Kure City," Joe said.

"That was our plan," the bishop replied, "but we discovered that the Prelate needs our help on another matter that will require us to stay in Nagasaki for a few more days. We were pleased to hear that because we wanted to visit you at least once more."

"I'm pleased to hear it, too. I was just thinking how great it is now for both of you to meet Hank.

"Yes. We already know Mr. Daniels, of course," the bishop said, smiling broadly.

Joe gave a surprised look but quickly put the previous visit by Hank together with the bishop's statement.

"Hey, I think we ought to move this reunion outta the hall before the nurses kick us out," Joe suggested. "The solarium should be big enough for us all and we can talk."

After Reiko gained permission, speaking in Japanese, at the nurses' station to use the solarium freely, the group filed into the sunny, plant-filled room, rearranging the chairs in a crooked circle.

The bishop, grinning broadly, said, "Well, I don't know about the rest of you, but I'd like to visit the cafeteria for some hot coffee. How about you, Hank?"

Hank agreed and left with the bishop, leaving Joe and Reiko together. Realizing that he was alone with Reiko, Joe suddenly could not find words. When he looked up, she smiled at him, he returned her smile, but he could still not find words to say.

Reiko, despite her natural shyness, broke the silence. "I am happy to be with you, Joseph."

"So am I—happy to be with you, Reiko. To me, you are what is wonderful about Japan. Without you, it would have all been a nightmare."

"It has been a nightmare. If I help you to see it differently, then I am honored." She hesitated for a moment before excusing herself and leaving the solarium for the restrooms.

Joe watched Reiko leave the solarium. He moved his wheelchair to the hallway and watched her walking imagining her barefoot and strolling across a field of grass in a sunny garden. When she was out of his sight, he quickly wheeled himself back to his room where he put a fresh hospital garment on and tried to comb his hair.

When Joe returned to the solarium, Natsume Toson was waiting outside the door. "Good, you're here, Natsume," Joe said, shaking Natsume's hand.

Appearing slightly embarrassed, Natsume chuckled, "I just came by to see how your recovery is progressing." He hesitated. And then he said, "I don't want to cause you any further problems while you are here in Japan. Of course, my newspaper readers are very interested in what happens to you," said Natsume with a smile. "Thanks for letting me stay."

"Are you kidding?" Joe asked. "If you hadn't set things in motion so the paramedics could get to me so fast, I wouldn't be here."

"I'm just glad I could help," Natsume said, following Joe into the room to add a chair to the circle.

~ ~ ~

In the hallway, Reiko became aware of a Japanese man staring at her. He looked directly at her, unabashedly following her every move. She felt targeted but refused to give the stranger the satisfaction of seeing the concern and hesitation that surged inside her. She walked directly into the restroom, and the man brazenly caught the door and followed her into the small space.

She felt a pang of great alarm when he reached into his pocket, but it subsided when his hand emerged holding not a knife or a gun, but an innocuous envelope. He handed it to her, saying in Japanese, "We expect you to act promptly with everything we are telling you in this letter."

His pronunciation was influenced by a region or tongue Reiko thought she should recognize but didn't. He seemed like any other man, not a terrorist or fanatic, and she was no longer afraid of him, but she was outraged.

"Read it carefully and obey!" he commanded, then placed his open hand on his chest and patted it with a gesture and facial expression she interpreted as satisfaction. Pivoting suddenly, he left the room, closing the door behind him.

Reiko, after a few seconds, opened the door and looked out into the hall, but the man had disappeared, so she went back inside and locked the door. She felt violated by the man's intrusion and deeply disgusted. The more she thought about the encounter, the angrier she became. She decided not to read the message, and when she reentered the hallway, she tossed the unopened envelope on a chair and left it behind. As she walked back into the solarium, Reiko noticed that her breathing rhythm had changed to fast and shallow, almost to the point of hyperventilation, and she realized she was both infuriated and scared.

Upon entering the solarium, she sat down beside Joe. "They are here, Joseph," she whispered. "A man followed me, right out there in the hallway."

Joe's eyes opened wide. Frowning, he asked, "Was he wearing mostly brown clothes?" He knew his kidnappers generally dressed in brown, he had surmised in his captivity, to indicate some clan or gang identity. He was at that time unaware of their Brown Dragons gang organization.

"Yes," Reiko answered.

A shiver of fear ran up Joe's spine. "Is he still out there?"

"I do not think so," replied Reiko. "I did not see him anywhere when I returned from the restroom."

"We need to tell the police," Joe said. "Let's go."

Leaving Natsume in the solarium, Joe and Reiko quickly found a security guard who hurried them to the security office, where they reported the details of Reiko's experience. After about twenty minutes with the police, they returned to the sunroom.

By that time, Hank and the Bishop had arrived back with coffees for all. Hank began to question Joe and Reiko. "Where'd the two of ya go?" he asked, switching his inquiring glance from one to the other. "I thought I saw you talking with a security guy."

Speaking rapidly and nervously, Joe said, "Yeah, well, it feels like trouble! One of the bad guys confronted Reiko right out there."

"Where?" Hank asked. "Here in the hospital?"

"Yeah, right out there in the hallway."

"He followed me into the restroom," Reiko said.

"What?" the bishop cried. Everyone's face registered shock and fear.

"Tell 'em about it, please, Reiko," Joe requested. The group fell silent and listened while Reiko gave a full account of her encounter with the man in brown.

When she had finished, Hank asked, "What'd the message say?" He leaned forward eagerly, ready to absorb every word. Natsume took out his notebook and pen.

"I did not want to read it. I left it there unopened," Reiko answered.

After a moment of stunned silence, Hank asked, "Where did you leave it?"

"On a chair between here and near the restroom," Reiko answered. Hank jumped to his feet and rushed into the hallway. Every chair on the way to the ladies' room was empty. Reaching the restroom, he clutched at his hair with both hands and rocked up and down on his toes. Then threw up his hands and returned to the sunroom to stand before Reiko.

"Didn't ya think ya had to read it so ya'd know what it said?" he asked her, trying to maintain a reasonable attitude but unable to hide his amazement and frustration. Natsume remained silent but his forehead was deeply furrowed.

She looked up at Hank in equal disbelief for a long minute before she answered. "You are different in the West, very different. What insults us does not insult you. What we consider important you seem to ignore." Her voice was calm. "Think of their threats to me this way, Mr. Daniels." She held out both her hands, palms down, fingers closed into fists. "This is how I react to those who would force their ways or beliefs on me. It is the way I have been since I was a little girl in the orphanage. I close my fists against them, and they cannot take or see what is in my hands. I could not react in any other way. I did not want to know what their awful letter said."

"Yes, ma'am," Hank said respectfully. "Maybe you're right. Maybe that's the way the whole world should treat the bad guys, as if they just don't count. Just don't listen to their bullish—excuse me."

Reiko nodded and Hank simply sat down on his seat.

"It all ties in," Joe said, looking around the circle. "Lemme give ya a quick rundown," Joe said. "There's this guy named Teach, a provocateur-type foreign agent with the Office of American Affairs in Tokyo, who seems to hate me. The morning of the day I was grabbed, he met me and a guy named Gould, an American who lives in Japan, at my hotel. Gould looks just like a movie star—well, actually, like John Lennon—and I felt for a minute I was in a Hollywood spy film. Anyway, this guy Teach told us both we had to get outta the country before we got hurt. They must send those government agents to acting classes because he sure was convincing. I just didn't make it out in time."

"Anyhow, last night Gould came to see me. When I told him, I was surprised he was still in Japan, he confessed that he and that gung-ho Teach had been working together, playing some kinda charade that was s'posed to scare me into leaving. Said he was sorry about my abduction. He said Teach wanted him to tell me I'm still in danger, that the bad guys are still enraged because the media made such a big deal about me being found."

"Who's that guy?" Hank asked.

"His name is Gould. He's and expatriated American or probably just another government agent."

"Okay."

"Somehow that wanna-be, would-be agent of adeptness, Teach, the jackass thinks I'm a threat to the prestige of the U.S. government here in Japan. He's convinced, so Gould says, that the elimination of any kinda controversy 'round me is essential. Agent Teach still wants me to leave the country. Gould said they might come after me again and they prob'ly know exactly where I sleep in this hospital. I thought it was just another scare tactic and told the guy to take a walk, but now—"

A buzzer sounded nearby, its harshness invading the rapt silence of Joe's attentive audience. Startled, the members of the group looked at each other with alarm but relaxed when nothing more happened.

"That's all of it," Joe concluded. "I don't understand it, but the note Reiko got, and Gould's message now seem to be connected." Heads nodded and a murmur arose as comments were made in low voices. Hank and Natsume got up and searched the hallway and around every chair again but came back empty handed.

"Just one more thing," Joe added. "Please keep your guard up. All of you. This isn't finished yet."

~   ~   ~

Reiko and the Bishop excused themselves, claiming to be hungry, and went to the cafeteria. Afterward, they walked to the center of the hospital to the interior Japanese garden. They settled themselves on benches, allowing their minds and bodies to absorb the sense of peacefulness that pervaded the spot. It was a good place to express private thoughts privately between friends who trusted each other...

"Excellency," Reiko began, "Joe McGrath brings trouble."

"Yes, it is scary."

"Hai, do you remember what Joseph told us yesterday about his belief that our world is in a totally new relationship with time?"

"Yes, I do."

"He said he believes the world is about to experience some great event, did he not?"

"He did indeed."

"And that he's had knowledge of this for a long time?"

"Yes."

"What do you think about what he said?" Reiko asked. "Is something mystical going on? Do you suppose it could be true? This fellow Joseph McGrath is mysterious. I feel safe when I was around him. It is hypnotic, this feeling, and it is beyond my explanations."

The bishop drew in a slow breath, emitting a serious contemplative sound. "I agree, Reiko, he is more of a mystery than he realizes—a mysterious fellow," he replied. "I get that same feeling. I just don't know what to do about it—or if anything should be done about it."

"I see." Reiko sat thoughtfully; her hands folded in her lap.

"Good will," the bishop muttered.

"Pardon me?" Reiko asked, wondering what the bishop meant.

"Those of extraordinary good will, like Joseph, wanting to go to Nagasaki and Hiroshima out of a sense of respect. There is more than what meets the eye. They always know. Everything is open to them and it always has been."

"Like Uncle Shiro, no matter what happens he is living, as he says, from the generous baskets of life?"

"Exactly," the bishop answered seriously, his eyes searching the tiny garden pond for the golden koi that hid under the rock ledge.

After a long period of silent thought, the bishop seemed to have made a decision. He drew a deep breath and said, most seriously, "I have something to tell you that very few know about. It's an extraordinary event that occurred during the bombing of Nagasaki. When I related it to my superiors, I was immediately placed in obedience to them and could not refuse their request to submit a record of the event to Rome. Rome responded with a letter of acknowledgment and an investigation of me as a mystic. The Pope believed in my experience and blessed it, but no one ever mentioned it again." The old priest sat perfectly still, staring into the water.

"Please continue," Reiko prompted, her eyes wide with curiosity.

"It is not easy to explain, but I will try," he sighed. "When I was in the bombing in Nagasaki, something happened to me. What the Pope called an opening, the doctors called *psychological conversion,* where symptoms of illness such as pain, fainting, paralysis, tremors, and so forth manifest without a physical cause. In other words, your mind makes you sick. My experience was just the opposite, according to the doctors. They decided I was hallucinating, and in my human weakness, I never really chose to believe either the scientific explanation or the spiritual.

"Sometimes I go back into the bombing and the pain. It's like breaking an arm -- it takes a long time to mend. A female victim in Hiroshima wrote, in an anonymous poem, 'If we catch a glimpse of hell and speak of it we are pulled back to hell,' and she was right. I can handle it if I have someone to talk it out with, but I prefer not to. I don't want to end up with my mind in a sling again like I did when I saw all those bodies floating in the East China Sea. My God, I went crazy!"

"Sometimes I forget you were in Nagasaki during the atomic bomb... that horrible time," Reiko said, almost whispering.

"I wish I were that fortunate," the bishop declared. "Since then, I have done my utmost to avoid even thinking of anything nuclear for fear it would trigger another hallucination. When the Tokyo press contacted me about Joseph, they wanted to talk about those war years. I didn't. I threw the letter away and blanked out the phone call. I always wipe out anything nuclear—except for Hank Daniels's story. That I could not ignore. I have even recently tried to forget Joseph McGrath, though I recognized his face as soon as I saw him again."

"Again? Please forgive my uncontrollable curiosity. Please, why do you say that? I thought you met Joseph for the first time when I brought him to you." Reiko was thoroughly confused. "I do not understand."

"Perhaps I should tell you what happened."

"Please do. I should like to hear about this. How could you have seen him before? Is that what you said?"

The bishop gazed out across the garden, and it was clear to Reiko that he was looking into the past. "It was August, a still morning, very hot, when an atomic bomb blasted Nagasaki to kingdom come," he intoned, "and I ended up on the floor trying to figure out who the person before me was with the flesh burnt off his or her face. One of our dead priests was trapped under piles of debris, with just his hand sticking up in the air. It was then, when I cursed God and all his creation, that I realized something cosmic, something supernatural, was happening. In the middle of destruction, extreme human misery, and agonizing deaths, I saw my surroundings enter a transformed state, unfolding like a beautiful new scene in a movie."

He raised his arms and spoke. "It was like a magnificent garden in an impressionist artist's most flawless painting. I remember seeing roses in a rainbow of colors, magnificent, perfected. I think I even conceived new colors. At the time it was glorious, and I thought it was real. The contrast with the Nagasaki bombing was beyond comprehension."

"It was a vision?" Reiko asked.

"Yes, but you have not heard it all. I was groping around the floor, which was covered with horribly wounded and dying Japanese people. At the same time, I am seeing this beautiful scene superimposed over everything, it was then that I saw a man of about your age standing amid the immediate aftermath of the explosion, the dust swirling around him. He was not Japanese, and somehow, I knew he was from another time and place. I was able to see what he was seeing, and it was not the beautiful garden, but the terrible destruction and death—yet his face was calm, and he exuded a sense of peace. It was all very mysterious. Then he and the garden disappeared, and I was back in hell with the survivors of the atomic explosions."

Reiko gripped the edge of the bench with both hands, "This is a shocking thing you are telling me!"

"I know. Was it a miraculous vision as the Pope believed? I have struggled with that from the instant it occurred. When I really think about it, I return to that mysterious state. All I know is that I had the vision, and Joseph McGrath was in it—but I don't think he had been born yet! How that could be?"

"You are telling this now! This happened? You and Joe McGrath were in the atomic bomb in 1945? Oh my God!" She stood up as one becoming uncontrollable.

"Yes, that happened, Reiko."

"They know about it in Rome?"

"Yes."

"God."

"Are you aware of such things?" the bishop asked.

"I know nothing about such things," Reiko mused, speaking slowly and thoughtfully. "It is as if you both died, at least for a moment, and your spirits met somehow."

Bishop Garvin turned to look at Reiko as he processed what she had said. Suddenly he leaped to his feet and stood bolt upright, startling her with his sudden movement. "That's it!" he exclaimed. "That has to be what happened! It *was* him; I know it! I can still see him. He, or his spirit, was in Nagasaki on August 9, 1945, *that nuclear August* we are remembering."

"And in all these years you never told anyone else?"

"No one but my spiritual director and the doctors. My feelings have always told me not to try to explain this to anyone else and I have been reluctant to speak to Joseph about it, even though I know that he was involved." He slid his hands into his sleeves the way religious men in cassocks do. It made him appear resolved with his words.

"I may never understand, Excellency," Reiko whispered. She gave the bishop a timid glance, then took a deep breath and set her jaw, as if she also came to a decision.

"I must tell you, Excellency," she said, "The night in Nagasaki after I brought Joseph to meet you, he and I sat under the trees at the hotel. There was a light rain which did not penetrate there below the leaves. I mention this because it created a stillness around us that made it easier to relax. We talked about many things, including our lives. Excellency, please understand, I thought I was falling in love with him. He is a sweet man, gentle and caring, but perhaps it was not him I loved. It was the way time stopped in the rain under the trees lit by only the night light and the understanding we shared in the depths of our souls."

"Are you saying I could tell Joseph about my vision and that he will understand?"

Reiko, certain that the bishop did not expect an answer, held her tongue. The bishop suddenly rushed toward the courtyard door, waving at Reiko to come with him.

"I've been dodging it!" the bishop muttered. "What a fool! I have to tell him."

~ ~ ~

Bishop Garvin hurried to the elevator and punched the number of the floor where Joe was a patient. After impatiently waiting for the lift to rise to his floor, he pushed through the gap made by the slowly sliding doors and walked quickly to the sunroom, followed closely by Reiko. He could see through the windows that Joe was alone.

"Joseph," he blurted, as his impetus carried him into the room, "I must talk to you." He signaled Reiko to take a seat as he approached Joe.

"Wha—?" Joe jerked his head up from his hands and regarded the bishop with bleary eyes, astounded by the unexpected interruption. The bishop noticed the silver Saint Michael's icon that dangled from Joe's neck, and Joe wondered what had sparked the man's suddenness.

"What's the matter?" Joe asked, looking around in alarm. "Is it them again?" Joe studied Reiko's somber face as she sat, hands folded, in silence.

"Oh, no, that's not it," the bishop answered contritely. "This is not about the Brown Dragons. I'm sorry I frightened you. I need to speak with you, but it has to be private, and I hoped this would be a good time."

"I guess it is," said Joe, rubbing his eyes. "Nobody came back yet, and Hank went to my room to grab some sleep. So, fire away."

The bishop went into the hallway, motioning to Joe to follow. Joe turned his wheelchair, which he was still under orders to use, toward the door and rolled after the holy man. "This will be more private," the bishop said, strolling along the corridor. "I have some things to ask you. Are you agreeable to my questioning?"

"Yeah, sure. Ask away."

"Thank you. Let's try this one first." The bishop was so filled with emotion he had trouble speaking and had to fight to keep from stuttering. "Have you ever seen me before, at any time before?"

"N-no," Joe replied hesitantly. "I don't think so." He saw that the bishop was puzzled but also seemed confident, as if he knew differently. "Did I?" Joe asked.

They stopped at a bench in front of a large plate-glass window, and the bishop sat down. He looked over at Joe, instinctively measuring his body language. Joe sat with his arms over the chair wheels, hands relaxed, and his head tilted slightly in a questioning manner. There was nothing defensive in his attitude. His body was sending a message of trust and the bishop was satisfied that he could be truthful.

"Have you ever been in Nagasaki before, at any time before?"

"No," Joe said, stiffening and crossing his arms over his chest. He started to feel uncomfortable with his answer and more so with the question. He caught himself looking away from the bishop. Turning back, he asked, "Do *you* think I have?"

"Have what?" the bishop said, confusing Joe.

"Been here before, like ya said. Now whadd'ya mean? What are ya getting at?"

"Well, Joseph, I'm sure this will sound strange, but I saw you in Nagasaki long before you came to Japan this year."

"How could you have seen me, Your Excellency?" Joe asked, his voice trailing off.

The bishop answered the question with another question. "Joe, since you were in those tests in Nevada, you would know what Nagasaki looked like after the atomic bomb exploded, would you not?"

"Ya really do know something, don'tcha, Father?"

"Perhaps. Can you tell me what you think I know? It's important, Joe."

"I think somehow ya know about the time I somehow saw – and I don't know how I saw --Nagasaki right after the bombing," Joe said cautiously, not wanting to give too much away. He was glad their conversation was private, for he had already been in enough trouble due to things he had said and people's faulty perceptions. He glanced furtively at the bishop, wondering what he would say next.

CHAPTER 16

"I must tell you, Joseph," the priest said gently, "that you and I had a shared experience. I, too, saw the destruction of Nagasaki because I was physically there. And I saw something else. I saw you, Joseph, having your vision."

"What? Now you're scaring me, Father," Joe nervously wiped his palms on the armrest of the wheelchair.

"No, no, there is nothing to fear," the bishop assured him. "It is nothing to be afraid of, I am certain. Please trust me, Joseph."

"But how couldja have seen me? I was in the United States, at an old Protestant black church up on a hill they call Buckingham Mountain, north of Philadelpha, and I was alone. How couldja know about that? I never told anyone!"

"I do not know how this extraordinary event happened; I only know that it did. As I said, I was in Nagasaki when it was bombed in 1945. I was only slightly injured, but I was surrounded by destruction, death, and the dying. It was during that exact time that I experienced a supernatural event. I saw another world formed around me. The atomic ruin was replaced by a recreation of all of life and the earth as well. This new world, like a garden of perfect flowers, was overlying the shattered remains of Nagasaki. And I saw you standing amid this new world, but not seeing it, surrounded by swirling dirt. Can you picture it?" the bishop asked.

"Yeah. Go ahead, Father."

"If I may, first I would like to hear your experience, Joseph. Please tell me what you saw when you were at the church."

Joe closed his eyes. "Dead children, and they had a dog. An old man with his clothes burned off. Dirt swirling everywhere, blocking the sun and suddenly making it dark as night. Everything enveloped in a strange blue light. Horror. Shock. People ducking and running all 'round me, their skin burned and blistering. Screaming, shouting, a babble of Japanese. It was a sensation of being suspended in an instant in time that left time that separated life from time or any other normal thing. I had no reference to anything." He opened his eyes and peered at the bishop.

"Ai-ee! Yes, it all fits!" the holy man said, his hands trembling with excitement.

"But I saw it just last year, Bishop, in 1968, and your vision was in 1945. How's that possible?"

"The Church has centuries of experience in such matters. It's called bilocation. The key is to simply be open to the graces God chooses to grant. God granted both of us a moment when time did not exist, when events were free flowing, with no markers to indicate past, present, or future. Within this moment we were on the same plane and our paths intersected. You had a supernatural sighting, as did I, and, although you did not see me, I witnessed you having that experience."

"Geez, Father! You're right, I didn't see ya. I do remember seeing the remains of like a monastery on a hill. Were you in there?"

"Yes. It had very thick walls, so not all of it was destroyed, and some of us survived. I had just passed a window when the blast occurred; I was thrown to the floor, and the church came down around me. Miraculously, I was unhurt, and the first thing I did was look out at the macabre scene before me.

"A-and—ya saw *me?*" Joe stammered.

"Yes. For all these years, I have doubted the authenticity of my vision, but I am sure of it now."

"What didja see?"

"A young man, your age, standing tall amid the immediate aftermath of the explosion, the dust swirling around him. He was not Japanese, and somehow, I knew he was from another time and place. I was able to see what he was seeing, as if I was looking at my world through his eyes. It was not a beautiful garden that he saw, only the terrible destruction and the dead and dying—yet his face was calm, and he exuded a sense of peace. I see it clearly, very clearly."

"Yeah. Right after the vision ended, I had these thoughts—maybe they were mine, maybe they were put in my head—but they were soothing and calmed me down."

"Do you remember what they were?"

"Unforgettable stuff, basically that everything is gonna turn our good, really good," said Joe. He then spoke boldly to the bishop: *"All evil has limits. Time will be a broom that sweeps it clean. It's all love."* He was smiling convincingly when he uttered, "It will happen one day when you least expect it."

"Ah, yes, it is as you said yesterday about expecting a miracle and the whole planet being in a totally new relationship with time. I knew you were trying to tell me about your vision, but I was not yet ready to discuss it, or my own. I am sorry I did not respond properly."

"I wasn't surprised, but I thought ya wouldn't talk about it cause ya thought I was nuts. Who wouldn't think that? I know these things are true—I got the certainty inside me—but I got no proof."

"We are proof. Have you had help with this, Joseph, a spiritual director, for instance?"

"Not up to now, but I'm beginning to think I might need one, ya know?"

"Well, as a Bishop, I would warn you as I was warned. Don't consider yourself more important than those who cannot claim such an experience. But I feel you are handling it well. Just stay as you are."

"Thanks, Father, but it seems a lot different now."

"If this becomes public—" the bishop warned.

"Nah, this won't go public, Father. My deal only lasted a few seconds, and I was alone. Who'd know?" Joe was surprised to see a spasm of pain cross Bishop Garvin's face. The priest hid behind his open hands and turned away, bowing his head and beginning to pray aloud. Joe waited patiently for the bishop to end his prayers. "Are ya okay, Father?" he asked when the man turned back to him.

"Flashbacks," the priest replied. "I have been dwelling on this for too long." He inhaled deeply and exhaled a shuddering breath. "One of the worst things I saw during that time, a thing I can never forget, was what had happened to one of the altar boys. He was between us when you were there. His entire head was burnt, and he was completely unrecognizable. He kept saying, 'Father, it is Oe. It is I, Father.' I could not have known him otherwise. Oh, so awful!"

The bishop's chin quivered as a tic began to flinch in his right eye. He pulled out a handkerchief to wipe his face, and Joe thought he had never seen a man look so vulnerable. "All that day I prayed for him and hoped he would not see his reflection," Bishop Garvin continued. "I never wanted him to see himself. No one would know him. He was dead the next day. I think he died of fright . . . poor little boy."

"Was he about this tall," Joe held his palm above the floor, "and was one of his eyes melted onto his face?"

The bishop stared at Joe in amazement. "Dear Lord, this is too much."

Joe dropped his gaze to the floor, realizing the bishop's need to stop the dialogue. The two atomic victims, made very special to each other by something beyond words and clear thoughts, sat quietly, emotionally, and spiritually arrested.

Outside, wind-blown trees slapped their branches against the windows as if the nuclear ghosts of Nagasaki were tapping their bony fingers, begging to be heard. The bishop placed a firm open hand on Joe's back and left with a nod. Joe said nothing, but also nodded.

CHAPTER 17

Joe, exhausted and longing for sleep, returned to his room, where Hank had already arranged himself in the recliner. The following day, Reiko informed them she had received an urgent summons from her uncle Shiro to come to Hiroshima as soon as possible and to bring the American. Until Joe made another visit to Hiroshima, the monk had said, they were all still in danger of being taken by the fanatics. Joe was willing to do what was necessary to eliminate the danger to his friends.

As they were leaving the hospital after visiting hours, Reiko and Bishop Garvin discussed her uncle's demands. "Why is Shiro so insistent that you bring Joseph to Hiroshima?" he asked. "One would think your uncle would want you far away from the American."

"My uncle said Joseph must go to Hiroshima to neutralize the extremists. Until he does so, the terrorists are still a threat to us all," Reiko answered.

"Are they going to get him again?" the bishop asked.

"Joseph?" Reiko sighed. "Any time they want him. I think they want to show how they can do whatever they want by making Joe give homage to Hiroshima."

"Your uncle wants him to make a well-publicized trip to Hiroshima."

"Yes, he said news of Joseph going back there may put an end to any leftover intrigue."

· "The public will realize that the Dragons forced him to give recognition to Hiroshima. Is that their goal?"

"Yes."

~   ~   ~

On Thursday morning, Joe was released from the hospital. Joe's tests indicated he was steadily gaining weight and fully hydrated, and his wounds were healing satisfactorily.

Hank Daniels, Joe McGrath, Reiko Fumioka, Natsume Toson, and Bishop Garvin gathered in the hospital lobby and exited the hospital as a group. Joe McGrath, abandoning his mandatory wheelchair outside the front door, joined the others in bidding the bishop goodbye. Waving additional farewells, the ensemble walked to the hotel so those with rooms could check out. They then fortified themselves with a quick brunch, and, led by Reiko and Natsume, walked to the train station, oblivious to the stares they attracted.

When they reached the train depot, Reiko helped everyone buy the correct tickets. During that time, Natsume called his newspaper and dictated an article, exacting a promise from his editor that it would be placed on the first page of that day's afternoon edition. The Japanese headline of the article translated to "Kidnapped American Nuclear Test Victim Returns to Hiroshima."

By the time they arrived in Hiroshima, most of those in the small troop of friends were trying to treat the trip for what it looked like, an excursion by a group of tourists. They laughed and chatted, pointed out different sights to each other, and purchased food from the swarming vendors. They knew better, however, than to ignore the fanatics' threats.

Joe wondered how much danger they were in, and, when he exchanged glances with Natsume and Reiko, he knew they were considering the same thing. If the terrorists wanted to capture or kill one of them, the fact that they were a group would be no deterrent. Joe knew, in this case, the idea of safety in numbers was a fallacy.

Signaling Reiko and Natsume and engaging them in quiet conversation, Joe asked their opinions of touring Hiroshima before they went to the monastery to meet Shiro. The three agreed that going to the monastery first would probably destroy whatever degree of authenticity, if any, their charade as Hiroshima visitors was affording. They decided to do sightseeing and save the visit to Shiro for last, since they were anticipating a sobering conversation with the old monk.

When at last they alighted from the train for the final time, Natsume and Reiko helped Joe find all the places he had seen during his first visit to Hiroshima. Joe was not surprised to see Reiko and Natsume avert their eyes from the grotesque Atomic Bomb Dome. He had noticed when he first toured the city that the Japanese did the same thing. Hank and Joe, however, walked away from the others toward the imposing monument and stood and stared at its nuclear melted shapes.

After spending time in the city and at the Peace Memorials, the group went to a local restaurant and partook of their evening meal. Afterward, Reiko led them to her uncle. When they arrived, they found him standing motionless by the garden gate, waiting impatiently for his niece to appear. He looked as if he had been waiting for a long time.

Reiko, Joe, and Natsume halted beneath the gate of the centuries-old monastery and executed courteous bows, which the old monk returned in kind. Tucking his hands chest-high into his saffron robe, Shiro asked Reiko to translate and then began to speak in Japanese.

"There is a boundless love for all beings, and it is the mission of this American to have been its emissary," he intoned, his voice filled with authority.

Everyone there listened to Reiko's translation with great interest. Surprised to hear himself referred to as an emissary of boundless love, Joe gripped the ancient gatepost. He turned his head away from the group, pretending to be avoiding the sunlight, as Shiro continued. Keeping his head averted and his eyes fixed on the treetops that stood between the small huddle of people and the distant tall buildings of Hiroshima, Joe absorbed the old monk's thoughts as if he knew what was being said before hearing the translation.

"Someday soon," Shiro concluded, "all grasping, and ignorance will truly cease, but now you are in immediate danger. We, ourselves, have little chance or time to clarify the minds of those who threaten. Do not take this warning lightly; the peril is still real."

With Reiko clutching his hand fearfully, Joe thanked the monk for his concern and assured him they would not disregard his words. After a few moments, the members of the group said their individual goodbyes to Shiro, aided by Reiko's nearly simultaneous translations. After making their parting remarks and gestures, they all stood motionless in the center walk of Shiro's garden, with the exception of Hank, who had already taken a few steps toward the ancient gate.

"We drive back to Tokyo early tomorrow, my dearest uncle," Reiko admitted reluctantly, with tears forming. "I must join Bishop Garvin in the Sekiguchi Archdiocese office in Bunkyo. He expects me in Tokyo tomorrow."

"Tokyo?" Shiro exclaimed in alarm. "You should not go there. The danger is great!" Joe, hearing the monk, frowned and nodded knowingly, trying to convey his understanding even as he looked at Reiko for translation. "No Tokyo, oh," Shiro repeated, perplexed by Joe's facial expressions.

"Thank you for the advice," Joe said as Reiko translated mechanically. Joe responded with a low bow. He could think of nothing more to say.

Natsume, who was standing behind the monk, spoke to the monk in Japanese, assuring the worried man that he would personally guard Reiko. Maintaining a tone of deepest respect, he confessed to Reiko's devoted uncle that they must go to Tokyo, since that is where he lived and where the Americans' plane connection was to be made.

"I understand," Shiro replied. "I do not like it, but I know you must go there, and that Reiko must go with you to meet her bishop, who is now taking direction from the Catholic hierarchy in Tokyo."

Cued by Reiko, Natsume told his friends in English that it was time to leave. They would need a good night's sleep, he added, as they would be leaving for Tokyo first thing in the morning. As Reiko translated for the old monk, Shiro's face contorted in fear, and he frowned a private warning to her. Her response, totally Japanese, was a silent and deep bow while very slowly walking backward and voicing her most honorific expressions to her uncle.

Everyone bowed to the aging monk, and the "Hiroshima tourists," reluctant to be so, turned and began to make their way back to the hotel they had booked earlier in the day. Disturbed by the warnings, they all spoke in subdued tones, no longer feeling safe.

~ ~ ~

Joe joined Reiko, Natsume, and Hank in the restaurant at eight o'clock for breakfast. No one had slept well, concerned as they were about Shiro's warnings. They discussed the old monk's admonition not to go to Tokyo, but, having no simple alternative, didn't feel they could heed his advice no matter how much trepidation they felt.

To be somewhat unpredictable about how they would travel, they had not bought return train tickets. Hank and Natsume rented a nine-passenger van, smiling when they were asked by the rental manager if they wanted a white or bronze van. "We've had enough of white vans," Hank said, pointing to the bronze one parked in the rental lot.

They all went along with Hank driving since he had driven in Tokyo several times. Natsume would point the way. The travelers loaded their suitcases into the vehicle and climbed in, settling themselves comfortably and issuing a collective sigh of relief when Hank put the van in gear and drove out of the lot.

"Homeward bound," breathed Hank.

"At last," Joe added.

Hank drove as fast as the posted limits would allow, eager to reach their destination but not wanting to be stopped for speeding. Just when everyone's tension dissipated as they neared the end of their journey, after they reached the suburban streets into Tokyo and the city loomed ahead of them, Reiko's eyes opened wide as she expelled a breath of concern.

A flatbed truck sped toward the rental van heading directly toward the driver's side on a course that would have resulted in a fatal collision had it not been for Hank's quick reflexes. Acting on instinct, he spun the wheel, turning the van until it was running side by side with the truck, reducing the impact of a "T-bone" to that of a sideswipe. Metal screeched on metal as the vehicles scraped together. The truck veered away and then swerved against them. Daniels could see two strong arms wrenching the steering wheel to the right and knew the truck driver was trying to push them off the road and over the embankment.

Protecting his passengers by allowing the careening vehicle to contact his side of the van only, Hank fought to stay on the road while he searched for an avenue of escape. Spotting an off-road paved area, he stomped on the accelerator and whipped the wheels to the right, breaking away from the truck and steering onto the blacktop at top speed. Alternating pressure from his foot between the brake and accelerator pedals, Hank managed to maintain the van's equilibrium so it remained upright, but he could not keep it from slamming into a parked bus. As the van crumpled and the sound of shattering glass filled the air, Hank and Natsume caught a glimpse of the white truck speeding off.

From the moment the truck had attacked, the passengers sat frozen in silence, hands and jaws clenched, terrified they would not survive. When the van came to a stop, and the motor shuddered, Reiko began to scream hysterically. Joe threw his arms around her and held her close, murmuring in her ear to calm her down, but to no avail. Casting sympathetic looks at the struggle, the others checked themselves for injuries. Reiko was holding her nose, which was bleeding.

Natsume, speaking in excited Japanese, held his forehead, which had been slammed against the interior roof; the skin was scraped and reddened, and some of his hair had been rubbed off. Reiko, noticing that Natsume's head begun to bleed, told him so as she reached out and gently touched her own nosebleed.

Everyone had suffered minor cuts and bruises. The police appeared a few minutes later, followed by emergency vehicles, and Hank, recognizing the flashing lights as a sign that their horrifying ordeal was over, subsided into quiet but deep breaths.

After giving their statements, everyone was transported to the nearest hospital, where their cuts were cleaned and bandaged. The emergency room doctors removed fingernail size pieces of glass from

Reiko's face and her elbows and sent her to radiology, saying they would keep her overnight.

After everyone had been cared for, Natsume went to the cafeteria to call the story into his newspaper. Joe and Hank stayed with Reiko until they were sure she was comfortable. When she said she was tired and wanted to sleep, Joe assured her he would return soon, and the two friends left. They walked out of the hospital and sat on a bench to discuss what had happened.

CHAPTER 18

TOKYO JAPAN

"That was no accident, Joe," Hank began, his tone intense. "Wait a minute," said Joe, looking intently at a skinny Japanese man dressed in a Western suit standing on the grass. It was the one he called the thin man, the man who acted like the gang boss throughout his abduction. "Where'd he come from?" Joe asked rhetorically as Hank glanced from one to the other in bewilderment. The thin man walked right up to the bench and past it, motioning to Joe to follow. His attitude was arrogant, as if Joe had no choice.

"Who does he think he is?" Hank asked testily in a low voice meant only for Joe.

"Back in a minute," Joe said after a brief hesitation. He got up and walked over to the man, who was waiting a few steps away, just beyond Hank's range of hearing. The two men stood facing each other without speaking for what seemed to be one or two long minutes. Joe was the first to break the silence.

"Ya tried killing us today," he accused, his voice bitter. "Whadd'ya think I've done to ya, and what's this all about, you damn maniac? D'ya understand what I'm asking?"

"You were told to leave Japan," the thin man replied, his attitude calm and casual. "But if we wanted to kill you, you would be dead. Maybe now you will leave our country, to protect you and your friends"

"If I was home, I'd bust your jaw and have ya arrested."

"Tough American," the man snorted, smirking at Joe's show of bravado. "If you tried, I would humiliate you."

"I'm asking ya again, what's this all about?" Joe balled his hands into fists.

"You seem like a smart man, but you have not yet figured any of this out?" the thin man asked with a condescending smile.

Sensing a confrontation, Hank got up and stood beside Joe. The Japanese man stepped back and sized Hank up. "So, you were both in atomic bomb testing, is that correct?"

Ignoring the man's question, Hank turned to Joe. "Who is this guy, Joe?" he demanded.

"My kidnapper, or one of 'em," Joe replied. "The head honcho, prob'ly."

"No shit?" Hank assumed a defensive stance.

"Another tough American," said the Japanese man.

"Ya might need your skull dented, Bones," Hank countered. "How come ya don't sound Japanese?"

The thin man sat down on the bench Hank had vacated and stretched his legs out. With an air of superiority, he began to explain himself. It was as if he had adopted a fresh attitude toward the two Americans. Looking at them through nearly closed eyes, his face contorted with what appeared to be pain, he said, "My American name was Michael." He folded his hands on his lap. "I was born in Eugene, Washington, the son of a sugar beet farmer. I was eighteen when the Second World War broke out."

Joe and Hank looked at each other with baffled expressions.

"I was planning to attend Oregon State. I wanted to become a math teacher and spend the rest of my life with Meredith O'Brien, who was going to become a Physical Education teacher. As different as our lives were, she was the only one I really believed didn't see me as another race. She looked and acted as if I was simply her guy, even after Pearl Harbor. To the other inhabitants of the white world, I became that putrid yellow, skinny son of a distrusted and hated nationality, even though I was born in America."

"So now ya hate the same way ya were hated?" Joe asked.

"Listen and you will learn of hatred, McGrath-*san*."

"And now ya teach violence instead of mathematics."

Hank started looking around for a policeman or security guard.

"Tell your friend to relax," the thin man said.

"Hey, ya play a serious game of being bad, and he's looking for somebody to get rid of ya," said Joe.

"You would be wise to listen. Do you know why the truck tried to run you off the road?"

"I think *you* can answer that better than we can."

"No, I cannot, McGrath-*san*. It was neither I nor anyone connected to me who attempted to take your lives today."

"I don't believe ya."

"Suspecting me leaves you unguarded from whoever did it and ignorant of the reasons for their actions."

Joe and Hank's eyes locked in a moment as they both realized that if what the thin man was saying was true, they had a new problem. Hank began to pace.

"Who else would want me outta the picture?" Joe asked.

"Have a seat," the man said, moving to the end of the bench to make room. Hank continued to pace, and Joe stood before the thin man in a challenging posture. The kidnapper shrugged nonchalantly and continued his saga.

"When my people came to America, they brought with them the knack of growing and caring for plants, especially earth plants like sugar beets and also strawberries. To them, plants were sacred, and they passed this reverence for growing things and the knowledge of how to care for them to their offspring. The whites hired and housed the Japanese because they knew how to care for the beet plants. Whole families, including first-generation Americans, worked the whites' lands. It was hard, strenuous work. Can you imagine planting acres, weeding, and harvesting them—all by hand?"

Abruptly Hank said, "Give us your fairy tales later, Slim Jim. What's going on?"

"Yeah, what makes ya think we wanna hear all about you?" Joe added. "Are ya nuts? You're still a maniac criminal."

He looked over the man's head and saw Hank walking backward, slowly edging toward the hospital. Seeing his friend's exaggerated wink, Joe surmised Hank was going to alert hospital security to the kidnapper's presence. But as the thin man continued his story, Joe saw Hank stop, stand still for a moment, reverse direction, and walk back toward the bench. Joe wondered what had changed Hank's mind.

When Hank passed him, Joe quickly whispered, "We got no choice, man, we gotta listen to this idiot."

"Yeah, he knows something. Let 'em talk, I guess."

They turned their attention toward their visitor, who was engrossed in his story and had not noticed their hasty exchange.

"Just when the land had become our own," the criminal continued, "when we were enfranchised to buy and possess, first small and then larger tracts of land, just when the sons of immigrant beet farmers could begin to think of themselves going to college and building a future, the war broke out. On December 7, 1941, Pearl Harbor happened, and in March of 1942, my family was imprisoned—and all that would happen thereafter began, like sentencing us to criminal status simply because of our race.

"All people of Japanese lineage were transported to a segregation prison camp in California. Born in America? Didn't matter. English-speaking from birth? Didn't matter. We were taken under military guard out of our homes and farms and towns. Practically everything we owned or held dear was left behind, including my Meredith. The rows of sugar beets were abandoned, and the sugar of our life was turned to salt. Meredith O'Brien and Oregon State University, and all we knew were lost to us, and much of that, forever."

"Lemme guess," said Hank from behind the bench. "Ya were in one of those desert camps, right? That was a sad story, and it's all coming out. And cause of that, now you're the lousy bastard who's locking people up?"

Joe looked across the grounds and noted the people—groups of nurses, individuals, and families—walking in and out of the hospital, conducting their business. Their innocence made the presence of a wanted criminal bizarre, yet Joe was sure the scenario he was in looked like three normal men talking in a relaxed manner. It was unimaginable that one of them was an expatriated terrorist and the others innocent prey.

"Perhaps, but then nothing like that ever happened to you, did it? So, I do not expect you to understand. It's too late now anyway, much too late, and there is no compensation for the injustices. We are still hated by many."

"So, when ya got out," Joe stated, "ya gave up being an American and came here to Japan."

"You come to quick conclusions, Joe McGrath," the thin man uttered with sarcasm. "You do not believe me, but I tell you I am no longer a threat to you. For now, think of this: I joined the United States Army when I was in the camp and still a teenager. In the 26th

Infantry, I was in a Japanese American weapons company for three years. We fought the Germans and Italians, and many of Japanese descent died for America. When the war was over and I came home, it was not to the home we lost to bankers and shrewd land investors, but to shanty places; for me, the back rooms of my parents' small store, one that could expect only a few very poor Japanese customers."

Hank stepped forward. "This is bullshit!" he shouted. "If ya know anything about that fuckin' truck, we wanna know *now!*"

People passed by and, like any big city, the crowd paid little or no attention to Hank's outburst in English. Fixing the men in a predatory glaring gaze, the wannabe teacher-turned-thug frowned deeply and held up one finger as if to both scold and command attention. Unmoved by Hank's demand, he continued his account of his life.

"Information about the bombing of Hiroshima and Nagasaki was being repressed by your government, and much of it was held secret. We learned of it from my Japanese relatives and people coming into the store sharing photos. My aunt, who came across the sea from Hiroshima, brought with her a little booklet printed in Japanese by survivors. It held survival discoveries and effective prescriptions. The U.S. government banned this booklet in Japan for about three years. I was struck most forcefully by the realization that the atomic bomb was for my yellow race, the hated people, in an act just like that of the camps. How few German Americans were placed in camps? For us it was a law that locked Japanese up as a race, just us."

"That was a sneak attack, the Pearl Harbor matter," said Hank, now an interested listener.

"But the Germans had planned their own Pearl Harbor: they intended to bomb New York," the thin man stated with conviction. "They envisioned the occupation of all of North America, using Volkswagens as touring cars for field grade Nazi officers. Why were they not treated as we were?"

The thin man's eyes were piercing hawkish eyes. Joe noticed that he and Hank avoided looking at them.

"We were incarcerated in the camps without due process," the thin man spoke more angrily, "We were caged without any concern for our humanity or our dignity as hard-working American farmers. In Japan, they were bombed by an experimental science of mass extermination because of their race and the insanity of war. But the weapon went beyond all sense of civilization, all sense of the continuation of the planet. It was the warfare of the white race at that time, the most dangerous racial warfare of all time."

"But it wasn't me that put ya in the camps or bombed your people," Joe protested. "Why'dja do me such an injustice, Michael, or whatever your name is? Ya held me, ya beat me, and now you've hurt my friends."

"My Japanese name is Tahsaku. And as I said, my Dragons are not the ones who attacked your van."

"Ya talk about me being a smart man. You're a smart man, so why are ya with this group of fanatics, or gangsters, or whatever they are?"

"Because some of you whites are diluters and greed merchants and slave traders. Look what you did to the Indians and the blacks.

THE GIRL IN JAPAN

What real importance do you place on lives other than your own race?"

A disdainful expression met Joe's as the small man raised his voice. "You are takers who would relegate all other races to concentration camps, reservations, and the so-called missions in Australia. Remember, the German Nazis were white. Some of you have been the bane of the world, but you all claim Christianity or Judaism or Islam and you all think it makes you look good. I came back to Japan because you brought more destruction to me and those like me than any other force.

"Your General Eisenhower thought dropping the atomic bomb was no longer necessary as a measure to save American lives. And Leahy, the fleet admiral of the U.S. Navy—even MacArthur—thought it was wrong, barbaric in one way or another, a tragedy, unnecessary. Ask yourself: if the Russians, who would overrun Japan, were coming into the war by mid-August, why did Truman drop the bombs one week in advance?

"Everyone knew the Japanese total collapse was in process. The war was over, and more than one hundred thousand Japanese, including woman and children, were dead toast in Tokyo from the incendiary bombs. Why were the bombs used on populated cities? Who could not imagine the Russians and their tanks and planes and the Chinese retaliation invading and killing nearly every citizen in Japan? Truman knew it would be stupid to invade a defeated Japan."

Joe said, "I dunno about all that, but with your rational mind when it comes to business and mathematics, how can ya live in the creed of an unbalanced equation? Japan's been as cruel to its neighbors as any nation has ever been. Look what Japan did to the Chinese! The only chosen people in the world are the people of the whole world, all of them. Imagine if ya'd never been brought to the camp in California."

"I can't."

"Well that's the kinda world we need. No Pearl Harbors or death marches, or any of it. God, you're wrong, man! Ya don't retaliate, not now, after all that's happened. It's insane to support any of it. No, ya wouldn't've been a good math teacher because ya don't make things add up. Going after past evils has never worked nearly as well as just trying to help people and be happy."

Tahsaku stood up, causing Joe to fall back a step. The kidnapper straightened his tie and looked from one to the other of them, his lips pressed into a line and his eyes placid. A group of people passed by the bench, and before Joe and Hank could react, the thin man glided smoothly into their midst. He was out of sight before Joe and Hank became conscious of how he had caught them up in his strange hypnotic persona.

The two friends looked at each other with surprise as they realized the criminal had slipped away. By tacit consent, they began walking toward the hospital to make a statement to the authorities about the encounter.

"Hey, Hank, didn't ya start to report this guy earlier?" Joe asked.

"Yeah, I did, but I changed my mind."

"How come?"

"Because I was afraid ya wouldn't be there when I got back."

"Oh." Joe thought about this for a second. "Thanks, good buddy."

~ ~ ~

Later Hank, gravely concerned for Joe's safety, was assured by both Natsume and the FBI agents that Joe would be watched over and kept safe until his flight departed. To be sure, Hank traveled with Joe, Natsume, and Reiko to an inexpensive, obscure hotel, where Joe booked a room and planned to stay until his flight. A plainclothes detective stayed with Joe, and two FBI agents were rotated as security bodyguards.

Satisfied that his friend was as safe as could be expected, Hank Daniels, who was beginning to feel quite ill, accepted a ride with Natsume and Reiko to the Tokyo airport, where they waited for his flight. Their attitudes were subdued, for—even though they had been told over and over not to—they worried about Joe, who still getting outpatient treatments, had not yet booked on a flight out of Japan.

CHAPTER 19

The following day, Natsume Toson resumed his regular routine. When not on a field assignment, he habitually worked in his downtown Tokyo office until eight in the evening, and today would be no exception. He was a very busy reporter devoted to his work. He always needed to stay on top of the news. Born and raised in the city, he had worked in Tokyo his entire career. He knew his job and was a great asset to his employers. He put in a full day preparing even minor articles for publication, and at eight o'clock he left the building and walked to the subway.

Tokyo, like Los Angeles, is a city always moving, always busy and one that spreads itself over a large region. Natsume preferred walking at this time of the evening, when fewer pedestrians and vehicles made it relatively quiet. As he crossed Chuo-dori Avenue north of the Ginza section, he heard a motorcycle revving its engine. It was a common and familiar sound, and he gave it no heed—until he realized it was coming too close. Alarmed, he instinctively raised himself on the balls of his feet and lurched away from the threat, filled with the fear of being hit. Taking a quick glance back, he caught a glimpse of a fiendish look on the face of the cyclist, as if the driver's mind was fixed on exacting revenge—but for what, Natsume had no idea.

The bike sped toward Natsume, almost touching him as it roared past. In that split second the driver, screaming hatefully, extended his arm full length and struck the reporter across the back with a metal bar; the force of the blow sent Natsume reeling to the ground. While the fallen Natsume clutched his shoulders and writhed with pain, the cyclist spun around and aimed his machine directly at him. Its front end elevated by rapid acceleration, the motorcycle charged the prone Natsume, striking him with its undercarriage and rear tire. The impact broke his nose and split his lips open. The undercarriage caught his clothing, and the motorcycle dragged and tumbled him down the street about twenty feet before his clothing tore away. The motorcycle raced away, leaving Natsume, skinned and bruised severely, lying unconscious in the street.

Not much goes unobserved in busy Tokyo, and in minutes Natsume Toson was in an ambulance being transported to the Tokyo Metropolitan Hospital, where he was treated and assigned a bed. Once Natsume had regained consciousness, he placed a call to his cameraman, Kanagaki, and asked him to come to the hospital to take his picture. He dictated an account of the attack to his editor and requested that it be published, with the photo Kanagaki would contribute the next day.

Kanagaki, marveling at Natsume's ability to remain level-headed after such a harrowing experience, rushed to comply with his request. After dispatching the exposed film to his crew by messenger with instructions to develop it prior to the publishing deadline, Kanagaki sat down to visit. He was enraged by the hit-and-run, for Natsume was his friend as well as his boss. Speaking in their native tongue, Kanagaki demanded to know all the details. Natsume, communicating in kind, told him everything he could remember.

"What do you think provoked this guy into wanting to hurt you, Natsume-*kun*? [close friend?]" the cameraman asked.

"By rights, Kanagaki, I should believe this was done by those who are after McGrath. If that's true, then I have also become their enemy."

"So, we are once again threatened by these criminals, just like what happened ten years ago when we covered the Dragon leader, Showa Auyoma."

"Yes," said Natsume, wincing with pain as he shifted his hips, "but I don't believe this was done by the Brown Dragons, or anyone Japanese."

Kanagaki was astonished. "Why not?"

"The guy was Chinese; I think from mainland Shanghai."

"How do you figure that out while you're being run over?"

"When I ducked down to prevent him from hitting me in the head, he cursed me in Chinese. Plus, we Asians know each other. You just know. True?"

"Well, yes, you do, in a flash sometimes. So what is he doing with the Dragons?"

"It can't be that; they hate each other. But whatever the reason, I'm going to find out. Tell no one, Kanagaki, that we know he was Chinese. No one! We have to know what it means first."

"Of course, Natsume, these men are dangerous. Only the public interest in our profession protects us, nothing else, and even that didn't help you tonight. But why would a Chinese guy,,,?"

"We'll find out." Natsume sounded grimly determined.

~ ~ ~

Joe made his way through the airport ready to go home. After Joe's conversation with the thin man, members of the Brown Dragons had been diligently guarding Joe, unbeknownst to Joe. They planned to do so until it was time for him to fly home. The Dragons, with powerful contacts everywhere, influenced the police, at the highest levels, to leave Joe's security up to them so that even the FBI presence disappeared. Diligently watching for troublemakers at Joe's hotel, Michael Tahsaku would not feel their job was done until they had put Joe safely on a plane. He was therefore, also at the airport, where he could watch Joe board with his own eyes.

Reiko had arrived earlier, eager to see Joe before he left. She was waiting for Joe at his departure point, and Joe was thrilled to see her again. His flagging spirits were lifted by her smile and her warm overtures of friendship, and he was delighted to have her company while he waited for his transport. They chatted quietly, recalling their experiences together.

Shortly before it was time for Joe's plane to arrive, Tahsaku stepped forward and asked to have a private word with Joe, but Joe insisted that Reiko be included in the conversation. "She knows everything I know," he said, "and I prefer her to be included." Reiko's face blushed and she reached her hand outward, touching Joe's arm.

Accepting Joe's terms with aplomb, the thin man said, "I want you to know that at first I thought you were in Japan in an attempt to somehow lessen the guilt of the American usage of atomic bombs on human beings. So, I tried to lessen you by taking away your freedom. Then, finding no one was paying any attention to you, I let you go. I am sorry for the beatings you received. I did not sanction them. I beg your forgiveness and beseech the spirit of Japan to strengthen and console you."

With a contrite expression, pointing his hands to his almost miniature torso, he continued, "I realized some time ago you were not against the Japanese but championed every one of my countrymen who died in Hiroshima and Nagasaki. You are a sincere, but perhaps naive man because you continue the caring for them. I tried to tell you this before. Do you remember the letter Reiko was given in the hospital to inform you of my revised outlook?"

"Yeah, there was a letter, but—"

Reiko interrupted. "That was my fault. I thought it was a threat and threw it away, refusing to read it. I apologize for my rashness, Joseph."

"Too bad," the thin man said. "Go home, Joseph McGrath, and know you may have added a thread to the fiber of a future state of sanity on this planet. I am sorry for what I did. In any case, you are a friend of Japan. And don't be afraid about Natsume Toson. We failed him the other night but from now on he will be carefully protected, I promise you.

Joe's senses pricked up in alarm. "Whadd'ya mean, ya failed him?"

"Natsume Toson has been injured?" Reiko asked with surprise.

"Have you not heard? It was in yesterday's newspapers," Tahsaku replied.

"Afraid I don't read Japanese," Joe countered somewhat wryly.

"Oh, yes. Sorry, I forgot. Toson was attacked by a man on a motorcycle. We did not know that the reporter was also in danger, and we were not watching him. He was beaten and run over, and he is now in the hospital."

"Will he be okay?" Joe asked.

"The reports say it will take time, but they expect full recovery. Apparently, he has all his senses, for he is the one who wrote the article for his own paper."

"Why didn't he call me?" Joe demanded, his fear making him sound angry. "I thought we were friends."

"I'm sure he wanted to, but he knows the phone lines at the hospital are not secure so he was probably worried they would be tapped. It was for your protection, I'm sure; he didn't want to lead your enemies to you."

"Well, then, why didn't someone call Reiko?" Joe asked.

"I know why," Reiko said as Tahsaku shrugged his shoulders. "He thought I had returned to Kure City, but I was still at St. Mary's

Cathedral, here in Tokyo, providing secretarial work in exchange for my room and board. It was a busy day, and I did not take time to read the paper. I wish I had!"

"Reiko?" Joe said, confident she knew his question.

"I will visit him today, Joseph," she answered, "as soon as I leave here."

"Please tell him how sorry I am he got hurt and that I would've gone to see him if I knew."

"I will," she promised.

"And can ya write to me and keep me posted about how he is?"

"I will be happy to. I will take your address in America before I go."

"Well," said the thin man, "your plane is due any minute, so I will leave you two alone. *Sayonara*, McGrath. I am terribly sorry. If it helps in any small way, my days of retaliation and meaningless violent acts are over for good. I might even go back to Eugene to become a simple strawberry and beet farmer—this time thinking in Japanese as I work the land."

He smiled and walked far enough away to give the couple some privacy, stopping beside a wide-shouldered man dressed in brown. Reiko and Joe had just enough time to say their goodbyes before the plane to America landed on the tarmac, tires shrieking.

"Here I am leaving Japan at last, Reiko, but I will remember you. I don't think I am really leaving you."

"You must leave this country. I am also leaving with the bishop to another assignment. We will never see each other again."

"Yes," Joe whispered, and frowning, he fixed his eyes on Reiko's lips.

"Yes," she whispered back.

"Is it possible that we should go somewhere, you and I? Should we go together, somewhere where there would be a place for us both?"

"You surprise me, Joseph . . . I don't know. We are different worlds, no?"

"No, and yes. The time to go is here, now."

"You must go, it is not safe for you."

"Not in Japan. Goodbye, Reiko."

"Goodbye, Joe."

Joe, his eyes filled with tears, began to walk but stopped and looked back sadly into Reiko's eyes, which were also rimmed in tears.

CHAPTER 20

Three days after the motorcyclist's assault, Natsume was surprised to see the bishop's secretary standing in the hallway near the door of his hospital room. Reiko recognized Kanagaki with a nod and a bow. Speaking in English, she said, "You are Natsume's cameraman, are you not? You were with him when he covered the Hato-age (Kite Wars) and Joseph McGrath's arrival at the bishop's residence."

Kanagaki bowed to Reiko, greeting her with polite Japanese expressions of honorific speech. She bowed again courteously to both men. Natsume said, in Japanese, "Please come in, Reiko. You honor us with your presence."

Reiko entered the room unhesitatingly and stood at the foot of Natsume's bed. Still speaking in English, she said, "I am shocked by what has happened. Now I know we are all threatened, all of us who know Joseph. We heard about your violent confrontation with the Brown Dragons, so I came to see how you are and to express my sympathy. Bishop Garvin sends you his benediction and prayers. We are told that the doctors say you will recover from your many injuries. Please excuse my simple curiosity."

"Thank you, and please tell the Bishop, I thank him as well. The doctors told you the truth: I am healing, if slowly. But do not worry. I am not too seriously hurt."

Kanagaki snorted. "Ho! That's what *he* says. In fact, he was bruised and cut all over his body, not to mention his broken nose and ribs!" he said angrily in English.

Natsume rolled his eyes and ignored Kanagaki's outburst. Deliberately continuing to speak in Japanese, he directed his comments to Reiko. "How are you, Reiko-*san*? I am happy to see you," he said, "although I am surprised you can recognize me, my face is so distorted."

"I knew you immediately, Toson-*san*," Reiko replied.

"I admit that I was startled at my first glance at myself when they brought me to the hospital. Perhaps it looks worse to me?"

She reverted easily to her native tongue, responding to Natsume's choice of language with its lyrical phonemes when spoken with kindness. The mere act of speaking and thinking in Japanese somehow made their conversation seem more personal.

Natsume was charmed by Reiko's demeanor and flattered by her concern. He had been studying her as they talked, noticing her traditionally styled hair, similar to the Geisha, only with a much fresher shampooed look. She had interested him the day he and his cameraman had first met her. He was curious about why such a beautiful young woman had chosen to live as if she was a consecrated layperson in the Japanese Catholic Church, sequestered and fully committed to her position.

He had also wanted to interview her when she and McGrath returned from Nagasaki, his reporter's sixth sense telling him she would possess the most interesting information about Joe McGrath and the Bishop. He also wondered if he could attract her. He thought that most women found him interesting.

"Please call me Natsume," he requested. "Everything will mend in time. It just looks terrible now."

"Your attackers are confusing us now, but what the Dragons did was cruel and criminal like everything they get away with. They are unpredictable cowards," Reiko stated with indignation.

"Yes. And always a great frustration," Kanagaki added, also switching to Japanese. "The fanatics are like the quick shadows of rodents. It seems they cannot be caught and eliminated."

The cameraman, sensing the personal interest his companion had in Reiko, followed this remark with the announcement that he would be back soon and slipped out the door. After watching him go, Reiko and Natsume resumed their conversation.

"Speaking of the fanatics, what are you and the bishop doing about these threats that follow you, Reiko?" Natsume asked, adopting a reporter's tone to mask his personal interest. "Don't you think it is dangerous for you to be in Tokyo alone?"

"I am with someone almost around the clock but being alone today in Tokyo may be safer than being in Kure City, where many strangers have been seen skulking about. The church officials need to decide on a satisfactory final solution, but until then they have told the bishop and me to keep moving from one place to another. They hope this will make it more difficult for someone to confront us."

"What do you think the final solution will be?"

"The bishop says we should expect to be transferred out of the country. I believe he is correct."

"You will be leaving Japan?" Natsume asked.

"Sadly, yes very sadly." She bowed her head, giving in momentarily to her unhappiness.

"Forgive my impertinence, Reiko, but before you leave, do you suppose I might have an interview with you about all this and your life in general?"

"An interview, Natsume? I would find that embarrassing," she said. Her mind told her that she was reacting without thinking things through. After a brief moment she raised her head and looked deliberately at Natsume, "If you wish, I would be honored by your interview," she said. "McGrath-*san*'s story has international value."

"It is I who will be honored," Natsume replied. "Thank you. I will contact you for an appointment as soon as I am released from this hospital."

Reiko said, as if overcoming her forgetfulness, "Oh, yes... I know you published an article about this terrible attack, but will your paper be printing news about anything else at this time?"

"We are. In the past few days, we have published more about the other, the first vehicular homicide attempt against Joe McGrath, plus more on the Americans' nuclear testing directly on their own people. Did you know, it is estimated they have exposed as many as two hundred forty thousand Americans to nuclear weapons, and there may be thousands of fatalities and serious illnesses from many different deadly cancers? The statistics are astounding!"

"Thousands of Americans, their own government bombing them. I am shocked to hear it!"

"And an unpublished and perhaps immeasurable spread of radiation throughout North America."

"How self-defeating, and the radiation in their own country. As for the articles, I will buy copies of your newspaper and take them to the bishop. The church officials expressed their curiosity about your paper's ongoing coverage. When I spoke with the bishop over the telephone, he asked me to find out what I could in order to help his superiors measure the continued danger to us."

"What do you mean? Did he send you here?" Natsume's eyelids closed slightly, and his lips pursed as trace evidence that he was disappointed.

"No, no one sent me. No one, not even I, knew how injured you were. When I learned of your troubles, I felt I had to come, as I wanted to see with my own eyes that you were all right. Besides, you have helped us all so much, it would have been ungrateful and unkind of me not to visit."

"I am very happy you did," Natsume replied warmly. "If you don't mind my asking how you found out I was attacked. I thought you had returned to Kure City."

"Oh, no, I knew Joseph was leaving today. I was with him, and I stayed at St. Mary's so I could see Joseph off. I thought he might need a friend at such a time. He did seem most grateful. He is a person you grow fond of as you get to know him. I think having made some good friends in Japan consoles him and offsets the madness he has encountered in our country. Do you agree?"

"I certainly hope we have made some difference," Natsume said. "How is Joseph?"

"He is unsure of himself and, like you, his healing will take time, but I believe he will mend."

Natsume nodded his head in agreement.

"But forgive me," Reiko apologized, "I have not answered your question. When I found Joseph at the airport, he was not alone. Several of the Brown Dragons were with him, including the one Joseph calls the thin man. Do you know the one I mean?"

"Yes; his name is Michael Tahsaku."

"Ah. Well, Tahsaku-*san* had ordered his men to guard Joseph all day and night until he boarded the plane. He said he came to the airport so he could see with his own eyes that Joseph was headed safely back to America. It is he who told us what happened to you. He apologized for not being there to help the night you were attacked, saying he did not realize you were also in danger. He promised Joseph that the Brown Dragons would watch over you and keep you safe from now on. He seemed quite concerned."

"Interesting, it seems Joseph's kidnapper is now his good friend," said Natsume.

"He did seem like a changed person. He spoke softly and vowed he was done with violence."

"Joseph must have been a good influence on the man," Natsume said.

"Joseph has many capabilities, many gifts," Reiko agreed, while Natsume's face became expressionless.

Reiko continued: "Joseph wanted you to know he was asking about you. He thinks highly of you and sends his regards. Oh, and he asked me to tell him how you are by sending him a letter. I have his address in America."

"Please tell McGrath-*san* I appreciate his good wishes and that I will be fine."

"I will be happy to give him your message. He is now on his way back to America, but I promised I would write to inform him of your condition. I do not think I will ever see him again."

"Nor I," Natsume concurred, with a look toward Reiko of barely hidden scrutiny in his eyes.

At that moment Kanagaki came into the room carrying several bags of snacks and cans of soda. "Please have a cold drink and some of these," he said, passing them out.

Natsume moved his hand carefully to his mouth, gently exploring the soreness of his swollen lips. Apprehensive about the sense of extraordinary pain he felt at even the slightest touch on his broken nose, he inserted a straw into the soda can and raised it carefully upward, using both hands to steady it against his mouth.

Reiko, seeing him wince as he sucked on the straw, silently berated herself that he needed his rest to heal and she felt guilty for having visited him. She felt that she must leave. Taking a few sips of her cola to be polite, she noticed Natsume's eyes on her and she flushed with embarrassment. With practiced Japanese cordialities and a very conscious desire to unlock his gaze on her, Reiko gracefully began to make her exit.

Natsume called her back saying her name twice.

She turned and came back. At that Natsume politely asked Kanagaki to let him and Reiko have time alone.

Kanagaki nodded and left.

Reiko was so embarrassed that it made her cast her eyes to the floor.

"Do you think the church will protect you and the bishop?"

"They will transfer us, far away."

"And you will go?"

"It is a matter of obedience."

"This will happen soon?"

"Yes, and it is an embarrassment to have to flee from brutal cowards," she continued, her voice emanating no small note of outrage. "It is true, of course, that the fanatics we have dealt with are only the froth on the sewage of this country's evil. A nation's fanatics are like its gangsters—they never recant their crimes in earnest, no?"

Natsume knew that she was mistaken, that it was no longer the Japanese, but the Chinese, she should fear, but he had not yet decided whether to tell her, since once she was gone from Japan the source of the danger would not matter. Deciding to leave her in ignorance for the moment, Natsume deflected her attention from the matter by paying her a compliment.

"Please sit down and be comfortable."

Reiko did so, placing her forearms on her lap.

"You should be a journalist, Reiko," he blurted. "You have the meanings and power of words flowing out of you." He was completely sincere, for her stream of Japanese had impressed him once again, and he felt she deserved the praise.

"No, Natsume," Reiko refuted. "It is my anxieties that dramatize everything. Does your paper see what this Joseph McGrath has brought to the nuclear issues?"

"I believe it does," said Natsume. "My editors commented that, in a miniature way, McGrath represents a new resolve to reopen an old, unsettled search for accountability with regard to atomic bombs."

"It is reassuring to learn your newspaper has some keen perceptions of the events. It is a wonder, is it not, that McGrath-*san* ever came to Japan?"

"Indeed so," Natsume agreed, "but I do not think McGrath-*san* has any idea how important he is—or could be."

Reiko quickly turned and leaned toward Natsume and laid a hand on his sleeve. "How true!" she exclaimed enthusiastically. "McGrath-*san* stands strangely with one foot in America and one in

Japan. He is oddly connected to them both, and he has paid a price for that, has he not?"

Reiko, realizing how easy it was for her to praise Joe to another person, began to examine her feelings.

"Most certainly, he has," replied Natsume, supremely conscious of Reiko's touch on his arm and the pleasant sensation it gave him, as warmth from a fire. "My editors want me to write about him as 'one walking on an isthmus of the global ideas of peace.' He has significant credentials regarding Nagasaki and Hiroshima—nothing you would expect from an American. Most Americans have only two thoughts: they created the bomb, and they won the war."

"An isthmus of ideas of global peace," Reiko paraphrased, weighing each word carefully. Each syllable she uttered fell on Natsume's ear like a note of angelic music. "Your editors are thinking about it all, that is good to know," she said.

Then, with a look of discovery, she said, "Joe McCrath has already turned the heart of the Brown's leader. I believe we have seen that."

Natsume nodded.

~   ~   ~

"You are such a good man," she said, looking him in the eye. "For me, your intellectual honesty adds to your reporting. Your writing, your journalism, is a great art and offers much to your readers. I always want to know more when I read what you have written." Natsume was mesmerized by her eyes and her almost musical intonations. "Whatever you do," she continued, "you must let your journalism be for those voices—for the voice of Joseph McGrath and the voice of our people, the *Hibakusha,* Yes?"

"If I were worthy of such a task, I would be honored to do so," Natsume replied.

"It is to them you will be giving honor. All art, Natsume—your art and that of the many great ones—is a confession, is it not?"

"Confession? That is an unusual choice of words," Natsume said as he watched Reiko release her hand from his arm.

"Yes, art confesses that man has pity for himself and, more importantly, that he pities his failure to change. Yet I believe that, in every expression of art, man *is* changed. Deep inside us all lay both our destiny and our transformation. In the end, my friend, when the desire in every one of us matches all truth, we are transformed. Perhaps it begins one person at a time, and then many are transformed, and then maybe all. But it starts with a confession."

CHAPTER 21

"Thank you for your thoughts, Reiko. I am always enchanted by what you have to say," said Natsume, biting carefully into one of Kanagaki's snacks, "We really should have had that interview."

"I believe we are having it now," she smiled, eliciting an answering smile from Natsume. Her face became serious as she focused on his scarred lip and the offset line of his nose. "It is dangerous for you, too, here in Japan," she observed. "Yet you will be staying, no?"

"Yes," said Natsume. "Once I returned from America, I knew I would never leave Japan again. Besides, it is not so dangerous for me. I have more protection than you and the bishop."

"How so?" Reiko asked, wrinkling her forehead.

"Because most of the time my work serves both the agendas of the good guys and the bad guys, so they want to keep me around."

"That sounds barely believable, but perhaps I understand: they both need you to write about them because the media serves their conveyance of otherwise unspeakable information, is it not so? But can that really protect you?"

"It has in the past, especially when the opponents truly differed," Natsume said with conviction. Reiko tilted her head and stared pointedly at the wounds on his lips. "Well," he said, "with this one exception, of course." He punctuated the statement with a dismissive wave of his hand, but a slight frown creased his forehead.

"You are still worried, no?" Reiko asked. "What is it you are not telling me?"

"There is one serious matter of concern," Natsume admitted reluctantly. "I did not correct you earlier when you named Japanese fanatics as the source of danger."

As he resettled himself in the hospital bed, he said,"Ths is a secret only my photographer, Kanagaki, and I share," Natsume informed her. "We have not told anyone. I am not certain how dangerous such knowledge could be for others, including yourself, or what impact it would have if I made it public. Besides, I promised I would not reveal it."

"Do you want to tell it to me?" she said with a wry smile.

"Yes, I do. It would be a great relief to tell you whom I trust," he answered, aware that he was easily returning her friendly smiles.

"Then please tell me," Reiko said, "and I will be grateful to listen."

Natsume tried to measure which of them had more control of this conversation.

"If what you have to tell me is a secret, perhaps you would prefer to speak in English, since probably no one else here understands it," she prompted.

"That's an excellent idea," Natsume agreed. He reached for her hand and clasped it warmly. Looking straight ahead, he began to recount his story. She released her hand from his, to sit back in her chair and make herself more comfortable.

"When we were sideswiped on the way back from Hiroshima, I discovered from the police report that the truck that hit us was driven by a man claiming to be a Chinese national. Whoever he really was, he rented it from a construction equipment rental company with what turned out to be false, but nevertheless Chinese, identification."

Reiko beginning to drink the rest of her can of soda said, "Not Japanese? That is odd."

"Further, when I was run over by that biker, I realized immediately that the man was not Japanese."

"How?"

"His language told me. He cursed me in Chinese," Natsume replied.

"Ahhh, I see," said Reiko, rocking back and forth in her chair. "That is mysterious. I thought all our troubles came from our own notorious Japanese fanatics. Even though the one Joseph calls the thin man apologized at the airport and promised he would protect us rather than cause us any more trouble, I believed it was still him—or at least his group—that was behind those incidents, and that the continuing threat of danger still came from them."

"I thought so, too," said Natsume, "but when the biker swore at me, both assailants being Chinese was too much of a coincidence. They were not the same man. I saw both of them, the one in the truck and the biker."

"Soo desu! [It is so!]" Reiko said.

"I wondered where I could go to learn what was behind the attacks, and I remembered Agent Reginald Teach, the U.S. government official assigned to McGrath who took charge at the cathedral when Joseph was released. I called Teach's headquarters and asked him if he knew what was going on. The moment I mentioned the Chinese on the phone, Agent Teach went into shock, as if I was suddenly a big problem to him. He began speaking suspiciously and insisted that we immediately find a private place to talk.

When I told him, I was still in the hospital he said that we should meet right away. He offered to come to the hospital. When he came, he pushed me in my wheelchair. We went down to the cafeteria. Our timing was perfect, for the lunch crowd was just leaving, and we soon had the place to ourselves."

Reiko listened attentively. Natsume provided her with a full description of Agent Teach, including the man's wrinkled beige summer-weight suit, his oily hair, curled and flattened on his scalp, and his habit of pushing his glass of ginger ale around in the rings of water it made on the countertop. Not surprisingly, Natsume was a consummate storyteller and, as he progressed, he could not restrain himself from embellishing his anecdote. He also explained that he didn't think Reiko would like Teach, describing him as long-winded, self-absorbed, and transparent. Reiko was amused.

Natsume repeated Teach's words as he remembered them, comically mimicking the man's gravelly voice and uncouth American accent: "*I wanna make sure ya understand that ya can't publicize your suspicions, not under any circumstances. Chinese involvement was the principal reason our government tried to keep the lid on the whole matter of McGrath. It all has international ramifications, and if your newspaper mentions it, it'll be like waving a burning torch around in a dynamite shed.*"

Natsume recounted how Teach, waving his hand for emphasis, had knocked over his glass, spilling ginger ale and ice cubes everywhere. He described the scene so clearly that Reiko could almost see the dripping counter and the agent's wet pants, and she giggled helplessly as Natsume, pleased with himself, looked on. When she finally got herself under control, he continued.

"I asked what he meant by Chinese involvement, and Teach said, '*I'm gonna make this quick. This was classified information, so don't spread it around. The Chinese, back in 1961 or so, anticipated a counterattack invasion by Chiang Kai-shek's Nationalists from Taiwan.*'"

Reiko's brow furrowed as she tried to remember that far back. "I know," said Natsume. "It was a long time ago. I was wracking my brain trying to remember what was going on. He must have noticed I was having trouble placing it, so he went into detail."

Once again impersonating Teach, Natsume repeated the agent's words: "'*The Chinese were afraid of a nuclear attack, an invasion on their mainland. So, at the same time they were publicly calling our test ban agreements fraudulent, they were trying to learn as much as they could about the atomic bomb. Somehow, they got their hands on all the available U.S. test data involving troops and tactical nuclear weapons—and we still haven't figured out how they did it.'"* Natsume interrupted himself, saying, "Teach was so egotistical, I swear he told me lots more than he should have, and I was into it and kept him talking."

"Kisha ga itsumo tsuika no jijitsu o sagashimotomete iru, nai? [Always the reporter hunting for additional facts, no?]" Reiko teased.

"That was when he told me that the Chinese were determined—fanatical about it, in fact—that no one should find out how or why they obtained the information. Even now, years later, Teach said, the Chinese think the disclosure would threaten their nuclear defenses—not to mention that it would be too controversial and would fly in the face of their recent heated accusations of past atrocities by wartime Japan. In any case, they want the McGrath issue—and all those connected to it—silenced, and they don't trust Japanese extreme nationalistic or gangster elements to do it."

"Oh, my," breathed Reiko. "This is, as the Americans would say, heavy stuff."

"That's for sure," Natsume agreed. "Teach definitely didn't want me to ask any questions, but I did anyway. I asked him how something as insignificant as a back-page news bullet about McGrath could be of any importance to the Chinese political scene."

"And his answer?" Reiko queried, her eyes squinting in anticipation.

"He said the Chinese are embarrassed about the discrete practice they used to source the information, and they've been very content with how the Americans have kept information about U.S. troops in atomic bomb tests at such a low-key level of publicity, almost always to the point of secrecy. *'If nobody cares or talks about it,'* he said, *'the Chinese won't have to explain anything and that lowers the chance of a leak about their nefarious spy rings, but you got to remember that the Tokyo hospital records show McGrath to be a mental case, experiencing severe psychological effects from exposure to nuclear explosives, and his solitary confinement.'"*

"In that context, I can see why they would be interested in silencing Joseph and all of us," Reiko said thoughtfully. "What more did you ask, and what did he say?"

"I asked him why the Chinese were specifically interested in the atomic tests with troops, and he told me what I would have never imagined—even though, being a reporter, perhaps I should have."

"One can't think of everything," Reiko said, as if defending him.

"I guess not," Natsume smiled. "Anyway, Teach said it was for one of two reasons: The first was that they had decided to use the films and reports they had secretly obtained to determine how to repel an attack or to explore strategies for a nuclear offensive, probably on the entire land mass of Taiwan. Secondly they needed to know how to destroy resistance with the use of a low-yield nuclear arsenal raining down ahead of their attacking troops."

"So according to agent Reginald Teach, the Chinese were planning to invade Formosa, which has since changed its name to Taiwan?" Reiko asked. Natsume was once again struck by the quickness of her mind and her ability to grasp the implications of what he was telling her, and his ego was bolstered by her close attention to his words.

"That's what he said," Natsume replied. "Using the stolen files, they could calculate the force necessary to launch a successful assault by computing the size of the enemy force that could be destroyed as well as the number of their own soldiers who would be too severely injured—hopelessly irradiated, that is—to continue the attack."

"The U.S. troop testing data gave them all that?" Reiko asked.

"That's how Teach described it," Natsume said, "and that's the *why* behind their stealing the information. Interestingly, though, Teach said it's not the *why* that the Chinese want to keep hidden, it's the *how*—and they think that any publicity given to McGrath about the tests might someday uncover their spying history."

"Did Teach say why that would be the biggest problem?" Reiko asked.

"He sure did," said Natsume. "'*First of all, buddy,*'" he quoted, dropping into a raspy laconic growl again, "*let me remind you that this is an ongoing investigation, and one you can't mess with. I'll tell you, but remember, this is in no way meant for publication; you gotta promise you'll keep it totally off the record.*' Of course, I gave Teach my word, and then he said the most astonishing thing: '*Those Chinese were also plugged into the Russians' nuclear developments. In fact, some of those tests might not have happened if the Chinese hadn't been involved.*'"

"What did he mean?" Reiko asked, her face troubled.

"That was my next question," said Natsume, "and he said, either directly or indirectly, the Chinese had high-level authorities in both the U.S. or Russia conducting tests on government troops. I tried to make my face stony so as not to betray the shock I felt but he must have seen something, for then he said, in a sly kind of way, '*Buying influence is as old as bamboo in China.*' I thought later that would make a great headline slug, but at the time I was too rattled to think of such things.

"I was dumbfounded after learning what the Chinese and their paid betrayers were up to, but of course I didn't want to show it, so I asked him another question to keep him talking and give myself time to regain control. 'So,' I said, 'is this *now* still so important that they will kill me and McGrath over it?' Joseph would probably be back in America by then, of course, but I wanted to know."

"And his answer?" asked Reiko, practically holding her breath.

Somehow, Natsume managed to growl and sound totally egotistical at the same time: "'*These problems are usually solved diplomatically, but that can't happen if somebody like McGrath opens the can of worms before the matter is put in a lock-tight can of its own. We do that canning every day, and we do it very well. Don't matter if it's the Chinese or the dumb-ass Russians or even little places like Cuba. This nuclear testing business is still a leaking container but, in the end, nobody beats us up on nothing.*'" He sat up and turned toward Reiko and gently placed his hands on her shoulders. "And that was the end of our conversation," he said in his own voice, smiling down at her.

"You did not ask him for the *identity* of the American and Russian authorities who sacrificed troops to the testing for the benefit of the Chinese?" Reiko asked.

"I thought about it but didn't think he would go that far—and I could tell it was time to stop asking questions. Teach left with a handshake and assurances that we would meet again, tossing both his paper money and change right into the puddle of ginger ale on the counter. I haven't seen him since."

Reiko's disgust at Teach's secrets and behavior registered on her face, convincing Natsume that she was a keen listener and that he had her personal interest.

Natsume said abruptly, "You should find your own place to live and stay clear of these Chinese and our own fanatics." He touched her knee, holding his fingertips there.

She stood saying, "You mean go live on my own, not with the bishop anymore?"

"Yes. If you did, I would care for you, and help you, wherever you live."

They smiled at each other, and then Reiko stood silently. Natsume looked on waiting for her reply.

Reiko whispered, "You are a good man and a great newspaper man. I should tell you I cannot accept your help. I am going to go with His Excellency to help him. He is an old man and he has been my refuge since the orphanage."

Natsume looked deep into her eyes. His voice husky with emotion, he murmured, "If you come back, please let me know and, if you stay there, and want me to, for any reason, I will go. My job allows me to go anywhere, and I will visit you."

"You are a very good and honorable man, thank you, I must go now"

"Thank you for your kind visit." He knew without saying what he told her would not be betrayed. He also had a look on his face that showed he knew he failed to arouse her romantic interests.

Reiko left the room quietly.

CHAPTER 22

KURE CITY JAPAN

A stack of packed suitcases on the entrance walkway cast a long, finger-shaped shadow toward the front door while the haunting sound of distant bamboo wind chimes floated through the mid-morning air. At the rear of the rectory, Reiko stood just inside a partially opened sliding door, savoring the fresh breezes that caressed her face.

For two weeks, after Joseph McGrath moved on with his life, Reiko had sheltered in the safety of the Hiroshima monastery, basking in Uncle Shiro's love and absorbing a sense of family. When she was summoned back to the bishop's residence at Kure City, she returned obediently but with a heavy heart, for she convinced herself she would never see her uncle again.

In the week that was to pass before she departed with the bishop and the rest of his staff, Reiko had kept herself busy overseeing the packing of her things and those of the bishop. Feeling the unthinkable, her detachment from her first home outside of the confined years in the orphanage, she was sending her soul out into the lush greenery of her garden and gathering the garden's essence in hopes that she could, in the best way, take the memory with her.

She looked out fondly at the traditional Japanese setting with its carefully tended plants, wooden foot bridge, and turtle pond. Hearing the new cleric greet someone, she presumed that the airport transportation had arrived for their luggage earlier than scheduled. She stood a while in silent reverie then, not knowing when she might see her beloved garden again, she decided to walk through it one last time.

As she leaned forward to slide the door fully open, a man's hand appeared from outside, pressing against the edge of the door to assist her. Startled, she discovered Joseph McGrath standing before her.

"Good afternoon, Mr. McGrath," Reiko whispered in English. "You are back in Japan." Her beautiful almond eyes, at first alarmed, darkened with pleasure as she gazed up at him.

"*Konnichiwa* [Good afternoon], Fumioka-*san*," answered Joe, emphasizing the Japanese greeting. He closed the door behind her as she stepped through, and they walked into the garden. "I am glad you are still here. When I saw your bags, I thought you might have gone on ahead and left them to be forwarded," he felt embarrassed and said, "The man at the front door pointed me back here."

"You came just in time," she murmured, modestly holding her head down. "The car from the airport should be arriving very soon. Why have you returned to Japan? Why?"

"I flew to Hawaii and just walked the beaches. I didn't want to go home."

"What do you mean, Joseph?"

"I don't think I am able to leave you. I kept thinking of you. So, I came back, what else could I do?"

"Me?"

"Reiko, if all the troubles were gone, never happened, would you want to spend time with me, with us?"

"Sadly, now there is no time for such a question. They are sending us out of the country, as I had feared, and we leave today. You are in such great danger. You must not stay in Japan!"

"How long will you be gone?" Joe asked, his eyes showed fear and longing at the same time.

"We have been advised to stay away for a year, maybe more, until we are forgotten, but unless the whole world changes, I think our exile will be permanent."

Joe's head bowed as his face filled with his great sadness, "So, y-you will g-go?" he stammered, his voice registering his regret. "You cannot change your mind?"

"It is not our decision to make," Reiko replied quietly as she surveyed the garden. "We are being sent away by our superiors. It is a matter of security and obedience." She focused on a nearby cherry tree. "We are threatened."

Breaking what he knew of Japanese mores and folkways by looking directly into Reiko's eyes, Joe held her gaze, allowing her to see his intense interest. He reached and touched her lightly with both hands. "I have often wished I could have rescued you from that orphanage," he said, watching her closely. "I have calculated that I was just leaving the Army when you were released into the adult world at the age of seventeen."

"You have?" Abandoning a lifetime of guarded behavior, Reiko reached out and laid a hand on his shoulder, which he immediately covered with his own. "You would have been a welcome sight," she smiled, bowing her head respectfully. "All the other girls would have been jealous." She continued to surprise herself by speaking her true feelings, "You will not stay in Japan Joseph, no?"

He smiled thinly and said, "No, I will leave."

As they reached the turtle pond, she bent down gracefully and extended her hand toward a curiously shaped paper prayer floating on the water. Scooping it up, she handed the intricately folded paper to Joe, who saw the message written in Japanese, handed it back. Reiko read aloud; her voice reverent. "*Behold I make all things new; I wipe away every tear.*" She carefully refolded the small piece of paper. "Just imagine. . ." she said, her voice trailing off.

Joe turned to face her, looking down on her lovely black hair and caressing it with his eyes. "I wish we had gotten to know more about each other, Reiko," he said. He watched as she stooped and set the paper prayer back onto the surface of the pond. It swirled around and drifted under the bridge and out the other side, slowing in the middle of the dark water. He was about to speak again when the new cleric appeared offering tea and rice wafers, stating, in Japanese, "*Ocha o nonde kudasai, watoshi no ocha o kudasai,*" that he wanted them to enjoy his tea. He discreetly slid the <u>Shoji doors</u> closed and then opened them again a few inches

Entering, the pair knelt on mats on either side of a low serving table, and Reiko poured the tea. Joe, gazing at her with obvious admiration for her gracious manners, accepted his cup and picked up a rice cake.

"You know, Joseph," she said, "it is not usually the uncelebrated person that newspapers study and react to. But we have been impacted by what the papers and television people, all the news attention, has stirred up, and the *Hibakusha* have a voice again. It may be weak right now, but we have no idea how many other voices will speak."

"The whole world needs to listen to such voices."

"I have heard those voices coming out of Hiroshima and Nagasaki since I was a child," Reiko declared.

"Where are you and the bishop going?"

"His new assignment from Rome is in Rawalpindi, Pakistan," said Reiko.

"No."

With true surprise now written on her face, Reiko answered, "I have decided to go to help the bishop for a while and then to leave. I do not want to go. I don't want to live in Pakistan, Joseph."

She began to pour him more tea in ceremonial fashion as she was trained to do as a child in the orphanage. Her hands were shaking. He bent his head down after she placed his tea before him. He was tearing up and pressed the heel of his palm against his eyes repeatedly. She was sobbing. They smiled at each other's distress, as some people oddly do when they do not have control of their physical reactions to emotions of sorrow or helplessness.

The wind chimes, made of hollow lengths of bamboo on leather thongs, drummed against each other, their random musical notes a mellow backdrop to their parting. The sound lured the two back out to the privacy of the garden, where they would be alone and out of sight of anyone else.

Her eyes followed tiny wind-blown petals as they tumbled in the air and across the ground. Near the small bridge, a wisteria tangled itself into a large but well-trimmed flowering shrub. The space was the most secluded area of the garden, shaded in stillness and there they embraced. They kissed as if it wasn't their first kiss, as if they had always kissed each other, no hesitation, uninhibited by their differences or previous expectations. She was suddenly his, and he was passionately hers.

"If you must go, when you are ready, call me, and I will come for you and take you to Philadelphia. Anybody from anywhere can get a start there. All you need are a few breaks, a few chances, and life will open to us. We will be in America together. Yes?"

"Yes, oh yes, Joseph, please do. Come for me and I will be with you forever."

"Forever?"

"Yes, forever."

"Wherever we are we will be happy."

She pressed herself into him, wrapped in his arms, "With you, I will always be happy. I know that now."

'So do I."

EPILOGUE
June 2019, Dayton OH USA

Joe McGrath, from Philadelphia, stood at a podium in the Midwest. He was speaking in current time of course, but what happened to him was a long time ago when he was nineteen-years old. Joe McGrath and the Japanese woman seated beside him had survived to old age. The Japanese woman was born in Hiroshima. Joe is an Atomic Veteran who suffered with many others from the radiation and betrayal when troops were used as a gigantic medical experiment by their own government. It was well over fifty years after his time with the atomic bomb detonations on Nevada's Nuclear Test site.

Reading his audience, those ex-servicemen who had been sent into atomic and hydrogen bomb tests, the international visitors and the participants from the media, Joe found himself discarding his prepared speech and the power-point presentation projected on dual screens, Joe began to speak, his voice louder than it needed to be, "We made a big mistake believing that the two atomic bombs dropped on Hiroshima and Nagasaki ended the Second World War and prevented an invasion of Japan. We were wrong to give any credit at all to those two filthy, horrible death bombs."

"I estimate they killed fifteen to twenty thousand children in each of those cities. We didn't just kill them, we fused their fingers together, blew their eyes out of their sockets." He breathed in deeply and said, "We had already destroyed sixty-eight Japanese cites and their children. We justified the two atomic bombs by what would never happen, the loss of thousands of American servicemen in an invasion of Japan. We were not going to invade Japan. Why would we invade a defeated Japan?" Joe noticed the silence of his audience. It was everywhere in the huge meeting room in Dayton, Ohio. There were people there from every nation that held nuclear power or that was victimized by atomic and hydrogen bombs and reckless science.

Joe McGrath was finally telling his sense of the truth. The tough audience of veterans, who were grateful to believe that the Second World War owed its conclusion and their victory to atomic bombs, were more than disturbed by his truth, squirming like irradiated worms beneath the soils of Hiroshima and Nagasaki.

"The invasion of Okinawa taught Truman and many of his advisers that the invasion of Japan had to be scrapped." He said that and paused, checking himself for steadiness and the will to continue. Expressionless up to that point, the Japanese woman, Reiko's face became reassuring. To Joe, her face was Japan, her eyes expressing the searching he and she lived since they met. They and their interracial Japanese-American marriage were the impossibility of reconciliation and union with which they escaped from the brutality of the Pacific war.

Now standing in front of the podium with his voice no longer unnecessarily elevated he finalized his speech, "Anyway, the invasion of Japan was going to be done by the Russians, and that made Japan seek surrender with the Allies even more than they were already seeking it." Rocking on the balls of his feet, and with the woman, Reiko standing, he said, "Those two death bombs did not win the Second World War. The army and the Marines and the Sailors and the Pilots of downed and returning airplanes and the people of the nations at war won the Second World War. The bombs were the runaway horrific science from monsters loosed by the rape of the innocent uranium molecular atoms of earth's creation, its elements, even plutonium, given to do good not to destroy life and the Japanese children of the earth."

He could almost feel the audience's discomfort with his proclamations. He spoke his mind steadied by determination and the raw courage to defy popularly held beliefs. He had found the fervor of discovery – a discovery that he was saying what he had to say, what he learned over the many years since he was irradiated by his own country on the Nevada desert with six hundred other infantrymen. He stood motionless and silent long enough for the audience to respond, but the audience gave no sign of believing him or accepting what he was saying

Later, with her Japanese accent, Reiko said, that Joe finally gave a truthful account versus the strange fiction that most Americans, whom she believed to be deceived, had long since professed.

She had once said of Americans, "The Americans only say, 'We made the bomb and we won the war.' They say nothing about how the Japanese civilians died so horribly and in such a nightmare of despair and disparaged death." Reiko's English was a second language, a learned language. She after all was the one who titled Joe's presentation. She called it, *A Young Soldier's Story by Joe McGrath* with the Japanese subtitle... "Watashi wa Amerika no genbaku hibaku-shadesu," (I am an American survivor of the atomic bomb).

She, by her words, joined Joe to the burnt children of Hiroshima and Nagasaki.

ABOUT THE AUTHOR

John A McCabe, a lifelong writer in all genres, is an active member of the Writers Guild at the Pearl S. Buck Writing Center. His novel, *The Girl In Japan - A Young Soldier's Story,* centers on his studies of Hiroshima and Nagasaki combined with his own experiences.

A short story writer, John has also authored several Short Story Collections. *Tracks Through Our Lives,* published in 2019 by The Pearl S. Buck Writing Center Press for international distribution, tells stories and tales of remarkable friendships formed in the neighborhoods of Philadelphia. The Second Edition is scheduled for release, Summer 2022. The second collection, Tracks Under Our Lives, further develops storyline and characters of amazing depth, is planned for release, Fall 2022.

John was published by the National Society of Collegiate Scholars 2010 as a University of Pennsylvania Chapter participant with *The Wedding Guests.* His works appear in PSB Literary Journals. He has also published poetry.

John is often a speaker at major literary and non-literary events. As a Presenter at the West Virginia University Gateway Conference honoring the legacy of Pearl S. Buck, he examined Buck's 1959 novel, *Command The Morning* - her historic fiction *exposé* of the Manhattan Project. John was also a speaker at the 2019 National Association of Atomic Veterans 40th annual convention in Dayton Ohio.

ALSO BY JOHN A MCCABE

Short Story Collections

Tracks Through Our Lives

First Edition, Pearl S Buck Writing Center Press, 2019

Coming Soon:

Tracks Through Our Lives - Second Edition, June 2022

Tracks Under Our Lives, November 2022

Lightning Source UK Ltd.
Milton Keynes UK
UKHW021404260522
403568UK00007B/1483